D1219883

THE VAMPIRE'S PRICELESS TREASURE
NOCTURNE FALLS, BOOK ELEVEN

KRISTEN PAINTER

THE VAMPIRE'S PRICELESS TREASURE:
Nocturne Falls, Book Eleven

Copyright © 2019 Kristen Painter

Welcome to Nocturne Falls, the town that celebrates Halloween 365 days a year. The tourists think it's all a show: the vampires, the werewolves, the witches, the occasional gargoyle flying through the sky. But the supernaturals populating the town know better.

Living in Nocturne Falls means being yourself. Fangs, fur, and all.

Half reaper, half vampire Kora Dupree has made big changes in her life. She's on good terms with her previously estranged father and taken on all kinds of adult responsibilities. But when an opportunity to find out the truth about her late mother comes along, she can't resist pursuing it. Even when it means returning to her somewhat dubious ways.

Vampire Greyson Garrett knows the bad but beautiful Kora is up to something. He's wise to her games. After all, her father has hired Greyson numerous times to save Kora from all the sticky situations she's gotten herself into. If she were just...better behaved he could see himself falling for her. Hard.

Even though Kora promises she's changed, Greyson has his doubts. So much so that he follows her one fateful night and gets pulled into her latest scheme. It's not like he hasn't been here before, but this time he swears it's her last chance to prove she's different.

Kora's new adventure sends them on a treasure hunt that takes them all over the globe, and in the course of their travels, they realize how good things are when they work together. But will that all change when the adventure is over? Are they really in love? Or just addicted to the rush?

*For all my readers who kept asking for Greyson
to get his own book.*

Enjoy!

Greyson Garrett loved the Nocturne Falls library, but he wasn't here to pick out his weekend reading. And not just because he'd already done that.

Instead, he was parked in the community wing, a three-room addition specifically meant for lectures, craft fairs, workshops, small conferences, and exhibits.

The space was bright and modern and beautifully designed. All paid for by the family who'd made the town the bustling tourist mecca and safe haven for supernaturals that it was, the Ellinghams.

But even being in such a well-appointed space wouldn't keep him from sighing with the kind of boredom that came from eight hours of doing essentially nothing.

Sure, he was getting paid for that nothing, which *was* actually something. He was working as a security guard. But the money was inconsequential.

The title amused him. Having a vampire as your security guard was pretty extreme. But the title also made him frown a little. Not because there was anything wrong with the job. There was nothing wrong with honest work of any kind. It was just that…he'd been a lot of things in his life. Security guard didn't really rank up there with the most riveting employment he'd undertaken.

But Elenora Ellingham had specifically requested him, and so here he was. One did not say no to Elenora, especially when complying could mean banking her goodwill for the future. Greyson wasn't a fool. Not when he lived in her town. For Elenora, he would be bored all day and all night.

Besides, he was technically an employee of Nocturne Falls, and the job would only last for five days. He looked at his watch. And the last day was almost over.

It had been numbingly uneventful, but given the circumstances of what he was guarding, that was a good thing.

He folded his hands in front of him and watched the tourists and locals alike who were wandering through the exhibit. *Touched by Magic: Gems and Jewelry with Mythical Connections*, to be exact.

Naturally, this was the kind of thing that Elenora swooned over. Her love of jewelry and priceless gems was no secret to anyone who'd lived in Nocturne Falls for any length of time. She'd opened the exhibit with a ribbon-cutting ceremony, but had held a private tour for a small group of VIPs the night before the official opening.

He'd been here for that, too, but his presence had

been mostly for show. At least that's what he'd assumed. The group had been Nocturne Falls's upper crust. Not the sort who were going to attempt to run off with Nefertiti's bejeweled and supposedly cursed mirror, or any of the other trinkets they'd all been oohing and aahing over.

Whatever. People got excited about weirder stuff.

But it was nice that a portion of the ticket sales was going to the pediatric wing of the hospital, so Greyson had no issues with any of it. Even if none of the proceeds had been going to a good cause, he still wouldn't care. Jewelry wasn't something that really interested him. Despite the pieces he wore. Sure, he liked some jewelry for its aesthetics, but there was only one piece that mattered to him.

And he wasn't sure that could even be considered jewelry.

That piece was the small cloth bag that hung on a leather cord around his neck, the contents of which kept him safe from the sun, thanks to the old Roma magic of his people. Well, mostly his great-aunt's ability to work that magic.

But the things in this exhibition? In his opinion, they were better left alone. Even if they weren't cursed. Which he doubted. When you were a vampire of Roma decent who lived in a town like Nocturne Falls, you had a tendency to believe in pretty much anything.

Life was a valuable teacher that way.

He shifted slightly, keeping his eyes on a man who was lingering a little too long near Medusa's headband.

The headband, when worn, supposedly kept one's curse at bay. Apparently, Medusa hadn't been wearing it when she'd turned all those poor Greeks into stone.

The man moved on, and Greyson scanned the crowd again. A few locals, but most of the visitors to the exhibit were tourists now. The locals had come early.

Most of the people in the wing were clustered around Elenora's own contribution to the exhibit, the Heart of Dawn, an extremely rare and valuable seventy-five-carat heart-shaped pink diamond that Elenora now claimed was cursed since it had been stolen during the ball thrown for the sole purpose of showing off the gem.

He didn't see how cursed the diamond could be given that it had also been recovered and returned. But if Elenora wanted to add it to the show, what did it matter to him? It was certainly bringing people in.

Although, if she really wanted to add something touched by magic, she should have added one of the amulets that each of the Ellinghams wore. The ones that kept them safe from the sun. They weren't Roma magic like what protected him. No, the Ellingham amulets were ancient witch magic. Not his area of expertise, for sure.

All he knew was that they were created by Alice Bishop, a very old and powerful witch whose life Elenora had saved in Salem when the trials had been going on. Alice had been Elenora's closest ally and companion since then.

Greyson didn't blame the woman. Having your life saved changed your perspective on a lot of things. He guessed. He'd never had his life saved in such dramatic fashion. He'd done some saving. But nothing that had resulted in a lifelong pledge of fealty and fidelity.

He snorted at the thought.

"What's funny?"

Greyson straightened at the familiar voice. "Hello, Hugh." Hugh Ellingham was one of Elenora's three grandsons. "Nothing, really. Just thinking about how your grandmother's diamond is the least-cursed thing in this exhibit, but the one that's drawing the biggest crowd."

Hugh nodded. "It's an impressive rock."

"It is. I'm sure a lot of women are leaving here with big ideas."

Hugh smirked. "I don't doubt you're right. Too bad Delaney's already seen it."

Greyson laughed. "Your wife has her own hoard of jewels. I don't think much in here could turn her head."

Hugh stuck his hands in his pockets and turned his attention to the crowd. "Not to mention, the shop and George keep her too busy to be bothered with such trinkets anyway."

"How is your son?"

"Brilliant," Hugh answered with a proud smile.

"Good to hear." There were days when Greyson wondered if he'd ever have the kind of domestic bliss each of the Ellingham brothers had. It wasn't something that gave him sleepless nights, but it was there, lingering at the back of his mind. Okay, maybe since breaking up with Jayne, his last girlfriend, he'd had one or two sleepless nights, but that was it. "So what can I do for you?"

"Nothing, really. Just wanted to see how this thing was going. You wouldn't believe the insurance nut we had to put up to host this exhibit."

"I can imagine." He couldn't really. He had money. Most vampires with any kind of age on them did. But the Ellinghams had been British nobility. They'd started out with money. And they had enough now to live the kind of lifestyles that allowed for things like seventy-five-carat diamonds, sprawling estates, a private plane, and, not to be forgotten, their own town.

Greyson didn't splash out quite so much. His big extravagance was his '69 Camaro. And maybe his wardrobe. But that was about it.

Hugh clapped him on the shoulder. "Have a good night. I better get back. I have to pick up dinner from Howler's on the way home. Delaney wants a bacon cheeseburger."

Greyson nodded. "Happy wife—"

"Happy life." Hugh shook his head. "You have no idea how true that is."

With a little wave, he was gone, leaving Greyson to contemplate that thought. And to remember the woman he'd thought had been the one. Winter elf Jayne Frost.

They'd had a parting of the ways, something that

had taken him a bit to get over, but in retrospect, he knew it had been for the good.

She was a princess, and he didn't mean that in the derogatory sense. She was the heir to the Winter Throne of the North Pole, which was an entirely separate magical realm.

He crossed his arms. Marrying her would have resulted in a very different life for him. A life that he knew now would fit him as poorly as another man's coat.

A soft chime rang, followed by an announcement in a woman's British-accented voice. "The exhibition will be closing in fifteen minutes. Thank you for visiting."

He uncrossed his arms. The exhibit's curator, Randolph Dillinger, would be along shortly to lock the doors. Then Greyson would do a sweep of the building to make sure that everyone was gone and—a familiar face in the crowd caught his attention.

And not because she was beautiful. Because she was trouble. And this was the third time she'd been here in as many days.

Kora Dupree. The half-vampire, half-reaper daughter of Lucien Dupree, owner of Insomnia, Greyson's favorite night spot.

He liked the club because it wasn't for humans. Which meant it was a tourist-free zone. Not that Nocturne Falls didn't have some supernatural tourists—it did. But they generally weren't a bother because they knew what was what.

The human tourists who came to Nocturne Falls

did so because they thought all the supernaturals were character actors, something encouraged by the town as a way of protecting those who lived here.

But there were times when Greyson felt he couldn't take being stopped on the street one more time and asked for a selfie. On those nights, and many others, he went to Insomnia.

Kora was now helping her father run the place as acting manager, but unlike her father, Kora spent a lot of time in the club. Who could blame the man? He was newly married, had moved into a new house, and had his daughter to take over things. The time off was well earned.

But because of Kora's presence at the club, Greyson had been a little scarcer there. It wasn't that he disliked Kora. It was just that she was the kind of woman who was constantly getting mixed up in something. Something Greyson would inevitably have to get her out of. And had, on numerous occasions. All paid for by her father, of course.

Someday, she was going to have to grow up and fight her own battles.

Or stop getting into battles altogether.

Since reconciling with her father, she did seem to be turning over a new leaf, but Greyson only trusted that for as long as the wind didn't blow. Something would happen to set her off again. He just knew it. People didn't really change all that much.

He slunk back into the shadows. That wouldn't keep her from seeing him, but it might buy him a few more minutes of calm.

Her gaze flicked from case to case with great curiosity. What had she expected to see? The Hope Diamond? Sure, it was cursed, but it was also the property of the Smithsonian. They weren't about to send that rock out on a road trip.

She moved through the exhibit with the same kind of detached attitude she'd had previously, making him question why she'd come back a third time. It certainly wasn't mandatory.

Would she return to the same item as she had before?

She stopped in front of a display at the end of one row. The same one as before. She stared through the glass, lips slightly parted, brow furrowed as if the world's balance hinged on her study of the object.

He didn't know what was in that case, but whatever it was, it continued to hold Kora's attention. He was going to have to see for himself now what it contained.

She leaned down to inspect the object more closely. He stayed where he was, watching and wondering what was so interesting about this particular piece. She pulled her phone out and snapped a few pictures.

She tucked the phone away, then straightened and looked around. He ducked behind the corner of the wall. Why, he wasn't sure. She had to know he was working there. He hadn't made a secret of it.

He didn't want to be caught watching her, though. Or do anything else that might incite a conversation.

But, really, he was being foolish. When he looked again, she was gone.

Well, that would save him from having to escort her out if she'd lingered any longer.

Then curiosity got the best of him. He wandered over to the display she'd been looking at to see what it was.

Half of a gold locket shaped like the sun. Date was approximately 1900. There was an inscription on the inside, but the ribbon looped through the top of the locket lay across the interior, making the words impossible to read. It was in Russian, too, and his understanding of Russian was nonexistent.

A mirror behind the piece showed off the front of the sun. Diamond rays spiraled out from a heart set with tiny rubies. The design meant nothing to him, but the gems were undoubtedly real. Probably real gold, too. All that considered, along with the piece's age and provenance, had to mean it was worth a tidy sum.

He read the little placard next to the piece. Apparently, the other half of the locket had been missing since the displayed half had been discovered. Anyone who owned the necklace was destined to come to a bad end, and it was rumored to have belonged to the Grand Duchess Olga Romanov, the eldest daughter of the last tsar of Russia. Tsar Nicholas II. That explained the Russian inscription.

It explained the curse, too. The Romanovs were the last of a royal dynasty who'd all been brutally murdered following the Russian Revolution.

A bad end indeed.

The story of the Romanovs had always upset him. And not just because he'd been living when it happened. To kill children just because of who their parents were... To kill an entire family because of what they represented... He shuddered involuntarily as he walked back to his station.

Why was Kora so interested in this locket? Was it just the story of the Romanovs? Greyson suspected not, but had no other ideas as to why it would have caught her attention so strongly. A broken locket couldn't be worth much, could it?

He thought about it a moment longer. Nothing clicked. There was no reason he could come up with that the locket would interest her.

Whatever. It was Kora's business. And he didn't need to be a part of that. He sighed. If only she wasn't so...Kora. She was staggeringly beautiful, intelligent, and half vampire. She was the kind of woman he'd normally pursue.

If she wasn't also a giant ball of crazy trouble. A relationship with her would end up with one of them dead or in jail. He crossed his arms. That seemed to be how it went, though. The brightest stars burned the hottest.

And sadly, he wasn't fireproof.

Kora was glad Greyson had slipped out of sight. That made her own disappearance much easier. The last thing she wanted to do was explain why she was at the exhibit for a third time. Or answer any of his questions.

She knew what he thought of her. That she was a wild child in need of discipline and growing up. A spoiled troublemaker who only cared about her own interests. He wasn't wrong. She *had* been those things. But not anymore. Not since she'd reconciled with her father, learned some hard truths about the past, and taken a long, introspective look at how she'd been living her life.

She'd grown up fast. Though, not entirely—she was definitely a work in progress. But she was on a new path now.

Or at least she had been before the package had arrived.

With accelerated vampire speed, she went straight

from the community wing to the reference section and used her keycard to access the door in the far corner marked Employees Only.

Beyond that door were the stairs to the Nocturne Falls Basement, the secret underground labyrinth beneath the town that provide passage for many of the supernatural employees. Doors to access the Basement were conveniently located all throughout town, like this one in the library. And the one just outside her father's nightclub, Insomnia. From there, she could go almost anywhere in town she wanted without ever having to step foot outside.

A very good thing when you were fifty percent vampire and a hundred percent UV intolerant.

As soon as she was down the steps, she stopped, pulled out her phone, and checked the pictures she'd taken. She leaned against the cool masonry wall as she looked at them, shaking her head in disbelief. The other half of the locket was really here. After nearly a year of looking, following every possible clue on the internet, scouring every historical document she could lay her hands on, calling antique shops across Europe…it was here.

Her hands trembled with excitement, but there was fear in her heart, too. So many unknowns swirled around this thing. Where would it lead her? Who was this Fox who had sent her the package in the first place? How had he known where to find her?

But most important, how did he know what had really happened to her mother? After Pavlina had disappeared, Kora and her father had always assumed

Pavlina had died, unable to find shelter from the sunrise. She'd lived her life impulsively, with little regard for her husband or child, indulging her own needs to the point that whatever had happened to her, death of some kind seemed most likely.

Perhaps inevitable.

Kora leaned back and took an unnecessary breath, trying to calm the flurry of emotions inside her. If only she could talk to her father about this. Or anyone. But the note that had accompanied the package had specifically forbidden her to disclose her mission.

If she did, the truth about her mother would never be revealed.

Kora questioned her need for such information. After all, it had been more than seventy-five years since she or her father had seen Pavlina. Why should Kora concern herself with this now? Especially when her mother couldn't be bothered to care about her only child.

But the truth was, Kora wasn't that hard-hearted. If anything, her new path had made her a lot more sensitive to feelings the old her would have brushed off. No longer could she be so cavalier. She wanted, no, *needed* the truth about her mother's disappearance and likely death. If only for the closure.

Then there was the rather intriguing locket. She loved jewelry, loved history, and loved adventure. With its combination of all three, this mission seemed made for her.

Which again brought to mind the question of how she'd been selected for it. Was it because she had a reputation for the kinds of activities that would make tackling this treasure hunt seem perfect for her? Was it because the Fox had the info on Pavlina? Or was that just a ploy to get Kora to track down the locket?

She scowled as she put her phone away and started moving down the passage toward Insomnia and her home. If this was all a ruse to recover whatever treasure it was she was supposed to recover and there wasn't any information to be had about Pavlina, Kora wasn't going to spare the person responsible.

For the Fox's sake, she hoped he remembered that while she was half vampire, she was half reaper, too. And while she might have very little of her father's side, she had his temperament about many things.

Including how justice should be served.

By the time she made it back home, she was genuinely angry about the task and its parameters. How dare she be expected to risk so much without any guarantee of reward? And without help. That was ludicrous.

She had half a mind to send a text via the burner phone included in the mysterious package and tell the Fox the deal was off.

Who called himself the Fox, anyway?

She went through the door that led down a dark hall and into her father's previous residence, the underground estate she now called home.

She shut the door behind her harder than intended. The sound brought Waffles, her cat, running. He meowed at her as he trotted down the hall.

"Hi there, sweet boy." She crouched down to pick

15

him up, snuggling him in her arms. She'd never wanted a pet, never considered having one, but when Chet, one of Insomnia's doormen, had told her there was a cat in the ground-level warehouse that wasn't doing too good, she'd gone up to see for herself. When she'd laid eyes on Waffles, a switch inside her flipped.

Waffles had been covered in fleas, so skinny his backbone was visible, his fur matted, and he'd been bitten by something that had left a horrible wound on his side.

Five months later, he was a gorgeous boy who'd filled out nicely, thanks to a steady diet of whatever he wanted. His wound was healed, his fur was thick and shiny, and if Kora was being honest, he'd taken up permanent residence in her heart. She hadn't known she could love another creature so much.

And she didn't want to be away from him for longer than necessary. Which was why, if she needed help with this mission, she was going to ask for it. For another thing, she didn't really have a choice. She couldn't read Russian, so translating the locket's inscription would require outside assistance.

She kissed Waffles's broad head. "Hungry, baby?"

He responded by butting his big noggin against her chin and making her smile.

For a third, she wasn't going to ignore her responsibilities for some quest. Besides Waffles, she'd made a commitment to her father to help at the club. She liked her job there. Liked doing it well. And she was enjoying her new relationship with her father. More surprisingly, she liked his new wife, too.

She'd never imagined her father would marry again, but what was stranger still was that she had genuinely come to like Imari. A reaper and a genie—such an unlikely combination, but they were very good together and clearly in love.

And if Imari made Kora's father happy, then that was enough for Kora.

But she liked Imari for more than the change in her father's outlook. Imari had given Kora's great-grandmother, Hattie, her life back.

Literally.

Hattie had been trapped in limbo between the living and the dead, a ghost by all appearances. And all because Lucien's reaper powers had gone haywire, and he'd accidentally reaped Hattie's soul.

That incident was the whole reason he'd retired. The whole reason he'd secreted himself away in his underground home. He couldn't trust his powers not to take a life, something no reaper could abide.

But that was all behind them now, thanks to Imari.

For that act alone, Kora gave the genie respect. She'd helped restore Lucien's happiness in many ways.

Something Kora had only caused to diminish for many years of her life. But that was in the past now, too. She had her family back, and she would fight to keep it.

She carried Waffles into the kitchen, then set him on the floor and fixed him a fresh bowl of Chicken Party. The food had been recommended by one of her father's friends, Jayne Frost. The winter elf just happened to be Greyson's ex-girlfriend, but Kora didn't care one way or the other who Greyson was or wasn't dating.

Not when it came to improving Waffles's life.

Jayne's cat, Spider, loved the particular flavor of food, and as it turned out, so did Waffles. Jayne and Spider had since moved to the North Pole, Jayne's hometown, so there weren't going to be any playdates in the future. Although Kora had begun to think it was time for Waffles to have a brother or sister.

As Kora filled his bowl, her mind returned to the locket. She knew part of her desire to see this quest through was her desperation to know the truth about her mother. What child wouldn't want that same thing? It was the kind of need that lived deep inside her, in a primal place that wasn't going to be denied.

So she would do what she could to fulfill the quest that had been laid out before her and hope that the Fox would honor his word.

But before she could do anything, she had to get the other half of the locket.

The packing up would start as soon as the exhibit was closed. Her plan was to head back to the library in the early hours of the morning before they came to load everything into the armored car to move on to the exhibit's next location.

She hoped the curators would think the locket had been swiped during the unpacking and setting up at the new location, which was in Miami.

If that wasn't what the curators thought... She'd cross that bridge when she came to it. Maybe she'd be able to return the locket by then. All she needed was the inscription translated.

Which should lead her to the next clue in the puzzle.

What that puzzle would reveal, she had no idea. She didn't care either. It could be a king's ransom in gold or a treasure map or proof aliens existed.

All she wanted was the truth she'd been promised.

She leaned against the kitchen counter, taking a long look around. Living in such a big space by herself was a little lonely at times. Having Waffles around really helped. Having another cat would be twice as good.

She smiled, imagining the pitter-patter of little feet.

So what if she was a little lonely? Having such a secure, safe place to call home was a gift. And it wasn't *that* lonely. Her father, Imari, and Hattie came over to visit every once in a while, or she'd go to their big Victorian on Shadows Drive. After sundown, of course.

She really enjoyed her time there, especially when Hattie showed off her gardens. It gave Kora great pleasure to see her mémé so happy.

But there'd be no visiting tonight. She was on duty at Insomnia until six a.m., which meant at some point she was going to have to slip out and make her trip to the library.

Hopefully, her absence at the club would go unnoticed. She imagined she could do everything she needed to in fifteen minutes or less, especially if she traveled at vampire speeds.

Having an alibi wasn't absolutely necessary,

especially if no one noticed she was gone, but it couldn't hurt in case the locket was discovered missing before Miami. She hoped it didn't come to that, but there was no way of knowing how all of this would unfold.

She left Waffles to his dinner and went to change. She dressed in her standard black leather, choosing leggings with knee-high, flat-soled boots and a bustier with a slim jacket over it. No dress and heels tonight. She had to be able to move quickly.

And while she'd normally have her little belt bag of supplies with her on a job like this, she wouldn't need it tonight. Or at least, she couldn't foresee needing it.

She did her hair and makeup, tucked a pair of gloves into the jacket's inside pocket, and went back to the kitchen for a little liquid refreshment. She needed to be fully fueled this evening.

Waffles was lying on the kitchen counter, cleaning himself.

She snorted at his boldness. "You know you're not allowed up there."

He ignored her, and she made no move to shoo him off. She was either a terrible cat mother or the best one ever.

She poured herself some sustenance, and as she drank her dinner, an image of Greyson popped into her head. She sighed. Her mind sure liked to bring him to the forefront of her thoughts lately. Probably a side effect of living in the same town with him. And she had seen him three times this week.

That was all it was. Proximity. Because she certainly wouldn't be thinking about him for any other reason.

Still, his image lingered.

Why? Was her subconscious trying to warn her?

Did he suspect something? She shouldn't have gone to the exhibit three times, but the first time was to be sure the locket was there. The second time was to map the place out and see what kind of security had been added, and the third time was because her nerves had gotten the best of her.

The need to double-check everything had overruled her good sense not to go.

But Greyson probably just thought she was fascinated by all the sparkly things. He knew she liked jewelry. No doubt that was all he thought. She'd been drawn by the glitter. There was no way he'd ever imagine why she was really there. How could he?

Too bad he was so critical of her. And so full of himself. And knew how attractive he was. If not for those faults, he would have been the kind of vampire she could see herself spending time with.

Actually, there was one more *big* fault that disqualified him for that pleasure: He was also her father's errand boy. Okay, that wasn't fair. Greyson was no *boy*. Not by a long shot. He was very much a man.

Kora exhaled at the sudden and unexpected heat that had built up in her belly. Dumb hormones. Greyson was not for her. He was too much in her father's pocket and knew too much about her past. And he judged her by it.

Always would, too. She knew the type. He thought he was superior because he'd come riding in on his proverbial white horse to rescue her. More than once. But not because he really was some kind of white knight. What he'd done for Kora he'd done because her father had hired him.

That was part of what colored his view of her. But what would he think if he knew about Waffles? Would that change his mind about her?

Didn't matter, though, because the days of needing rescue were over. She could rescue herself now. No, wait. She wasn't going to need rescuing, because she wasn't doing dumb things anymore.

Except for tonight's little robbery. And the upcoming adventure to follow. But after that, she was utterly and completely done with those kinds of shenanigans.

"Keep a good thought for Mama, Waffles. I have to do a little breaking and entering, and I don't want to get caught."

But she couldn't back out now. She had a valid reason for needing that locket. She drained the last of the liquid in her glass, then ran her tongue over her fangs.

If you could call doing the bidding of someone named the Fox *a valid reason*.

Whatever. She had to stop second-guessing her decision to go along with this task. She was doing it, and that was that.

She gave Waffles a quick pat on the head, then went back to her room, put on a pair of diamond stud earrings and a bracelet of jet beads and diamond rondels set in platinum, then tucked her phone into her jacket pocket. Time to get to work.

Something told her it was going to be a long night. And not just because she was planning on breaking the law in a few hours.

Greyson sat at the bar at Howler's, nursing a beer he wasn't really interested in. He just wasn't ready to go home.

He couldn't shake the feeling that Kora was up to something. Call it instinct, call it experience, call it time spent with a woman who'd never met a rule she thought applied to her, but his vampire senses were tingling with concern.

What the something she might be up to was, he didn't know, but a safe guess said it involved the broken locket she'd stood in front of for so long. And come to see three times. Why on earth would she want that thing? Especially when it wasn't even whole.

That didn't seem like Kora's style. He knew she liked antique jewelry, but all the pieces he'd seen her with had been in mint condition.

Maybe her tastes had changed. Anything was possible. But he doubted it was as simple as that.

Was it because the locket had belonged to the Romanovs? Was there some connection there? He vaguely remembered something Lucien had once said about his ex-wife being of Russian decent. But had he meant by human birth or vampire siring? Because most vampires, once turned, considered their sire's bloodline first and their human one second. In fact, some vampire bloodlines were far more prestigious than any human ones could ever be.

But a reaper might not have taken that into consideration.

Greyson pondered the situation a little more, allowing his mind to go down some unlikely rabbit holes.

The most unlikely was that Kora thought her mother was a descendant, vampirically speaking, of the infamous Rasputin, the mystic to the Romanov family and the vampire who'd turned the eldest daughter in time to save her from the fate of the rest of her family. Or at least that was the story.

If that was the case, did Kora think the locket was somehow a piece of her mother's history? That it might give her some insight into the woman who'd abandoned her? Or entrance into that particular vampire family group?

Stranger things had happened. In fact, Kora had done stranger things. On more than one occasion.

Bridget came by, tossing a bar towel over her shoulder as she stopped in front of him. "You look lost in thought."

He nodded. "I wasn't aware it was that obvious."

She grinned. "Well, I asked you twice if you want another beer and didn't get an answer, so I figured I better come over here and check on you."

"You did? I didn't hear you." He sighed. This thing with Kora was bothering him more than he'd realized. "Sorry. I'm good on the beer."

"No worries. Just making sure you're okay. That you're, you know, not going to walk into the sun, or whatever a vampire like you might do." She winked at him.

He laughed. "No, that's not going to happen. Promise." She'd probably winked because she knew the sun wouldn't have any effect on him anyway. Not unless he took off the little bag that hung around his neck. But most people in town knew he was one of the rare vamps who could daywalk.

"All right. Good to know. Can't have my place getting a rep for depressing vampires." Still smiling, she went off to check on the next customer.

He took a pull off the bottle in front of him, realizing too late it had gone warm. That was all the sign he needed that it was time to go. He left some money on the bar and took off, giving Bridget a wave as he went.

As he walked toward his car, his brain continued to work. The exhibit was being packed up, but it wasn't going to be loaded on the truck until very early in the morning, which left plenty of time for something to happen.

And maybe, if he hadn't been working security on the exhibit, he wouldn't have cared. Maybe, too, if

Kora hadn't been involved, he could have left it alone.

But he had and she was and he couldn't.

He climbed into his Camaro, started it up, and drove out to the library. He slowed as he approached. Security lights were on, but there was no sign of anyone in the building that he could see. No cars in the lot either.

He pulled in and drove all the way around, just to be sure. The library had a loading dock in the back along with a man door, and there was no way to see anyone parked back there unless you made the trip around.

But that part of the lot was empty, too. Not like Kora drove an inconspicuous car either. Her black Ferrari was a gift from her father. A little much, in Greyson's opinion, but prodigal kids tended to get spoiled like that.

He stopped at the exit to the parking lot. She wouldn't have been so dumb as to actually drive her car here anyway. Not when there was no reason to. She had a keycard to access the Basement, just like he did.

And the library had an access door.

If Kora wanted, she'd never have to step foot outside to get into the library.

He tapped his fingers on the wheel in frustration. That left him with only one option. He had to find Kora. And he had to keep an eye on her.

At least until the exhibit was loaded and on its way to Florida.

Good thing finding Kora was easy.

He turned toward home. If he was going to Insomnia, he had to look the part. But he also didn't want Kora to think he was there specifically to keep an eye on her. He needed some cover. Fortunately, he had a pretty good idea where he could get some.

A few hours later, he rolled into the club with Undrea Seely on his arm and two more of her friends around him. Not only was Undrea unnaturally beautiful (being a mermaid had its advantages), but they'd established a while back that they weren't destined to be anything but friends.

She'd installed an aquarium for him at his place. That was her business. She ran a place called Tanks A Lot that not only set aquariums up for people and businesses, but also maintained them.

After breaking up with Jayne, he'd needed a distraction. Undrea had helped with that and become a friend in the process.

But that was all the chemistry they had. Just friends. It was fine with him. Gave him someone new to hang out with.

Tonight, however, he might be fighting the men off her. Undrea had worn a rose-gold sequin jumpsuit that matched the color of her long hair. She'd highlighted her skin with more gold glitter. Even her chunky platform sandals were gold. She looked like a disco queen—in the best possible way.

Her friends, Mattie Sharpe, a green witch who kept bees and made magical honey, and Caroline Linzer, a feline shifter whose family owned the pet store in town, both looked pretty spectacular, too.

The ladies had shown up in a big way. There wasn't a chance their group would go unnoticed. Even in a place like Insomnia, where the supernaturals let it all hang out.

But that was pretty much what he wanted. For Kora to see that he was there and that he was occupied.

As soon as they were in the club, he found a server, handed her his credit card, and asked to be seated in the VIP lounge. That would keep them visible, but not too visible thanks to the sheer white curtains that draped the space.

With the women dressed as spectacularly as they were and him in black, he'd be easy to overlook, making it simple to assume he was there even if he wasn't. Also part of his plan.

When they were settled into a spot, he ordered two bottles of excellent champagne, a fruit tray, and a dessert tray. And he let the server know to refresh whatever ran out until the women told her otherwise.

The women gave him a round of applause, and Undrea lifted her glass to toast him. "This is incredibly nice of you, Greyson. Whatever the reason."

He shrugged it off with a smile. "I just thought you lovelies needed a night out."

"No argument there," Mattie said. "Thank you for including us in this impromptu celebration."

"Thank you for being available." He leaned against the leather couch, resting his arms along the back. "I've been promising Undrea an evening out since she installed my tank. I figured it would be more fun if she had her girlfriends along."

"Sure," Undrea said. "More fun for me."

He laughed. "Is it a crime to enjoy being surrounded by beautiful women?"

They all grinned and shook their heads.

Caroline smiled shyly. "I've never been out with a vampire before." She suddenly went pink. "I mean, I know we're not on a date. We're just out. In a group. But we're together." She squeezed her eyes shut suddenly and exhaled loudly. "You know what I mean."

The other women laughed good-naturedly. Greyson thought she was adorable. Far too young for him to even consider dating. If anything, she was prime little sister material. He gave her a warm smile as she opened her eyes. "I know exactly what you mean, Caroline. But you have nothing to be afraid of, I promise you."

Her blush subsided. "That's very kind of you to say. But I'm not afraid." Her pupils narrowed into vertical slits, and she waved her fingers at him, the tips of which now sported the long, curved claws of her kind. "I'm not exactly defenseless."

He put a hand to his heart as if taken aback. "You are not. None of you women are, which, I might add, makes you especially enjoyable company." He raised his glass to them. "To strong women and the men they allow in their presence."

That got them toasting and laughing and drinking their champagne. It also put him firmly in their good graces, although truthfully, he was certain the drinks and nibbles had already done that.

As their server arrived with the fruit and dessert platters, he excused himself to head toward the main bar. He hadn't seen Kora yet, and he was a little concerned that he'd miscalculated.

If she'd already gone back to the exhibit—

"Greyson."

He turned at the familiar female voice. "Kora." He raked his gaze over her outfit. "Don't you look Goth?" She did a bit, but not fully with that icy-blonde hair. But black leather was black leather.

She would have been beautiful covered in mud.

A smirk greeted him. "Says the man dressed like a Johnny Cash impersonator."

He glanced down at his clothing. "This jacket is a very dark burgundy velvet, I'll have you know." But his pants, shoes, belt, and shirt were black. He frowned at her. He wasn't about to admit she had a point. Even if she had a point.

Her eyes narrowed. "Isn't your harem missing you?"

So she'd noticed. "I'm sure they are."

"I'll let you get back to them, then. I have actual work to do."

Impulse took hold of him. "You must have really enjoyed the exhibit. I saw you there again today."

Something flashed in her eyes, but it was gone too quickly for him to interpret. The falseness of her smile, however, was easy to read. "You know how much I like sparkly things."

He wasn't buying that. "Uh-huh. But you know that stuff's not for sale, right?"

The smirk returned, a little haughtier this time. "I think I hear the sound of vacuous laughter and empty champagne glasses."

Was that edge to her voice jealousy? He grinned without even trying. "Now, now, Kora. The green tinge to your words is terribly unbecoming. Those women are lovely. You might even try getting to know them. Friends are a wonderful thing to have."

Her mouth dropped open, then snapped shut as her gaze smoldered with indignation. "You really think a lot of yourself, don't you, Vampire?"

He shrugged with all the nonchalance he could muster. "I know what I'm capable of, if that's what you're asking. But then, I suppose you know that based on Rome alone."

The smolder burst into flames. "That's never going to happen again."

"Good. It's about time you grew up."

"Why did you come here tonight? It's been so peaceful without you around."

His brows lifted. "To show my friends a good time. Which means I'm spending a lot of money in your father's establishment. I'm good for business, Kora. Maybe try to remember that."

That seemed to give her a moment of pause. She considered his words, then schooled her expression, raising her chin slightly. "Well, then. I hope you and your friends have a wonderful evening, Mr. Garrett."

"I'm sure we will. If we can be left alone to do just that."

"Don't worry. I won't be on the floor much tonight. I have plenty of work in the office to keep me busy." She sent one last searing gaze in his direction, then took off toward the other side of the club.

He watched her for a moment. Hard not to when she had a body like that. But she was on edge. That much seemed plain to him by the instant reaction she'd had to his presence. She'd shown more than her usual disdain when she'd seen him. And to Greyson, that spoke volumes.

It also confirmed his suspicions. It was interesting, too, that by telling him she had to work in the office, she was already explaining her future absence.

But Greyson knew where to find her. He planned on being there, too.

He went back to the VIP lounge and settled in. His gaze remained on the club floor, but Kora was as good as her word. There was no sign of her.

Half an hour later, it was time to move. He excused himself from the party again, telling the women he had a phone call to make and that he'd be back as soon as he could.

Then he used his vampire speed to slip away unnoticed. By the time he reached the Basement, the thumping bass from the club had faded and his mind was all business.

The business of Kora and the locket. He wasn't quite sure what he was going to do if she took it, other than confront her and get it back.

The rest would just happen as it happened. He inhaled deeply. Kora's distinctive scent lingered, but very faintly. If she'd passed this way recently, it would have been stronger.

He sped to the stairs that led up to library. At the door, he slipped his keycard through the reader, then slowly opened the door, every sense alert for Kora's presence.

The library felt empty. Good. He'd gotten there first.

He kept out of the pools of light spilled by the security spots, hugging the walls as he made his way through the reference section and into the exhibit hall.

Then he stopped. The locket wasn't in there anymore. Nothing was. It had all been packed up. He changed direction toward the back of the library and the loading dock.

The crates were all there. Neatly stacked, marked with the codes assigned by the exhibition company. He had no way of knowing which one the locket would be in. Did Kora?

It would be interesting if she did. To him, that would imply a much deeper involvement. Could she be pulling some kind of insurance heist with one of the curators? Nothing was impossible. But if that was the case, why not take something more valuable?

Unless the locket was just a ruse.

He sighed. Whatever she was up to, he would do his best to keep her from making this huge mistake. Not for her so much as for Lucien and Hattie. And for Elenora. Having her exhibit robbed would turn her livid.

She'd take her anger out on Greyson first, no questions asked. Once Kora's involvement was revealed, she'd feel Elenora's wrath, too. Possibly Lucien, too, if Elenora really went ballistic. There was no telling how much damage Elenora would do if something her name was attached to had this kind of trouble.

He found a dark corner of the bay. The ceiling was open above, just HVAC lines and steel beams. He leaped up, landing on one of the cross sections. Dust puffed up where his feet touched. He walked to the far wall that was in shadow, leaned against it, and settled in to wait.

Waiting was boring, but easy. Passing time was nothing to a vampire who'd already seen more days go by than most monuments. There was a mode vampires shifted into, a kind of half-on, half-off limbo. Not sleep, but not fully awake either.

Like a motion sensor waiting for something to break the plane of stillness.

And so Greyson slipped into that mode, shutting down but not off. Conserving energy until he needed it.

Awaiting the woman who, once again, was going to need him to rescue her.

One thing led to another, and before Kora knew it, hours had passed. Some nights were like that at the club. One small fire after another needing to be put out. But she was getting antsy now. She had to go. Had to get to the library before the armored truck arrived and everything was loaded and gone.

She finished the schedule for next week, hit save on the computer, then headed out to the club floor to pass the word that she needed some time alone in her office. The bar manager was already headed toward her with an obvious problem.

Kora started to shut the man down, then took a breath and hoped it was something that could be dealt with quickly. "What's wrong?"

"There's a group of tourists at a high-top in the bar, shifters by the scent of them, and the credit card they gave me won't—"

"Will, you can handle this." She smiled, trying to

convey her confidence in him. "You don't need me for a credit card issue."

"But they're saying they're friends of your father's and —"

"Lots of people say that. Just be polite and handle it. If polite doesn't cut it, get one of the bouncers to back you up. Now I must have twenty minutes alone in my office, or I am not going to get this payroll done. You do want a check this week, don't you?"

"Yes." He looked mildly subdued. "I'll handle the shifters. I'll get Bret to go with me if they give me any more grief."

Bret was a bear shifter and doorman Chet's younger brother. He'd just moved to Nocturne Falls, and Insomnia had hired him immediately. "Great. Let everyone else know I'm not to be disturbed, okay?"

"Yes, ma'am."

She smiled. "Thanks." Being called *ma'am* was weird. She was not used to that at all. With a single glance toward the VIP lounge, where Greyson's party was still thankfully in full swing, she slipped back to her office, out through another door, and down the hall that led to the Basement.

Fifteen minutes. Twenty, tops. She could do this. She had to do this. She sped forward, the Basement passing in a blur until she reached the library steps. She paused there for just a second, absorbing a scent that lingered nearby. Cinnamon. She wrinkled her nose and glanced up. Someone was baking something somewhere, but then, it was a little after four a.m., and that was about the time places like Mummy's diner and Zombie Donuts started work on their goodies.

Neither of those places was near the library, however. Must be traveling through the air vents.

Whatever. She had work to do. With as much speed and quiet as she could manage, she went up the steps and into the library. She took a moment as she eased the door open, listening hard for any sound that might tip her off to someone else's presence.

Nothing that she could hear, but that didn't stop her nerves from pinging like crazy. She forced herself to ignore them. The old Kora would have done this just for the kicks, but now that she'd gone straight and had a purpose, she was nervous.

Go figure.

She closed the door quietly, then made her way to the loading dock. The crates were all there, ready to go. Unfortunately, she had no idea what the locket's inventory number was.

She did have a place to start looking, though. The prefix 0079. It was what the exhibit company used as the code for Slavic antiquities. She'd learned that much when digging around online. The Romanov locket fell into that category.

She took the gloves out of her jacket pocket and put them on, then got to work. The loading area was dark, lit only by a single security light over the man door.

As much as she would have liked to turn on more lights, she couldn't risk it. Instead, she had to rely on her vampire eyesight. But things would have moved faster with more light.

It didn't help that the numbers on the boxes weren't all showing either. Some she couldn't read until she moved another box off the top. Others had to be turned around.

All in all, it took her a good couple of minutes of careful hunting to locate the Slavic boxes. Then she had no choice but to open them all to examine the contents.

Her fifteen- to twenty-minute time frame was rapidly disappearing.

She could only go so fast with the individual items. She didn't want to damage a piece and be responsible for that. After all, she wasn't here to steal the locket so much as borrow it until such time as she no longer needed it.

Maybe a day or two. The inscription merely needed translating. That was it. At least, that's what she imagined. But what if the locket was a bigger part of the puzzle than she knew? Maybe the inscription's translation would help her figure that out.

Using brute strength, she pulled the tops off the sealed crates. The nails squealed as they came out of the wood. She dug through the packing material and started unwrapping items one by one. When she didn't find the locket, she replaced the items and sealed the crate back up, using her fist to pound the nails into place again. That way, when she found the locket, the cleanup would be done. The idea, after all, was to leave everything as she found it so that the missing piece wouldn't be discovered until the exhibit was unpacked in Miami.

But it was tedious work. And all the while, minutes kept ticking away.

She'd seriously underestimated how long this was going to take. Finally, she found the half of the locket. She got the lid quickly back on the crate, peeled off her gloves, and stuck them back in her pocket, then held the piece up to the light for a moment.

"At last," she whispered.

A soft *whoosh* filled the space behind her.

"I knew you'd come for it."

She turned, snatching the locket into her hand. "Greyson. What are you doing here?"

He scowled. "Keeping you from doing something foolish."

Panic welled up in her. "You don't understand."

"I understand enough. You're about to steal that locket, but I can't let you do that."

"I'm not stealing it, I'm—"

"Spare me the lies. I know you, remember?"

"You knew the old me. I'm not like that anymore."

He rolled his eyes. "Sure." Then he held out his hand. "Give it to me."

"No. I need it. Just for a day or—"

Metal screeched against metal as the loading bay's overhead door started to roll up.

Kora froze, realizing too late that arguing with Greyson had caused her to ignore the arrival of the armored truck.

She could not get caught stealing the locket. That would entangle her in too much drama to finish her task.

So as the door revealed them, she did the only thing she could think of to buy herself an excuse.

She grabbed Greyson by the collar of his jacket and kissed him.

Greyson almost managed to sputter out a question, but his words died against Kora's soft, lush mouth. He couldn't even remember what he was about to say. Just that she was kissing him and running her hands over his torso like she couldn't get enough.

It was heady stuff, to say the least.

He was vaguely aware of the men from the armored truck. Still held rapt by the kiss, he raised a hand, finger up, asking the people with the armored truck for one more minute. Whatever had caused this kiss, he saw no harm in letting it play out a moment longer.

After some inscrutable length of time, Kora broke off the kiss. She smiled coyly at the men. "Um, hi. Are we, uh, in your way?"

Deputy Jenna Blythe stepped forward. "Greyson, what's going on?"

He had a split second to make a decision. A choice that would color everything that happened from here on out. But no decision was without consequences. He picked the one he thought had the fewest. "I thought I should be here to keep an eye on the loading. And then..."

Kora laughed. "Then I showed up and surprised him." She grinned at him, trailing a finger down his cheek with surprising tenderness. "I guess our little secret isn't a secret anymore, huh, sugar lips?"

Sugar lips? He struggled to keep his top lip from curling. Instead, he smiled and pulled Kora close, his grip on her hips anything but loving. "That's right, snuggle button." He shrugged at Jenna. "The heart wants what the heart wants."

Jenna looked unconvinced, and Greyson couldn't blame her. His lack of love for Kora was no secret. Nor was Kora's reputation for getting into trouble.

The deputy approached them. She cocked a finger at Kora. "Come over here and turn around. I'm going to frisk you."

Greyson almost groaned. This was it. Kora would be found out, and chances were, he'd end up going down with her. He could spit he was so mad. He should have known better. She was nothing but trouble. Lucien was going to owe him.

Kora pouted. "What for?"

"Because there's too much money on the line not to." Jenna put her hand on her Taser. "Now, Ms. Dupree."

If Greyson had needed to breathe, he would have held his breath. He wasn't sure what Kora would do. The truck drivers were human. Doing anything that revealed her true nature would result in an even worse conclusion to this mess.

For a second, Kora didn't move. Then she lifted her chin, sauntered over, turned around, and put her hands on top of her head. She certainly knew the drill. She gave Greyson a smug look. "Go ahead, Officer. But you're not going to find anything. I just came by to surprise my lover."

Greyson choked back a retort.

Jenna frisked Kora with the kind of thorough intent Greyson had previously assumed was reserved for the most severe offenders. But all she produced was a pair of latex gloves from inside Kora's jacket. "What are these?"

"Gloves."

Jenna frowned. "Why do you have them?"

"Have you ever worked at a club like Insomnia? You never know what you're going to find. I like to be prepared."

Jenna stuffed the gloves back into the jacket pocket. "You're free to go. You, too, Greyson. I appreciate you showing up, but I've got this covered. And Deputy Cruz is on his way over. He's escorting the truck to the state line. Anyway, it might be best if you saw Ms. Dupree back to wherever it is she came from."

"I'll see to it." Greyson wasn't sure how Kora had hidden the locket so efficiently, but they were definitely going to talk. But not about the kiss. He never wanted to talk about that. Not about why it had happened, not how it had warmed him from stem to stern, not how he was thinking about doing it again just to see if his first reaction had been some kind of fluke.

None of it.

He took Kora by the elbow and ushered her through the library and back to the Basement access door. He swiped his card through the reader and got them down the steps. When they hit the Basement level, he spun her around. "What the hell was that?"

"Self-preservation," she snapped right back at him.

He glowered at her. She wasn't making any sense. "What are you talking about?"

She crossed her arms. "What are you talking about?"

"The locket."

"Oh."

He snorted. "You thought I meant the kiss?"

Her eyes narrowed ever so slightly, and her head tilted to one side. "Still on your mind, I see."

"Only because it was so utterly revolting."

"Oh," she said, making a big show of smacking the heel of her palm against her forehead. "I didn't realize you were still pining for the blue-haired elf princess who tossed you aside for the necromancer."

The muscles in his jaw locked up. He forced himself to relax. "I'm *not* pining. That's long over. I just don't want your mouth on mine. Understood?"

She shrugged. "I had to do something to cover why I was there. And I did. So cool it. Jenna's none the wiser."

"None the wiser? Really? She *frisked* you. Or did you forget that already?"

Kora put on an obviously fake smile. "But she didn't find anything, did she?"

"No." Greyson stared at her. Hard. "And why is that?"

"Because I'm smarter than Deputy Blythe." Kora leaned in, putting her hands on his chest. Then one hand dipped down into his jacket pocket and came back with the missing half of the locket. "And also, apparently, you."

A litany of curses filled Greyson's head. He snatched at the locket, but Kora yanked it out of reach just in time.

"Nope. I need this."

He growled at her. "It doesn't belong to you."

"I'm not keeping it. I'm just borrowing it."

"Right."

"I am."

He gave her his best skeptical look. "So you'll be returning it, then?"

"That's the plan."

"You're lying."

She had the audacity to look miffed. "I am not. And as much as I'd like to stand here and debate this with you, I don't really care, and I have to get back to the club."

She started to walk away from him, but he grabbed her arm. "Not until you hand over that locket."

She pulled her arm away, but turned to face him. "Greyson, it's not going to happen, so let it go."

"Then I'm reporting you. To the sheriff, to your father, to Elenora. I'm not going to be on the hook for this. I'm done pulling you out of the fires you start. You want to walk around dousing everything in lighter fluid, be my guest, but deal with the consequences on your own."

She stared at him for a moment, then sighed long and hard. "Why can't you just leave me alone? Just let me do what I need to do."

"I should just turn a blind eye to your thievery? Really?"

"I told you, I'm not stealing the locket, I'm—"

"Borrowing it. Right. You mentioned that. And then I called you a liar. We've done this." He put his hands up, at his wits' end with her, and started backing toward the library stairs. "I have to go speak to Deputy Blythe."

A low, guttural growl spilled out of Kora. "Fine. I'll tell you the truth."

He stopped walking. He'd listen. But he was fully prepared for another of her stories that would be as full of crap as a baby's nappy. "Go on."

She frowned and sighed again and shifted from one foot to the other. "I just need the full inscription on the locket so I can get it translated. As soon as I have that, I'll get the locket back to the exhibit."

He shook his head and stared at the passageway's lights. "You don't even see the giant hole in that tale, do you?"

Her brows bent in consternation. "What are you talking about?"

He snorted. "You stole *half* of a locket. How on earth can you get the inscription translated when you don't have the whole thing?"

One side of her mouth curved up in an irritatingly charming grin. "Oh, but I *do* have the whole thing. The other half is already in my possession."

A few wheels turned in his thought process, and he realized something that made him angrier than he already was. "Then this is the second criminal act you've committed. That only reaffirms my need to turn you in."

"I didn't steal the other half of the locket. It was sent to me." Her eyes widened a little, like she'd realized she'd revealed too much. "Anyway, I have to go."

He flashed forward to block her path. "You expect me to believe that?"

"I don't care what you believe, but it's true. And that's all I'm going to tell you. Now get out of my way."

"Who would send you such a thing? And why?"

"This conversation is over. Besides, don't you need to speak to the deputy?"

She was uncommonly resolved. He calmed his tone. "Kora, what's going on? Why don't you want to talk about it?"

Her mouth pursed, and for a moment, he thought he was about to get kissed again. Then she scowled at him. "Greyson, don't act like you care about what's happening with me all of a sudden. I know how you feel about me. What you think of me. You've made that abundantly clear."

"Those feelings are mutual, and you know it. Doesn't mean we can't put those feelings aside for a moment if you really need help." He shrugged one shoulder. "Despite what you think of me, have I ever done anything that wasn't to help you?"

"You mean, have you ever done anything to help me that my father wasn't paying for?" She raised her brows. "No."

"Help is help." He crossed his arms. "What's going on?"

"I can't tell you."

"What do you think will happen when I let the deputy and your father in on your theft?"

She glared at him, the anger in her eyes almost visible as flames. "For someone who purports to be such a bad boy, you're a complete suck-up, you know that?"

"I'm not going to apologize for being an adult. You should try it sometime."

"Shut up, Greyson. I'm being very adult, for your information."

He was getting to her. He smiled. "Then keep it up and tell me the truth."

She glanced around. "Not here."

Now that was interesting. "Where, then?"

"Back at the club. My office."

"Fine." He held his hand out. "But until you explain everything, I'm holding on to the locket."

"You promise not to turn me in until you hear my side of the story?"

"I promise."

With a much put-upon sigh, she handed the locket over. "Don't lose it, though, okay? I'm not going to get a second chance at this."

Kora was happy for the silence that accompanied them back to Insomnia. Not that she didn't enjoy the verbal sparring she and Greyson engaged in, but she needed to get her head together and figure out what she was going to tell him.

The Fox had commanded her silence about this mission, but she had to tell Greyson something. Would the Fox truly penalize her for needing help? Surely he didn't expect her to do this completely on her own?

For the first time in her life, she was concerned about breaking the rules. Who was she that it bothered her? Or better yet, who was she becoming? An adult, apparently. Wouldn't Greyson be proud if he knew?

Well, maybe not so much proud, but surprised at the very least. Maybe as surprised as he'd been by that kiss.

A little smile bent her mouth, but he couldn't see her and wouldn't know what she was smiling about anyway.

That kiss had been a stroke of genius on her part. It had been the perfect cover. And as kisses went, she'd had worse. Much worse, truthfully. Greyson, once he'd recovered from the shock of her impulsive action, had turned out to be pretty talented in the kissing department.

A fact that pleased her and mortified her in equal parts. The mortification was all due to how pleased she'd been with his response. The way his mouth had known exactly how to set fire to every nerve in her body.

Almost as if he'd imagined kissing her before. Was that…was that possible?

"What now?"

She glanced at him. "What do you mean?"

"You sighed."

"No, I didn't."

"Yes, you did."

"I was just…breathing."

"Vampires don't need to breathe."

"I'm half reaper, you know."

He shot her a look, then shook his head and went quiet again.

She picked up the pace, stopped thinking about the kiss, and tried to figure out what she was going to tell him. She wasn't sure she could get away with less than everything. It wasn't the kind of situation that could be explained piecemeal. One detail would lead to another, and before you knew it, everything would be out.

Maybe she'd swear him to secrecy first. Impress on him how he absolutely had to keep everything she told him in confidence. But would he? He was her father's man, after all. Could she trust him not to tell Lucien?

She had her doubts about that.

"I'm going in this way. Where are you going?"

She turned to see him stopped at the Insomnia exit. "There's another door a little farther down. Leads into the offices."

"You go that way, then. I'm going to check in with the women who came with me this evening, make sure they're all right. Then I'll come back to your office."

She hesitated.

He frowned. "I'm not going anywhere else, I promise."

She didn't like it, but she didn't have much choice since she'd handed over the half locket. "Please don't take off with that locket. You don't understand yet how important it is to me."

His frown evened out to a hard line. "I said I promise. I can't do more than that."

Kora had said *please*. Greyson hadn't been aware she actually knew that word. Even her kiss hadn't shocked him quite so much. Whatever was going on with this locket was serious business. He hoped she would tell him the truth about it and not another of her wild tales, like she usually did when she had to explain her ridiculous exploits.

He went back into the club and up to the VIP lounge.

Undrea greeted him with a smile. "Long phone call."

He nodded. "And it's only led to more business I have to attend to. Listen, the tab is taken care of. You ladies enjoy what's left of the evening. I'm very sorry, but I have to go."

Mattie lifted her glass, which he saw was now water. "I need to go home anyway. This is about the latest I've been out since I moved here. But it was so much fun." She smiled at him. "And very generous of you to cover the bill. If you ever need any honey or beeswax, you just let me know."

"I will." Although he couldn't imagine when that might be. He smiled at Caroline. "I hope you had fun as well."

Her grin was instantaneous. "I did. Very much. Good thing I have today off, because I plan on sleeping until dinner."

Just like a cat, he thought. "All right, ladies. Get home safe. We'll do it again sometime."

With that, he left and went straight to Kora's office. He knocked once, then opened the door.

She wasn't alone, but after glancing at him, she went back to whatever business she was dealing with. "Just get the inventories in by this afternoon, all right?"

"Yes, ma'am." The man left, closing the door behind him.

"Lock it," she said to Greyson. "I don't want to be disturbed again."

He turned the bolt, then took a seat across from her desk. "So. What's the story I need to know?"

She settled in, hands on her desk. "Not long after I made the decision to stay here in Nocturne Falls, all due to the reconciliation with my father, I received a package. It contained the other half of the locket. The one that's supposedly been missing all these years."

"And?" Because there was no way that was all the package had held.

She stared at the desktop for a moment. "There was a burner phone, too, and a note with the locket.

54

Addressed to me. It said that I needed to find the other half of the locket, get the full inscription translated, then follow the clue that was revealed. And that I should keep doing that until the final treasure was revealed. That I would know what that final treasure was when I found it."

"And you were supposed to do all this why?" He could already guess that it was some kind of blackmail. She certainly had a past ripe for that sort of manipulation.

"Because if I did…" She held his gaze. "You have to swear to me that you'll keep this secret. I'm not supposed to tell anyone what I'm doing. I could lose what I've been promised."

"I can't do that. What if the next clue has you breaking into the Tower of London and stealing the crown jewels? I'm just supposed to keep quiet about that?"

"Yes. But I don't think it will."

He leaned in. "What are you so eager to keep hidden that you'll go to such lengths?"

"I'm not trying to keep anything hidden. I'm trying to find something out, actually."

Intriguing. "Such as?"

She closed her eyes for a moment. Trying to decide what to tell him, perhaps. At last she opened them, her gaze full of resolution and resignation. "Such as the truth about my mother."

That wasn't remotely what he'd thought she was going to say. "I thought your mother was dead."

"She is. I don't doubt that. But how did it happen?

When? Maybe…maybe something happened that prevented her from getting home that wasn't her fault. Maybe…she was trying to get home and…I don't know. But I want to know."

In that moment, he felt for her. He also understood. That longing to believe something different about your past, about the past of someone as influential as a parent, that was a driving force. He nodded. "Okay."

"Okay?"

He reached into his pocket and took the locket out. "You can have it back. But on one condition."

She looked wary. "What kind of condition?"

"I'm doing this with you. To make sure you don't get in over your head. Any more than you already are."

"You can't. That's a clear violation of what the note said to do."

"You realize that if you follow this through and find this treasure, you then hold all the cards? If the person behind this wants the treasure from you, they'll have to give you what you want."

She hesitated. "I suppose that's true. But what if they get mad that I've involved someone else and stop communicating?"

"Then you're off the hook for finding this thing and in no different a position than you were when you started."

She sighed. "Meaning I still won't know the truth about my mother."

"No. But…" He was about to make her an offer he'd probably come to regret. "Maybe we can look into it ourselves. I have a few contacts on the European Vampire Council who owe me favors. I can reach out to them."

It was her turn this evening to be shocked, judging by the look on her face. "You'd do that for me? Why? What do you want?"

"I don't want anything. I just understand what it's like not to have closure. Although, it would be nice if we could live peaceably in this town together. Especially since it seems like you're here to stay."

Her mouth quirked up in a wry smile. "That's asking an awful lot."

He gave her a similar look in return. "I realize that."

"We can work on it." She stood and stuck her hand out. "Deal."

He got to his feet and shook her hand. "All right, then. Let's get that inscription translated."

"You can read Russian?"

"No, but I know someone who can."

"Can they be trusted?"

"Absolutely."

"How soon can we—"

A knock on the door ended the conversation.

"Who is it?" Kora asked.

"Your father."

She looked at Greyson. "Unlock the door, please."

He did as she asked.

"Come in," Kora called.

The door opened, and Lucien walked in. "Hi, honey."

"Hi, Dad."

Lucien looked at Greyson, then back at Kora. "Everything all right?"

Greyson answered, knowing Kora wouldn't want anything revealed to her father. "Just seeing if I can get a discount on my tab. I ran up quite the bill this evening."

Kora rolled her eyes with clear disdain. "And I told him no."

Amazing how quickly she returned to her usual self.

"Kora." Lucien's tone had an unusually soft edge to it. "I think for Greyson we can offer a little—"

"No, that's fine." Greyson shook his head. "If that's how she wants it, I'll abide. Now, if you'll excuse me, I need to get some sleep." He made eye contact with Kora. "It's been a long night. And I have a feeling the next few days are going to be just as long."

As Greyson shut the door behind him, Kora grimaced. The man was still insufferable, even if he had offered to help. Which was just an offer at this point. She'd believe it when it came to fruition.

Her father sighed. "I wish you two didn't have such an adversarial relationship."

"Dad, stop trying to play matchmaker."

"I am *not* trying to play matchmaker. The last thing you need in your life is a relationship."

"Well, don't worry, because it's never going to be Greyson. He's a modern-day equivalent of a sellsword. And a man who rents himself out to the highest bidder is never going to be the man for me."

Lucien snorted. "You realize that highest bidder is usually me, and the work he's done has been to come to your rescue."

She frowned. "Don't remind me. In fact, let's not talk about Greyson anymore, all right?" She moved the mouse on her desk, bringing the computer monitor to life. "The evening's reports aren't done yet because I'm still waiting for cash-outs on a couple of the registers."

"I can handle it. Get some rest. You look tired."

She was exhausted, actually. Both from the stress of the evening's events and spending time with Greyson. Spilling her guts to him the way she had wasn't something she ever wanted to do again. She hated that his having so much information about her gave him leverage.

If he told anyone what was going on, this whole thing would come crashing down, and the answers about her mother would disappear forever. Because despite Greyson offering to help dig into the truth, Kora questioned how hard he'd really work on something like that.

Especially because it had just occurred to her how little Lucien would care for it.

If her father knew what she was doing and why, he'd shut it down. He despised his late wife. Kora knew that. And she understood. But Lucien would only think he was protecting his daughter.

He wouldn't comprehend how important finding out what had really happened was to her.

So she just smiled and nodded. "I am a little beat. Sunrise always does that to me."

She came out from around the desk, leaned in, and kissed him on the cheek. "Have a good day."

He put his hand on her arm. "Rest well. Mémé would love for you to come to dinner this evening."

"I'll call you later and let you know if I'm up to it."

"Okay." He smiled at her, his eyes filled with the kind of love they always had been, though she'd been too stubborn and bitter to appreciate it.

"Love you."

His smile widened. "Love you, too, honey."

She slipped out the side door that led to her underground home. She took the locket out as she walked toward her bedroom, eager to compare it to the half currently hidden in her underwear drawer.

But when she walked in and flipped on the light, something was off. "Waffles? Where are you?"

He was usually passed out on the bed, waiting for her.

"He's right here."

She jumped, whipping around to see Greyson standing in the doorway behind her, Waffles's bulk cradled in his arms like a baby.

The cat had the nerve to also have his eyes closed in bliss as Greyson rubbed his tummy.

"What are you doing here? Why are you holding my cat? Waffles, are you okay? Is the bad man bothering you?"

Greyson laughed. "That's a lot of questions. Now I have one for you. Waffles? Really?" He looked at the cat like they were suddenly best buds. "Women, am I right?"

Waffles stuck his front paws in the air and started kneading.

She huffed out a breath for punctuation. "What are you doing here? And put my cat down."

"I thought you wanted to get the inscription translated."

"I do, but why are you in my house?"

"Because it's where you are." He gave her an incredulous look. "Where else would I go?"

"But you're *in* my house."

"Right. Because you're here. Try to keep up."

She closed her eyes for a moment, attempting to preserve the calm he was eroding. Was he being deliberately obtuse to annoy her? If so, he was doing a bang-up job. Still, he had someone who could do the translation. She needed him for that much. She opened her eyes with new resolve. "*How* did you get in here?"

He held up his hand. A key dangled from one finger.

She frowned. "You can't have a key to my house."

"I wasn't aware you'd purchased this domicile from your father."

She ground her teeth together to keep from snapping his head off. "You know what I mean. I live here now. It was different when it was my father's place. It's not right."

He waggled his brows. "Worried I might sneak in and ravish you?"

A curse slipped out. Followed by a second one. She felt marginally better. "You really are full of yourself."

"For good reason." He put Waffles on the floor. The cat wound around Greyson's feet before sitting beside him. "I get things done."

Rotten little furry turncoat, Kora thought.

Greyson leaned against the doorjamb. "Do you want this thing translated, or don't you?"

"I do."

"Then let's go. I've already arranged it."

"You realize the sun's just about up." She put her hands on her hips. "Or are you trying to toast me?"

An odd look of concern crossed his face. "I'd forgotten about that. Hmm."

"I take it this individual isn't reachable through the Basement?"

"No. He lives up in the hills." Greyson rested his hand on his chin. "We could go in my car, if you're willing to use an umbrella to get from the car to his door."

"You want me to risk the sun?" She felt a little weak suddenly. Light-headed, even. Sounds went tinny, and the floor seemed to tilt beneath her. She reached out for the dresser a few feet away.

And found Greyson instead. "You okay? You got really pale. Which is saying something, all things considered."

She shook her head, unsure of her ability to form words in the moment.

He helped her to the bed and got her to sit. "What's going on? Are you okay?"

She put both hands on the bed to steady herself. "I'll be fine."

"But what happened? Was that all because of the idea of going out in the sun?"

She nodded. "It started not long after I got to town. Right after my dad and I made everything right." She swallowed. "The thought of being in the sun..."

He sat beside her. "Do you think it has something to do with your mother?"

"Oh, yeah. Definitely." She stared at the floor. "But why now? Why after so many years?"

"I don't know. Maybe reconciling with Lucien made you finally accept your mother's death?"

She thought about that. "Could be."

"Hey. It's okay. Everyone has something they have to deal with."

"Right." She gave him some serious side-eye. "What's your thing?"

"Oh, I don't have a thing. But most everybody else does." With a grin, he got back to his feet. "I'll make a phone call and see if we can meet this evening."

He turned and took his phone from his pocket.

She stuck her tongue out at him. Maybe being saddled with him was her penance for all the mischief she'd caused throughout her life.

If so, when this ordeal was over, she ought to be starting with a clean slate.

Greyson returned to Kora's house a few minutes before sundown. She'd be up. Probably had been for at least half an hour or so. Vampires, even those who were half reaper, could sense the sun's cycle. But he didn't let himself in this time. Instead, he rang the bell at the garage entrance, like any other visitor.

Although it was unlikely this house had seen many of those in its time. Lucien had built this place specifically to help him avoid people.

While Greyson waited, he looked around at the wealth of cars still parked in the massive underground space. But then, where else would Lucien keep his collection? The Victorian he and Imari had moved into was large, but only had a standard detached garage. And Greyson doubted the retired reaper would trust any of these machines to such plebian accommodations.

He glanced at the door. Then his watch.

By the time Kora came to open it, nearly ten

minutes had gone by. She either hadn't been up or had decided to make him wait.

He forgot all about complaining when he saw her. She looked...different. Maybe because she wasn't wearing black leather for a change. Instead, she was in gently distressed jeans, a white T-shirt, and a pale pink leather jacket, which while still leather, was a far cry from the dominatrix stuff she normally favored. Even her makeup was softer and more natural.

She could have been the girl next door. The incredibly beautiful girl next door, but still. The change was remarkable. "Wow."

"What?" she asked.

"You look different. That's all." He couldn't stop staring. Was she really wearing lip gloss? And why was he noticing that?

She didn't move out of the way to let him in. "Different good or different bad?"

So they were going to do this. "Different good. Softer. Less like a vampire. More like a lady who lunches."

She frowned. "Great." She stepped back, letting him in. "I'm trying to be more approachable."

"A more approachable vampire. Sounds like a recipe for disaster." He wasn't kidding either. A more approachable Kora could only lead to those who approached her getting spanked. Metaphorically speaking.

"Mémé said my look probably scared people. That it was all right for the club, but for everyday life, I should lighten up."

"She said 'lighten up'?"

"She did."

"Well, for what it's worth, I like it."

"Thanks." She smiled, but only for a second. Maybe she'd been hoping for a bigger reaction?

He didn't know what else to say. If she were his girlfriend, which was a weird thing to even think, he would have elaborated. As it was, they were barely friends. "You ready to go, then?"

She sighed. "Yeah."

"Listen, I like it. I really do. You look nice. I'm just not used to it. It's like a shark wearing a bow tie. Kind of makes you forget you're dealing with an apex predator."

She rolled her eyes. "You're just full of compliments."

"Hey, I get what you're going for, and I approve."

"Like I care about your approval."

And there was the Kora he knew.

She walked away from him into the house. "I have to feed Waffles, then I'm ready."

Greyson followed her. "Where is my boy? I bet he missed me."

He could have sworn he heard Kora growl softly under her breath. He grinned. She was too easy a target. He really should lay off. But why, when it was so much fun to spin her up?

In the kitchen, Kora pulled the top off a can of food and tipped it into a bowl. "Here, kitty, kitty."

Waffles came running into the room so fast he skidded halfway across the tile.

Greyson almost laughed at the scene. Kora was wearing pink and had a cat. He was living in opposite world.

Except nothing else about Kora was different. She still had a mouth on her. Still excelled at getting herself into trouble.

Still was as beautiful as ever.

He took a few steps toward the door. "Maybe I should wait outside."

"I'm ready." She grabbed a small handbag off the counter and slipped the long strap over her head, adjusting it to hang across her body. "I take it you're driving?"

"Yes."

They left the house together, walking out into the space that was more dream-car museum than garage.

In the midst of so many expensive, imported machines, Greyson's Camaro still held its own. At least in his mind. American muscle cars were a class unto themselves and a very different animal than the high-end European sports cars. Didn't mean he couldn't appreciate all the horsepower around him, but he didn't have any real envy either.

They got into the '69, and he took off.

She shifted in her seat so she was turned slightly toward him. "Are you going to tell me who we're about to see?"

"Ivan Tsvetkov. I don't think you know him."

"No, I don't. Should I?"

"He's a good guy. Worth knowing. So yes, you should. You might even try to be friends with his wife.

She's very nice. She's a Will-o'-the-Wisp."

"Interesting." Kora seemed unmoved by that. "I take it from his name that he's Russian?"

"Yes. He can translate. And he can keep a secret."

"Good. Because I need him not to say a word of this to anyone." She faced forward again.

But Greyson wasn't done talking. "How many times have you been contacted by the person who sent you the locket?"

"Just once. He calls himself the Fox."

"And you contact this Fox via the burner phone?"

"Yes, but it doesn't mean I'll get an answer. I've texted a few times since getting the package and not heard back. I'm guessing he'll reach out again when I get closer to the prize. If I get closer."

He nodded, thinking. "Why you? Just because he has information on your mother?"

"That's a question I've been asking myself." She stared out the window as the town went past. "I'm aware I could have been chosen because of my old reputation for being willing to break laws and that the promise of information about my mother could be a ruse just to get me to do what he wants."

He almost laughed. "Your *old* reputation?"

She glared at him. "You might not believe it, but I'm working hard to be a different person. More responsible. More aboveboard. More adult."

He shot a quick look at her. "Well, you look different, but as for the rest of it, good luck."

She huffed out a breath. "Thanks for the vote of confidence."

"You forget I've seen you at your worst. Several times. And the leopard doesn't change its spots."

"Just because that's a saying doesn't mean it's true. And I'm not a leopard. If I want to change, I can. And I will." She shook her head. "I *am* changing. I already have. I'm working a steady job, taking on responsibilities. I have a pet, for crying out loud."

"True." Maybe he should cut her some slack. But he still wasn't sure he believed all this new-leaf business. Didn't mean he wanted to rile her up right before they saw Ivan, though. He changed the subject. "How did you end up with Waffles, anyway?"

She leaned an elbow on the door, sliding her fingers around the back of her neck. "You know Chet?"

"The doorman at the club."

"Yes. He called my office one night and said there was a wounded animal in the warehouse entrance and asked what he should do with it. I went up to see what it was and found Waffles. He was a mess. He'd gotten into a fight with something and had a gash on his side. He was skin and bones, covered in fleas, fur matted up and filthy. Really struggling. But somehow he'd made it into the warehouse."

She put her hands in her lap and stared at them. "I think he was looking for a safe place to die."

A knot formed in Greyson's throat. He'd never considered himself an animal person, but the suffering of any innocent creature was hard to take. "Yeah, maybe."

"I'd never cared for another creature in my life at

that point. Animal or otherwise. Not outside of my mémé, anyway. But I'd just made things right with my dad and been spending time with my mémé—"

"Hattie is amazing."

"Yes, she is." Kora smiled for a moment. "Something inside me kind of broke when I saw that poor cat. I couldn't let him die. Maybe…because I'd just gotten a second chance, and I thought he deserved one, too."

Greyson's brows lifted, but he stayed quiet. Was it possible Kora had changed? He'd never imagined that she had this side to her.

"I don't know if he sensed that I wanted to help him, but he let me pick him up, and I rushed him to the twenty-four-hour emergency vet." She let out a dry laugh. "Long story short, nearly two grand later and he's doing great. I had to borrow the money from my dad, but I paid him back."

Greyson chuckled. "That must have been some conversation."

"It was. He didn't believe that I needed the money for a cat until I put the vet on the phone. And even then, I think he was skeptical. Not that I blame him."

Greyson didn't either, but he kept that to himself. "How did you end up naming the cat Waffles?"

"He was at the animal hospital for four days while they got him stabilized and healthy enough to have a fighting chance. When I went to pick him up, I put him in the new carrier I'd just bought and had him sitting by my feet while I paid the bill. There was a little girl there with her parents. Their dog was getting spayed, I think. They were picking him up, too. Anyway, the little girl came over to look at Waffles."

Kora's smile returned, a little distant and dreamy with the memory. "She was sticking her fingers through the front gate of the carrier, and he was leaning in, letting him pet her. Then she looked up at me and said, 'Waffles is a nice cat.'"

Kora shook her head. "I hadn't named him. I hadn't even really thought about keeping him at that point. I mean, I hadn't been sure he was going to make it. And me with a cat? Anyhow, I looked at the little girl and asked her how she knew his name was Waffles. She said that's what he told her."

Kora shrugged. "So that's how he became Waffles. Kind of fits him. He is warm and comforting."

Greyson smiled. "How about that? Not only did you gain a cat, but you met a certified cat whisperer."

"Right?" Kora laughed before staring at her hands again. "It's weird, though, isn't it? Me having a cat?"

"It is, but I like it. Makes you more…human."

She didn't react like he thought she would with some kind of outrage. Instead, she just nodded. "Yeah, I suppose it does. I'm even thinking he could use a feline friend."

"That's how it starts, you know." He turned onto the dirt road that led to Ivan's long paved drive. The paved section didn't start until after the bend, something Ivan had done as a way of disguising the entrance to his home in the hills. "Before you know it, you have twelve."

She raised one brow and looked at him. "Well, I have the room."

They both laughed, and for a moment, Greyson was so charmed by her he almost forgot how many times she'd nearly gotten him killed.

Kora hadn't intended to reveal so much to Greyson, but besides the sartorial advice she'd received from Hattie, her mémé had also told her to stop putting up walls. To let people get to know her. To be willing to be vulnerable.

Not only was that hard, but Kora had no idea why she'd chosen Greyson to practice on. Maybe because after all these months in Nocturne Falls, she still didn't have any real friends. Acquaintances, yes. People who said hello to her because they knew who she was, or really, who her father was.

Beyond that, her circle of friends was her father, his wife, Imari, and Hattie. The only other numbers in her phone's contacts list was the vet's office, some of the club's distributors, and Salvatore's delivery line. Even vampires had pizza cravings on occasion.

That contacts list proved she was living a pretty sad existence. But she was determined to change that. Just as soon as she put this mission behind her. In fact, finding out the truth about her mother felt like the perfect way to close out the final chapter of her old life.

With that information, she could stop looking behind her and focus on the future. On making real changes.

And with those changes, she hoped that she could make friends. As pathetic as that sounded. She was tired of being alone. Tired of being lonely.

A second cat wasn't going to solve that. Although Waffles could definitely use a buddy.

Greyson parked, and she looked up at the big log cabin in front of them. "I knew there were cabins in these hills, but this is my first time seeing one. Pretty impressive. Looks more like a chalet than a cabin."

"This one is sort of the cream of the crop. Most of the rest of them are more standard fare."

She got out of the car. "Compared to this, how could the rest not fall short? It's really beautiful."

She was used to wealth. Her father was one of the richest people she'd met in all her years. But knowing she was about to meet the man who lived in this house suddenly intimidated her a little. After all, she needed his help. And he needed nothing from her. Would he even agree to do the translation? Would he want payment?

She judged everything by her past. By what she would have done. It colored her world. How on earth was she supposed to move forward when she was so flawed?

"What's wrong?"

THE VAMPIRE'S PRICELESS TREASURE

She glanced at Greyson. "I don't have anything to offer him. And I can't afford to pay him."

Greyson's brows bent. "Van won't want payment. He's just reading some Russian. We're not asking him to do anything crazy."

"You're sure?"

Greyson nodded. "Absolutely."

That made her feel a little better, but some of the nerves remained.

Together, they walked up the stairs to the front door. The porches on the house ran all the way around it, providing incredible views of the surrounding hills and the town below. The lights made it seem so inviting.

One of these days, Kora was going to have to play tourist, take a night off, and see what Nocturne Falls was all about. More than she had, which wasn't much.

The door opened before Greyson could knock.

A huge man stood there, smiling at them. "Hello."

Behind him sat a large Doberman, tongue out.

"Hi, Van." Greyson shook hands with the man. "This is Kora Dupree. Lucien's daughter. She's the one who needs the translation."

"Nice to meet you, Kora." Van's accent was subtle, but very present.

She nodded at him, remembering to smile. "Nice to meet you, too. Greyson speaks very highly of you."

Van's smile broadened. "He is a good man. Come in." He patted the dog on the head. "Do not be afraid of Grom. He does not bite unless commanded to do so."

"Good to know," Kora said with a little laugh.

They went in, and Kora couldn't help but look around. "Your home is really great."

"Thank you very much." Van led them into the kitchen, where a gorgeous redhead was cleaning up. She was in leggings and a tunic-length T-shirt, showing off a very trim figure, and sneakers.

He put his arm around her. "This is my wife, Monalisa." Then he spoke to her. "This is Greyson's friend Kora."

Kora smiled. "Hello. Thank you for letting us come over."

"Nice to meet you, Kora." Monalisa folded the towel she held. "Van is always happy to help, and it's always nice to meet new people. I understand you haven't lived here very long?"

"No, not that long. I really need to meet new people, too." As hard as that was.

"Can I get either of you something to drink?" Monalisa asked.

"I'm fine," Kora said.

"So am I," Greyson added. "But thank you for the offer."

"No problem. And I know you have work to do with Van, so if you'll excuse me, I'm going to take Grom out for a walk. I hope we see you again, Kora."

"Thank you."

Monalisa headed for the door and took a leash off a hook on the wall there. Grom got to his feet instantly, his tail wagging excitedly. She hooked the leash to his collar, and the pair left the house.

Kora almost sighed in relief. With Monalisa gone, she wouldn't see the locket. Of course, there was nothing to stop Van from telling her all about it, but Greyson had said the man could keep a secret. Whether or not that included keeping it from his wife, Kora didn't know. But she imagined Greyson had made it clear that this was a delicate situation.

Van held his hand out toward the other half of the house. "Let's go to the living room, and you can show me this inscription."

They followed him into the next room and took seats on the overstuffed leather furniture. The sofa and chairs would have looked gargantuan in any other space, but in Van's home, with his size, they seemed perfect. Perhaps even custom made.

Greyson and Kora took the chairs while Van sat in the middle of the couch opposite them, making the thing look more like an oversized chair.

Greyson leaned back. "Really appreciate you doing this, Van."

"You know I am always happy to help." He scooted to the edge of the couch, resting his elbows on his knees and clasping his hands together. He looked at Kora. "Greyson tells me this matter must be kept quiet. I assure you, I will tell no one. I understand such matters, so you may trust me."

She nodded. "Thank you. That's good to hear. I'm really glad you're doing this for me, too."

He shrugged, his mountainous shoulders rising. "This is what friends do for friends." He held his hand out. "What would you like me to read?"

She reached into her purse. She'd put both halves of the locket into a small jewelry box. She took it out and opened it, then removed the two pieces. "There's an inscription on this locket that can only be read completely when the pieces are joined."

Van took his hand back. "You join them. My fingers are too large and not so nimble."

"Sure," she answered. She'd examined them earlier and had seen how they fit together. She held one piece perpendicular to the other and slid them together, then turned the first piece to align with the second.

They snapped together so seamlessly it was hard to tell they'd ever been separated. She tested the hinge to see how the locket opened. It worked perfectly. The locket hadn't been broken, but deliberately separated.

She left it open and held the now complete sun shape out to Van. "Here you go."

He took it from her and studied the words inside for a moment before looking at her again. "You have no idea what this says?"

"None. That's why I need you." She got her phone out, ready to type in the translation for safekeeping.

His eyes narrowed ever so slightly before his gaze returned to the inscription. He cleared his throat. "Seek the witch's heart in the dragon's hoard, but beware the pain of untrue love."

Greyson looked at Kora, whose thumbs were flying over the phone's screen. "What on earth is that supposed to mean?"

Van frowned. "I do not like this."

"Why?" Kora asked.

"Why do you think?" Van retorted.

Greyson shifted forward in his seat. "Van, she doesn't know what you are."

A little niggle of panic set Kora's inner alarms off. "Why does what he is matter?" It was clear Van was some kind of supernatural, but she hadn't bothered to ask. What mattered to her was his ability to read Russian.

Van's scowl creased his mouth and brow. "I am a dragon. But no one is seeking anything in my hoard. If I had a hoard. Which I am not saying I do."

Kora leaned back. "Okay, I don't know anything about any hoard. I just needed the translation. I don't think it really means—wait, do you *have* a hoard?"

Van glared at Greyson. "Vampire, this is not what we bargained for."

Greyson sighed. "Everyone just relax. Van, we had no idea what the inscription said. None. And, Kora, a dragon's hoard is a very private, personal thing. You don't just ask about a thing like that."

"Okay, I'm not asking. But the inscription does make it seem like I should be."

Van held up the locket. "Where did this come from? Who wrote this?"

Kora shook her head. "I have no idea who wrote it, but the locket's provenance says it's connected to the Romanov dynasty. Legend claims it may have belonged to one of the daughters. Perhaps Olga."

Van's expression changed to something much more haunted. "The Romanovs?"

"Yes."

He handed the locket back to her, then sighed heavily. "That was not a good time in Russian history."

"No, it wasn't," Greyson said. "And from a supernatural side of things, we know they were vampires. Turned by Rasputin. But I'm sure you know that since you're Russian."

"*Da*," Van said. He frowned again. "I mean to say yes, but sometimes my tongue slips. I also know of the line of Rasputin. And of the vampires turned by him who claim him as their sire. But I have not thought of such things in many years."

Kora's curiosity ticked up a notch. "Do you know anything else about them? The Rasputin vampires? Any stories you might have heard growing up?"

"What I know, I will tell you." Van rubbed his chin. "They say that Rasputin turned the Romanovs and a few of their servants right before they were murdered by the Bolsheviks. But the murders were successful anyway, because the Bolsheviks suspected they'd been turned. The Bolsheviks drenched everything in holy water and made their bullets out of blessed silver, etching crosses into the metal."

Kora cringed, realizing a second later that Greyson looked equally as ill.

Unfazed, Van continued. "Legend also says Rasputin foresaw the Bolsheviks' plan and informed the family, but also told them that because of his power, they would remain unharmed. The legend goes that one of the maids overheard all this and went running before the Bolsheviks came for the family. She took with her untold wealth in jewels and the source of

Rasputin's power and protection over the family."

He held up a finger. "She was not supposed to take that source. Because of her, the family was left vulnerable. Because of her, the family died."

Kora shuddered. "That's a horrible story."

Van sat back, almost looking pleased. "It is. But in Russia, these things happen."

He said it as though murdering whole families was commonplace. But then, they were talking about vampires and Bolsheviks, so maybe he had a point.

"Do you have any idea what that source of power was?"

Van shook his head. "None. But with Rasputin, I would say it was something valuable. He liked very much the money and power of the Romanovs."

"So…" Kora's mind spun with possibilities. She looked at Greyson. "We could be on a hunt for that source."

He nodded slowly. "I suppose it's possible."

She looked at Van again. "And if you have a hoard, I'd assume it's filled with valuable things. Could the source be among the treasures in it?"

Van's expression clouded over again. "*Nyet*. My hoard—if I have one—is my business."

"Van," Greyson started. "Dragon's have hoards. It's a known fact. And she's not looking to steal anything from you. But whatever this thing is that Kora's been tasked to find, it's very important. Not because of the thing's value, but because the person who wants it has promised to tell Kora what truly happened to her mother."

The hard line of Van's mouth softened. "I did not know." He sighed. "A dragon's hoard is a very personal thing."

"I understand," Kora said. "And I don't need to see it. I just need to know if this...witch's heart, I think is what you read, if that's in there."

Van made a face. "If I had a heart in a jar, I would know."

Kora gritted her teeth. "I really hope that's not what we're looking for, but my guess is the inscription refers to a shape. A witch's heart is almost like a typical heart shape, but the tail points to the right. They were very popular in Victorian times. They were meant to ward off evil spirits, that sort of thing. They could be made of tin, but they could also be made of gold and jewels. Anyone with a collection of valuable things might have one."

She pulled out her phone and brought up images of some, then turned it around to show Van what they looked like. "Do you think you have anything that looks like these?"

He peered at the screen. After a moment, he shook his head. "No. But...if one were to have a large collection of valuable things, they might not remember everything that is in it."

She tried to keep her smile to herself, but a small grin turned up the corners of her mouth despite her best efforts. "No, they might not."

Greyson paced a line in the carpet of Kora's living room. Why this was making him nervous, he had no idea.

"Sit down, will you?" Kora shook her head. "You're making Waffles jumpy."

Greyson stopped. The fluffy beast was standing on the arm of the sofa, looking a little unsettled. "Sorry, puss, but I know the feeling." He sighed at Kora. "I'm not the most patient man. I don't like waiting. If Van finds that he has the heart, that would mean we have the next clue."

"We?" Her brows rose. "Also, you realize that of all the dragon shifters in the world, the odds of him being the one who has the right witch's heart in his hoard are astronomically low."

Greyson raked a hand through his hair. "Yes, I know. But sometimes these things align."

She snorted softly. "Not in my life, they don't."

Waffles jumped off the arm to curl up on the sofa cushion.

Greyson sat next to him and dug his fingers into the animal's long fur, stroking him until he rolled over and showed his belly. "I'm just saying, you never know."

"No, you don't. But in this case, I kind of have a feeling. It would be too coincidental. And that would be a pretty easy clue, telling whoever reads the inscription exactly where to find the next piece of the puzzle. Something tells me it's not going to be that simple."

"No, I suppose not." He sighed.

She crossed her arms and her legs at the same time, sitting very straight in her chair. "Go back to the *we* you mentioned. Are you saying you want to take this journey with me? I know you mentioned that the other night at the club, but I didn't think you were serious."

He kept his eyes on the cat. It was easier than looking at Kora while he answered her. "We do work well together."

"That's not really an answer."

No, it wasn't, but he'd hoped it would be enough. So much for that. "I can keep you safe." He glanced at her. "Your father would appreciate that."

The downturn of her mouth and the narrowing of her eyes were pretty much what he'd expected in response. She uncrossed her arms. "You always think about him, don't you?"

Not lately, if he was being absolutely truthful. Lately, all he thought about was her. "You really think your father is going to give you his blessing to pursue this thing?"

"I hadn't planned on telling him."

"So much for being responsible and becoming more adult."

The perturbed look returned. "I hate when you're right." She rested her head against the chair and stared at the ceiling. "I have to tell him. I guess. Unless Van has the heart I need in his hoard. Then this is over, and I'm done. I'll have the truth about my mother and the closure I need."

"You realize if Van has the heart, it belongs to him. He's not just going to give it to you." Then Greyson paused. "I suppose he might, but I think if a dragon gives you something from his hoard, you owe him a large favor in return. Something like that."

"I'd be okay with that. He doesn't seem the type to ask for anything too outlandish. Although I'm not fond of being beholden to anyone." An odd gleam sparked in her gaze. "Present company included."

He snorted. "Please. I can't even count how many reasons there are for you to be beholden to me."

"You were paid. I owe you nothing."

"Yes, paid by your father. I'm not sure you've ever even said thank you."

She opened her mouth to say something, but his phone rang.

He grabbed it. "Hello?"

Van answered. "I do not have good news. No such witch's heart exists in my…possession."

Greyson sighed. "Okay." He looked at Kora and

shook his head while he continued to talk to Van. "Thank you for checking."

"Of course. I am happy to help. I hope Kora finds what she is looking for."

"So do I. And if you think of anything else that might help, even the smallest thing, let me know."

"I will."

They hung up, and Greyson sat down, slightly defeated.

"I told you," Kora gruffed. "Not sure why you thought it was going to be so easy." She swallowed as if something were caught in her throat. "He wouldn't lie, would he? Never mind, I already know the answer to that."

"I know you're frustrated. I am, too."

She cut her eyes at him. "You have no reason to be. In fact, you should be happy. A dead end means no more for you to worry about."

She was hurting. He could see that from the pain in her eyes. She wanted this information about her mother, maybe even more than she'd admitted to herself. "Hey, I'm not happy you've hit a wall."

"Why? Why should you care? You don't even like me."

"That's not true." But it had been. Why had it changed?

"Yeah, okay." She snorted as she got to her feet. "Thanks for hanging out, but I have a job to go to."

He stood and moved into her path to keep her from leaving. "I do like you, Kora. I like the changes you've made. The ones you're trying to make.

You're not the same vampire I rescued in Rome."

She stood inches from him. "You're just saying that."

"No, I'm not. I have no reason to lie to you. I still have a lot of reservations about you, but I can see the differences. They look good on you."

The muscles in her jaw tightened, and for the briefest of moments, it looked as if tears were edging her lower lash line. Then she lifted her head. "Thank you."

Realization shot through him like a punch to the solar plexus. About how hard she was trying. How lonely she must be. How much her mother's abandonment and death had damaged her. And just like that, he cared about her. Too much. Far more than was safe.

The moment swept over him, tumbling him along like a piece of driftwood caught in a rogue wave. He took hold of her shoulders, pulled her close, and kissed her.

She didn't resist like he'd expected. Instead, she shocked him by leaning in with a ferocity that seemed true to her old self. The Kora who took what she wanted with no concern for cost or consequence.

That was the woman who'd always secretly intrigued him, and now that she was in his arms, he was enflamed by her wildness.

She slid her hands up his sides until they griped his rib cage. All the while, little mewls of needy pleasure slipped from her throat.

He broke the kiss to rake his fangs down her neck, making her cry out.

She suddenly pushed away from him. Her eyes glowed white-hot, as he was sure his own did. "We can't do this."

"You mean we shouldn't do this. Adults can do whatever they please."

She dragged the back of her hand across her mouth. "You're just trying to distract me."

"Wrong." Her rejection hurt, but had he really thought there would be a different outcome? Well, maybe, after that first kiss. "I wasn't thinking about you at all."

A slow smile spread across her face. "How about that? You're not the completely tamed vampire I thought you were."

He scowled. "There is nothing tame about me."

She shrugged. "I don't know. The princess had you just about domesticated."

If she was trying to make him angry, she'd succeeded. "Good night, Kora."

She tipped her head to one side, still clearly amused with herself. "Night, Greyson."

He stalked out of the room and out of the house, the persistent image of her coy smile stuck in his head.

But not nearly with the same plaguing tenacity as the feel of her mouth on his and her hands on his body.

Why in Hades had he kissed her? Because he'd wanted to, that was why. She'd brought it out in him by making him care. By showing him that she'd finally stopped being a spoiled child and become a woman.

A woman he wanted.

In that moment, he knew one thing with great certainty.

He was doomed.

Kora held on to her casual, devil-may-care grin until she heard the front door slam. Then she let out the gasp she'd been holding in and sank down on the couch, as weak as Waffles had been the night he'd been discovered.

Her fingers went to her lips, which were still buzzing with Greyson's scorching kiss. Then they traveled to her throat, where he'd scraped his fangs across her skin. To her utter embarrassment, she'd thought he was going to bite her, and she'd never wanted anything so much in her life.

She squeezed her eyes shut against the thought. That did nothing to erase it from her brain. If anything, it brought his face to the forefront of her mind. He was too damn handsome for his own good.

Too male and full of himself and too…too… perfect.

She bumped her head against the couch a few times. What was wrong with her? She was *not* interested in Greyson.

Except she was.

No. It wasn't interest. It was common lust. That was all. She was exhausted from being so responsible, and her defenses were down. She was weakened by all the adulting she'd been doing, and that weakness was making her see Greyson as desirable. That was it. End of story.

But how could it be when he'd essentially offered to help her with her quest? She didn't have to accept, but having him along would make things easier.

Waffles climbed into her lap and pawed at her to pet him. She obliged, mindlessly running her nails down his back as her brain kept spinning.

Greyson was right, too, that her father would be a lot happier if the vampire was involved. No doubt so Greyson could keep an eye on her and report back on what she was doing. Because what else did her father pay him for but to be her minder?

She let out a frustrated sigh. She had no time for this right now. She had to get ready for work, and her current look wasn't going to cut it.

"Waffles, you want dinner?"

He let out a chirp at the word *dinner*.

"I thought so. Let's get you fed, then Mama has to get moving. No work means no check, and no check means no Chicken Party."

He hopped down and looked back at her to be sure she was following. She let him lead her to the kitchen.

At least she had one man in her life who thought she was all that.

She got him fed, then dressed for work. Black leather tunic minidress with thigh-high black leather boots. Part of her hoped Greyson would show up at the club again. If he did, this outfit should remind him that she was not a lady who lunched, but a very powerful vampire.

Just in case he'd forgotten.

With a kiss to Waffles's fluffy head, she headed out of her house and around to the main entrance of the club. She didn't like to use the secret side entrance all the time, lest it stopped being a secret.

She came through the main entrance and found her father on the club floor speaking with some guests. She waited until he was through, then greeted him. "Hi, Dad."

"Hi, Kora. How was your day?"

Full of Greyson. But that wasn't about to be her answer. "Good. Nothing exciting."

He nodded. "How's the cat?"

"He has a name, Dad." She laughed. "Waffles is fine."

"Your grandmother expects to see you for dinner tomorrow night, since you didn't make it tonight."

"Okay. Tell Mémé I'll be there. Sundown?"

"Sundown."

She tipped her head toward the entrance she'd just come through. "I'm going to run upstairs and check in with the doorman. You can go, though, if you want. I won't be long."

"I'll go up with you. Imari and your grandmother are waiting. We have tickets for the playhouse."

Together, they walked to the elevator. Kora pushed the call button.

Hattie loved the theater. So much so that Lucien

had become the new playhouse's main sponsor. "What show are they putting on?"

"*My Fair Lady*."

The doors opened, and they got on. Kora couldn't see her father at a musical, but it was amazing what he'd endure for his wife and grandmother. Still, Kora couldn't help but smirk. "Sounds like fun. Have a good time."

"Thanks." He sighed. "The things I do…"

She laughed. "I was just thinking that."

The doors opened, and they got out. He kissed her cheek. "Have a good night."

"You, too."

He gave Chet, who was at the door, a nod as he went past.

Kora went to stand beside the bear shifter. "Evening."

"Evening, Ms. Dupree."

"How's it been up here?"

"Pretty regular. Same as always."

"Need anything?"

"Nope, I'm good." He grinned. "How's the boy doing?"

She smiled back. "Waffles is doing really well. In fact, I think I might get him a buddy."

Chet's eyes lit up. "That would be nice. Everybody needs a friend."

"I suppose they do." She just wasn't sure she wanted hers to be Greyson. Not when her feelings toward him went beyond ordinary friendship.

Greyson should have gone home from Kora's, but he couldn't. Not yet. Not while he was strung out on thoughts of her and restless with the need to do something, anything that wasn't going home. He was wound up with the residual energy from the kiss. The kind of energy that needed using, or it would drive him mad.

But he couldn't figure out what he wanted to do, so he settled for parking and walking around town. People watching was always entertaining in Nocturne Falls. The distraction worked. He started to relax. He thought about going to Howler's, but he'd just been there. He wanted something different.

So he kept walking. And thinking. He forcibly turned his thoughts from Kora to the inscription on the locket. Had they missed something? Was there some small clue that they'd overlooked? A way to figure out which dragon's hoard held the witch's heart? How many dragon shifters were there in the world?

The more he thought, the more impossible finding that witch's heart seemed.

Maybe the riddle was so vague because it was supposed to be unsolvable. But then, why leave a clue at all?

He sighed and muttered to himself and almost ran into a few tourists, so after another hour of aimless wandering, he went into the closest restaurant that wasn't Howler's, found a seat at the bar, and ordered a pint.

He was halfway through that pint when he really thought about where he was. The Poisoned Apple pub.

The location suddenly seemed important, but he had no idea why. Maybe because he hadn't been here in a long time? Maybe because his brain was working on something? What the connection was to the Poisoned Apple, he didn't know. But it felt like being at the pub should register in some way. So he drank the rest of his pint and ordered another and kept thinking.

As the second pint was delivered, he sensed the woman next to him wanted to talk. Or flirt. For reasons that had nothing to do with Kora, he wasn't interested in that at all, so he pulled out his phone and pretended to be busy.

But there was only so much social media he could take. So he switched over to his search engine and, on a whim, plugged in the words *dragon's hoard*.

He didn't expect to learn much, but on the second page of results, his interest perked up.

A pub in Ireland was called the Dragon's Hoard. Had he known that? He'd spent a good many years in Ireland, enough that he still carried a slight lilt in his speech. Was that why being in a pub now had seemed relevant?

He clicked through to the pub's website and browsed through the photos and info. The place was old, which wasn't so unusual for pubs. Or places in Ireland. It had all the markings of a typical pub. Dark wood, brass fixtures, dart boards. It also had dragons carved into the wood above the bar.

Something else was carved into the wood, but he couldn't quite make it out. He tapped the picture, then enlarged it with his fingers.

Hearts. There were hearts carved into the wood. And at regular intervals around the bar. Even on the paneling. There was no way this was coincidence. Was there? It had to mean something.

But he wasn't going to figure it out here. He put his phone away, then caught the bartender's gaze to let the man know he was leaving. He tossed a few bills on the bar and headed out. He had to tell Kora about this, but he wasn't going to just send her a text. Actually, he couldn't, since he didn't have her number. But he wasn't going to call Insomnia either.

No, he wanted to see her face when he told her what he'd found. When he proved to her that he was genuinely interested in becoming part of this quest for the adventure of it and not just to keep an eye on her.

That was it. He wasn't going to the club because he

wanted to see her again. Or because her kiss still lingered in his head.

In fact, there wasn't going to be any more kissing. They were still very much opposites, even if she had matured a lot in the last year.

He needed a very different kind of woman. How that woman was different from Kora, he couldn't immediately answer, but he knew that getting involved with her would lead to all kinds of trouble. So no more kissing Kora. No more thinking about her in romantic ways.

They were going to be partners on this quest. At most, they would become friends. And yes, he was doing it to keep her safe. As a favor to Lucien. Who didn't know any of this was going on, but that was beside the point.

He got in his car and headed for Insomnia, ignoring the fact that the last time he'd been this excited about seeing a woman, he'd been dating a blue-haired winter elf with a royal lineage longer than summer in the Sahara.

As he drove, he worked out all the ways Kora was different from Jayne. For one thing, Kora would never fall in love with a necromancer. Vampires knew better. For another, Kora didn't have a life of privilege and protocol awaiting her in another magical realm.

But best of all, Kora was a vampire like him. Sure, she was half reaper, but the vampire genetics mostly overruled the reaper ones, putting her firmly in his camp. She understood what being a vampire meant.

Then he questioned why he felt the need to make such a comparison.

After all, they were only going to be friends.

Just friends. Just. Friends.

He parked and got out, repeating those words to himself as he walked into the abandoned Caldwell Manufacturing building that housed the entrance to Insomnia. He kept up the mantra as he greeted Chet at the door, as he rode the elevator down to the club level, as he strolled through the club, looking for Kora.

But he completely forget it when he found her.

She was in the VIP lounge, talking with some guests and being oddly smiley. Seeing her in work mode amused him. He had a feeling she'd scowl when she saw him.

But his thoughts died there as he took in what she was wearing. A slinky, black leather minidress that hung off one shoulder like a big T-shirt. It wasn't particularly body conscious, but her shape was still visible.

Where the dress stopped, a pair of thigh-high black leather boots began, leaving about an inch of thigh exposed.

She was almost completely covered except for her arms, one shoulder, and that glimpse of thigh.

And yet his mouth had gone dry and his head blank.

She was a vampire goddess. A fanged dream in black leather. The kind of trouble he no longer wanted to avoid.

How had he thought they could just be friends?

Had being near her turned him into an idiot? That was a very real possibility.

She came down the steps from the lounge and stopped halfway when she saw him.

To his great surprise, she smiled. Then she continued toward him, the sway of her hips drawing the eyes of nearly every male in the vicinity.

Greyson's fangs descended at the thought of all those men—whoa. He blinked and pulled his fangs back. He was *not* jealous. He couldn't be. That was an emotion reserved for people who cared. People who already felt things like love.

She stopped in front of him, her grin kicking up on one side, the way it sometimes did when she was feeling especially proud of herself. "Couldn't stay away, huh?"

"I...uh..." What had he come there for? The quest? Right. The quest. "I know where the Dragon's Hoard is."

The amusement left her face. Her mouth dropped open, and her eyes rounded with excitement. She grabbed his arm. "My office. Now."

They sped through the club. Not at top vampire speed, but faster than a power walk. Once in her office, she shut the door. "Where is it?"

"I think it's in Ireland."

"You think? You just said you knew."

He took out his phone to show her the pictures he'd found. "Well, what's your take?"

She looked at the photos, expanding them the same way he had. "Holy sunrise, that's a heart. A witch's heart. And they're all over the place." Then she made a face at him. "Hang on. This heart is supposed to be in a dragon's hoard. How does this mean anything?"

"Look at the name of the pub."

She glanced at the pictures again. This time, a real curse slipped from her mouth. She swallowed. "You found it." She stared at him, her eyes shining with excitement. "You did it. I don't know how, but you did it."

He was about to respond with something urbane and witty, but then he couldn't speak. Because her mouth was on his.

The kiss was over so fast he never had a chance to shut his eyes.

"Thank you!" She punched both fists into the air, raising the hemline of her dress to a scandalous level.

She put her arms down again, saving him from having to tell her he knew what color underwear she had on.

Black. But then...what else?

He felt like he'd been spun in a centrifuge. Up was down, black was white, Kora was being nice to him, and she'd kissed him again.

"So when do we leave?"

He stared at her. "What?"

"For Ireland? For the pub? When do we leave?"

"Oh. I...I don't know." He mentally shook himself and focused on something that wasn't her bare shoulder or mouth or thigh. "We can't just go. You need to tell your father. You need to get your shifts covered. We need transportation, and the trip has to be timed right, because we can't arrive in the middle of the day—"

She waved her hand. "Details."

He frowned. "Important details." He turned and took a few steps away from her, just to give himself some thinking room. "It's too bad your father doesn't have his own plane."

"I agree. He really should. Maybe I can get him to buy one? But the windows would have to be UV coated, and that would take too long. I want to leave as soon as possible."

He knew he shouldn't say what he was about to say, but his mouth opened, and he couldn't stop himself. "The Ellinghams have a plane."

Her smile as she sidled up to him told him everything he needed to know.

He put his hands up before she said a word. "Forget I said that. I am not asking to borrow their plane."

She rested her hands lightly on his chest and gazed at him with a look he couldn't turn away from. "Please?"

Wow. Was she actually fluttering her lashes at him? Who was this devilish creature trying to seduce him to her will? Where was the woman who would have grabbed him by the collar and told him to make it happen?

"I guess I could ask." Son of a—had he actually just said that? He had to get out of here before he promised to speak to her father, too.

"You're the best, Greyson. Do you think you could say something to my dad about—"

"*No.*" The word came out a panicked bark. He ran a hand through his hair. "Stop it. Whatever you're doing, stop it."

She frowned. "I have no idea what you're talking about."

"You're using your feminine vampire wiles on me, that's what."

Her frown flipped. "You think I have feminine wiles?"

He sighed. "You talk to your father. Let him know what's going on. As much as you can, anyway. Get your shifts covered. I'll talk to the Ellinghams. But no promises. You understand?"

She nodded. And looked very suspiciously like she might kiss him again.

He backed up, bumping into her desk. "I'll let you know when I find something out."

"We should swap numbers. So you can text me."

"Okay. Then I have to go."

"To talk to the Ellinghams?"

He nodded. "Yes."

Because for once in his life, asking for a favor from the vampire family who ran the town seemed like the easier option.

11

Greyson's discovery had left Kora giddy, and that wasn't something she was used to feeling. In fact, she wasn't sure she had felt it since she was a child.

It was like champagne bubbles and helium all rolled into one, and while it was wonderful, being so light-headed with happiness had caused her to kiss Greyson again.

That's what she was blaming it on, the impulsiveness caused by such sudden happiness. What other reason could there be?

The necessity of talking to her father, however, had taken the edge off that dizzy feeling, and now that she sat alone in her office, phone in hand, she was having all kinds of doubts.

Her father wasn't going to like what she was about to tell him. She knew that much. He'd probably think that going off on this quest in the hopes of getting the truth about her mother was a waste of time.

Or worse, he might forbid her from going.

Would he really do that? She certainly wasn't a child anymore. She was old enough to be someone's mémé herself. But she *was* living in her father's house and working at her father's club so... He might not be able to stop her, but he could make her new life here in Nocturne Falls very difficult.

She sighed. Postponing the call wasn't helping anything. She tapped her father's name on her short contacts list. A list that now included Greyson. That was enough to make her smile as she listened to the phone ringing on her father's end.

"Hello, Kora."

"Hi, Dad. How are you?"

"I'm good." There was concern in his voice. "Is everything all right?"

"Yep. Everything's running smoothly. But I need to talk to you about a personal thing." She could practically hear him tense up. "It's nothing bad, I promise."

"I can come by."

"That would be great. Thank you."

"See you shortly." He hung up.

She didn't know if *shortly* meant an hour or five minutes, but his impending arrival was already triggering her nerves. She made herself busy with cleaning and straightening her office. Might as well. It would make a good impression.

As it turned out, *shortly* was twenty minutes.

She greeted him with a smile and a kiss on the cheek. "Thanks for coming on such short notice."

"For you, Kora? Anything."

103

She hoped he still felt that way after what she was about to tell him. "I first want to say I really appreciate everything you've done for me since I got here. I hope you're pleased with the job I'm doing."

He nodded as he sat in the chair across from her desk. "I am. Not only have you proven to be a fast learner, but your being here has enabled me to spend more time with Imari."

She went to her desk chair and sat. "I'm glad for that. I like Imari. We owe her a lot as a family."

He smiled. "Trust me, I am making sure she wants for nothing."

Kora nodded. "I have no doubt. How's Mémé?"

"She's doing very well. And looking forward to seeing you at dinner."

"Right, tomorrow night." She folded her hands on the desktop.

He crossed his ankle over his knee. "You didn't ask me here to find out about Hattie. What's going on? You said it was something personal."

"It is." She paused, gathering her thoughts. "I need some time off. And I'm not sure how much time. But there's something I need to do. Something that will bring me the closure I've been missing all my life."

His gaze darkened. "This is about your mother, isn't it?"

How he'd sussed that out so quickly, she had no idea. Maybe she was just that obvious. Nothing she could do about that. She held on to her cool as best she could. "Yes. I've been given the chance to find out the truth about her death."

He frowned, his countenance now as dark as his eyes. "From who?"

"They haven't revealed themselves to me yet."

"So you have no idea if they're a credible source or not."

"No, I don't. But no one else has ever had any answers, so while this might be a long shot, it might also be my only shot."

His brows knit together, and a breathy, grumbly noise vibrated out of his throat.

He hated it. That was plain.

"This person is just going to give you this information?"

She'd been hoping to gloss over that part, but her father was far too smart for that to happen. "No. I have to find something for them. Something we think is in Ireland."

His brows pulled even closer together. "We?"

Great. She hadn't meant to mention Greyson. But then, her father liked him, so maybe his involvement would be a plus. "Greyson Garrett is helping me."

Her father stared at her for a few uncomfortable moments. "Greyson has agreed to this?"

"Don't look so surprised. We've kind of become friends."

But that did nothing to change the look on his face. "Friends?"

"Sort of. We're not joining a bowling league together or anything, but we're not exactly at each other's throats anymore." Unless Greyson was literally at her throat, scraping his fangs down her neck in that way that caused little goose bumps to—oh, that was not a line of thought to engage in with her father sitting across from her. No way, no how. "Anyway, he's agreed to go with me."

More silence from her father, who as a reaper, excelled at silence. Finally, he spoke. "I want to talk to Greyson."

"I'm sure he'd be happy to speak with you."

"Are you paying him to help you?"

"No, he's doing this on his own. I couldn't afford to anyway, you know that. Not that my salary here isn't more than generous, it is. But I don't have that kind of bank account."

With a nod, Lucien rose from the chair, about as concerned as she'd seen him lately. "I'll talk to him, then I'll make my decision."

She stood as he turned toward the door. "Dad."

He looked at her.

"I need to do this. I don't want to seem ungrateful at all, but I am an adult, and I don't need your permission. However, I would very much like your blessing. And if I can't get that, I would settle for your understanding."

His expression softened a little. "I do understand. As for my blessing…I don't know. I worry about you, Kora. About what could happen to you."

"I know, because of all the trouble I've gotten into before."

"No." He shook his head. "Because I've only just gotten you back, and I don't want to lose you again."

"You won't, Dad. I promise. I'll be careful."

His nod was terse. "I would hope so. I'll give you my answer as soon as I speak to him."

"Thank you."

He left, and she grabbed her phone, texting Greyson with the info that her father would be reaching out. And that everything hinged on him.

Greyson knew how important this was to her, and besides that, he'd seemed eager to go. He'd convince Lucien, wouldn't he? Because if he didn't, and she went anyway, she'd be back to square one with her father. Hattie would probably be mad at her, too.

Was finding out the truth about her mother worth losing the rest of her family over?

The quick answer was no. But would she resent them for stopping her?

The quick answer to that was maybe.

Greyson was leaving Hugh Ellingham's house when Kora's text came through. Hugh had promised to check with the rest of his family to be sure that no one was going to need the plane, but otherwise he was fine with Greyson and Kora using it.

Greyson had made it clear he'd take care of the fuel bill, something Kora didn't need to know or worry about.

He jumped in his Camaro and texted her back to let her know he'd speak with Lucien immediately. Then his next call was to the man himself.

"Garrett."

"Lucien. I understand you spoke with Kora."

"Yes, and I was just getting ready to call you. Come by the house, and we'll talk."

As was Lucien's style, he didn't so much ask as he directed. Was it any wonder Kora had the same tendencies? "I can be there in fifteen minutes or so."

"Good. Until then." He hung up.

Greyson drove over to Lucien's new house. It was one of the truly impressive Victorians on a street of impressive Victorians. He parked in the drive and got out.

Despite the late hour, Hattie greeted him at the door. "How are you, Greyson?"

"Just fine, Hattie. How are you?"

"I'm wonderful. Thanks for asking. Would you like something to drink? I have coffee, tea, lemonade, water. No blood, sorry. But I have cookies, too. I made a batch of oatmeal butterscotch chip this morning. Or I could get you a nice slice of lemon pound cake."

He kind of wanted to hug her. He just smiled instead. "That is very kind of you, but I'm fine."

A deeper voice came from down the hall. "I don't think he'll be here long enough for refreshments, Hattie." Lucien walked out of the shadows.

"Well, there's always time for a glass of lemonade and a cookie. You boys go talk. I'll bring it in."

Lucien shook his head in gentle amusement. Then he gestured toward the French doors on the opposite side of the hall. "Let's go into the sitting room."

Greyson went in after Lucien, and they both sat.

The bookcases that lined the east and west walls were filled, giving the room more of a library feel that was no doubt Lucien's doing. But the pale green silk upholstery on the matching couches felt like either Hattie's or Imari's influence.

Lucien leaned back against the couch and gave Greyson a hard stare. "I want to know what's going on. Kora was light on details."

"She had no choice. The letter she received detailing the quest demanded she tell no one."

"She told you."

"She had no choice in that either."

"I see." Lucien frowned. "You're under no such obligation."

"No, I am not."

"Then explain."

Hattie came in with a bamboo tray. On it were two tall glasses of lemonade and a china plate piled high with cookies. Two smaller plates and two linen napkins completed the service. She set it on the square tufted ottoman that served as a table between the couches. "Here you are. Holler if you need anything else."

"Thank you," Greyson said.

When she'd left, Lucien sighed and picked up a cookie. "You're helping me with these. She'll be disappointed if we don't make an effort."

"Can't have that." Greyson put two cookies on a plate and took a glass of lemonade. "But she knows I'm a vampire."

"She also knows vampires can eat if they choose to."

Greyson wasn't going to argue further. He wasn't all that interested in sweets, but for Hattie's sake, and the sake of staying on Lucien's good side, he'd eat and drink until he was near bursting. He took a big bite of a cookie to prove he was a team player.

Lucien sipped his lemonade. "Now explain what's going on."

Greyson washed the cookie down with some lemonade, thankful it was more tart than sweet, and began to explain everything Kora had told him.

When he was done, Lucien sat without speaking for a bit.

Greyson used the silence to finish his cookie, plus two more. He'd nearly emptied his glass of lemonade when Lucien spoke.

"Do you think this quest is something that can be accomplished safely?"

"I don't have any reason to think otherwise. There are probably other people who want whatever this final treasure is, but Kora's got the sun locket. Without that, there's no way to even get started."

"Doesn't mean you won't be watched."

"I'd already assumed we would be. I also won't let her take any unnecessary chances. Part of the reason I want to go with her is to keep her safe."

"She told me she's not paying you."

"She's not. I don't want her to. I'd much rather go with her as a friend than hired help."

Lucien's eyes narrowed in thought, and he went quiet again.

Greyson finished his lemonade and set the empty glass back on the tray.

Lucien swirled the ice in his glass, but didn't drink. "Is there anything romantic going on between you two?"

If there'd been any food in Greyson's mouth, he would have choked on it. "No."

Was that true? He wasn't sure. Did a few kisses constitute something romantic? Or had those kisses just been reactions to the moments that preceded them? He didn't know. And didn't want to analyze any further. Mostly for fear of making his answer a lie.

"Good. Keep it that way."

Greyson frowned. "Can I ask why?"

Lucien set his glass on the tray, then stretched his arm along the back of the couch. "You're a good man, Greyson. It's nothing personal. But Kora's just getting her life on track. A romantic involvement would complicate that. A breakup would be even worse. She needs a solid year of working and keeping up with her responsibilities before she should even think about getting involved with someone."

"Right." On the inside, though, he was bristling. In Greyson's opinion, Lucien was overstepping. But then, he was Kora's father, and he had paid dearly over the years to extricate her from all kinds of trouble. So maybe...maybe Greyson could understand.

"I'm glad you agree. Bring her home safely. And still single. And I will make it worth your while."

"I don't need—"

"By which I mean a million dollars. Cash, gold, gems, stocks, however you want it, I'll deliver."

Greyson blinked as the reaper's words sank in. He was well-off. But in the world of supernaturals, there was rich and there was Ellingham-level wealth. Greyson wasn't at the level of the Ellinghams. And he wasn't sure the Ellinghams, except maybe for Elenora, were at the level of Lucien.

So even though he was pretty comfortable, a million dollars was still a lot of money. He made himself respond, but he couldn't bring himself to agree. "That's very generous of you."

"My daughter is the only treasure that matters to me."

Greyson nodded. "I will keep her safe."

"Then I'm fine with her going. Perhaps not *fine*. But I understand her need to do this. How are you traveling?"

"I've already arranged for the use of the Ellinghams' plane."

"That was kind of them."

"I'm sure Kora being your daughter played into it."

He grunted. "I suppose I'll owe them, then."

"I think I might be the one that will owe them." Greyson shrugged. "But then, who in this town isn't beholden to them in some way?"

"True." Lucien stood, ending Greyson's visit. "When will you leave?"

Greyson followed suit and got up. "As soon as Kora can. I know she wants to go soon, but she has to work out everything at the club."

"I'll speak to her and tell her that's handled. The sooner you two leave, the sooner you can return."

"Agreed."

"Thank you for coming by." Lucien walked him to the door, but before he opened it, he turned to Greyson. "You have my number. If you need anything while you're away, call."

"I will."

Lucien's hand was on the knob, but he still didn't open the door. "And I want updates. Understood?"

"Understood." Greyson made himself smile. But what he really understood was that no matter how old Kora was, her father was never going to lose his need to protect her.

And while that was a commendable trait in a parent, Greyson also realized that having Lucien as a father-in-law was a daunting proposition.

Bringing Kora home safe might not be easy. But bringing her home single was going to be a piece of cake.

12

Kora could barely contain her excitement as the Ellinghams' plane touched down at the Weston Airport outside of Dublin. It was a little after eight thirty in the evening, and she'd woken up only an hour earlier. Not only had sleeping on the plane helped to pass the time, but she'd needed to sleep so she'd be ready for this next leg of the quest.

Greyson had been up about the same amount of time, but while she was looking out the window, he was on his phone.

She glanced at him. "What are you doing?"

"Hiring a car to take us to the Dragon's Hoard. It's about forty-five minutes from here as best I can tell."

"Shouldn't we be getting a hotel?"

He didn't look up from his phone. "I'm hoping not to be here that long."

"You really think we're going to figure out this next clue and go after it in a matter of hours? The locket doesn't work that way."

He put his phone down. "You make it sound like you don't think this is going to be the location of the final treasure."

"I don't. That would be too easy."

"I suppose that's true." He picked his phone up again and started tapping the screen. "There are a couple of dead-and-breakfasts' here, one in particular that I remember. Been a while, but if it's still around, we'll go there."

"Sounds good." D&Bs were vampire-friendly boutique hotels. They also supplied rooms to other supernaturals, but vampires were their main clientele. Nocturne Falls had a few. They'd have blood on hand, windows that were UV tinted, blackout curtains in all the rooms, an understanding staff, and most had secondary and tertiary exits, a throwback to the days of angry villagers with pitchforks.

Even if such threats didn't exist in current times, there were new ones. Extra escape routes were never a bad thing.

She snuck a look at Greyson again. Having a handsome, capable vampire at your side wasn't a bad thing either.

And while Greyson had been exceptionally kind and accommodating since they'd gotten their trip underway, he'd also been a little…aloof. Almost like he'd decided that while they were on this trip, he needed to be all about the business of the quest.

She'd seen him like this before. Every time he'd come to rescue her from some predicament. It was a mode he went into where he was hyperfocused on his surroundings and keeping them safe.

And while she understood and even appreciated that part of him, they were still on the plane. There wasn't anything that could happen to them here.

It made her inexplicably sad. Like she'd become a client to him again. A job to be done.

She much preferred him as a friend. A friend she really needed to stop kissing. Although there was little danger of that happening again when he was keeping her at arm's length.

Wait a second. Was that *why* he was keeping her at arm's length?

He hadn't seemed particularly upset by the kissing. In fact, he'd initiated one of the kisses. And had done so in a way that had made it seem like he'd been driven by desire and unable to stop himself.

Kora had found that rather flattering.

So this change in him was a little baffling. What could have caused it? Since his discovery of the pub and them getting on the plane, not that much time had passed. But something in that span of hours had shifted his attitude toward her.

What had done that? Had he made the decision on his own to treat this like any other job? Could be. But why?

He'd met with Hugh Ellingham to ask about using the plane, but she doubted Hugh would have had anything to say about how Greyson approached this mission. She could see him making a remark about returning the plane in one piece or something like that, but the plane was staying at the airport.

Not much chance of it running into trouble there.

After Hugh, he'd gone to see her father. And really, that meeting had all the makings of a game changer, but Greyson had acted like it had been a whole lot of nothing. To the point that she hadn't given it much thought.

Now, however, she realized she'd been wrong to do that. Her father had agreed without any stipulations to let her do this quest. At least none he'd mentioned to her.

That didn't mean he hadn't put stipulations on Greyson.

There was no point in asking him, though. She doubted he'd confess the truth of that meeting to her. Chances were good he couldn't anyway. Lucien probably had made Greyson's silence part of the deal.

Whatever deal it was that had been struck.

The plane came to a stop, and the pilot announced their arrival.

They got up and got their backpacks from the overhead storage. The backpacks didn't hold all that much. A change of clothes, a few odds and ends. The bulk of their luggage would remain on the plane.

The backpacks were more about completing their look since they'd chosen to dress like traveling students rather than centuries-old vampires. It would make blending in easier. And no one was likely to look at them more than twice.

Greyson's hair was pulled back in a short ponytail, and he hadn't shaved, giving him a little shadow on his jaw. He was in cargo pants, a T-shirt, and a flannel button-down left open. He looked exactly like a college student. Kora hadn't been able to stop staring at him when she'd first seen him. It was so different than the way he usually looked.

She could almost forget he was a vampire. But then, that was the point.

She'd opted for jeans, a T-shirt, and a lightweight jacket with a drawstring waist. The jacket had a lot of pockets, making it great for traveling. She'd pushed her hair back with a headband and wore very little makeup.

He pulled his backpack on and faced her. "The D&B is all set up, but I'm assuming you want to go straight to the pub."

"I do." She smiled. "I really want to find this next clue."

"Then that's what we'll do. The car should be out in front of the terminal by the time we get there."

"Thanks for taking care of all of that."

"That's what I'm here for."

She tipped her head. "No, it's not. You're here to be my partner in this. I didn't ask you to come so you can handle all the admin. I mean, I appreciate it very much. But in my mind, we're equals in this."

He looked at her without saying anything for a moment, then broke his silence. "Thanks. I don't mind doing the admin stuff."

"I just...I don't want you to think you have to take care of me. I can handle myself. Maybe that wasn't the case a while ago, but I promise I'm making smarter choices these days. The kind that don't involve breaking laws and risking life and limb." She grinned. "After all, I have Waffles to look after now."

Only a hint of a smile played in his eyes. "Glad to hear it. And while I can see the changes in you, they aren't going to stop me from protecting you."

He was still being aloof, and it frustrated her. She wanted to lean in and kiss him, just to see what he'd do. Instead, a spark of her old self flared up inside her, filling her mouth with words better left unsaid.

But she hadn't changed that much just yet. She went a different route. "Why? Is that what my father told you to do?"

His reaction was immediate and told her that her father had said something, but the look disappeared instantly. "What father wouldn't want his daughter protected?"

She narrowed her eyes. "What else did he tell you to do?"

"Nothing. We should go." He pushed past her to the now-open door.

She followed. She'd definitely struck a nerve. Greyson was holding something back. What that was, she didn't know. But she'd find out sooner or later. If Greyson didn't come clean, she'd work it out of her father.

And if he wouldn't talk, Mémé would be the next best source. All Kora needed was some alone time to make a phone call.

Greyson hadn't been back in Ireland in a long time, but going into the pub still felt like coming home. It was exactly the kind of place he used to hang out in when he wasn't with Catherine, his wealthy sire and the woman he'd been romantically involved with for most of his vampire life.

Her death at the hands of a necromancer had changed everything, but he didn't have time for wallowing in the injustices of the past.

Now was all about the present—and a very different woman.

Still playing their roles as trekking students, they found a table in one of the dark corners and settled in. Greyson went up to the bar and ordered two small beers. Guinness, naturally. He also got two packets of crisps, which seemed like the kind of thing students would do.

He took the beers and the crisps back to the table and sat down.

Kora leaned in, voice low. "There are witch's hearts all over this place. They're carved into everything like a motif."

"I see that. They're even behind the bar on the paneling."

She picked up a bag of crisps and looked at it. Her top lip curled. "Pickled onion?"

"We're students. We're trying new things. You don't actually have to eat them."

"Good. Because yuck." But her tone held a teasing note, and her eyes were full of amusement. She lifted the glass of Guinness. "I will drink this, however."

"A real sacrifice, I'm sure." He lifted his own and knocked it gently against hers in a toast. "Here's to a successful trip."

"Absolutely." She took a sip, then set it back down. "The good news is, this has to be the place."

He frowned. "Is there bad news?"

She nodded. "I have no idea how to find what we're looking for. For one thing, there are too many witch's hearts to look closely at them all in a single visit. For another, how will we know which one is the right one? And what do we do with it when and if we find it?" She sighed. "This is a lot more complicated than I thought it was going to be."

"Okay, let's try to break down the locket's inscription," he said. "Seek the witch's heart in the dragon's hoard, but beware the pain of untrue love."

Kora moved her chair a little closer to his. "The witch's heart, we know."

"You're sure it can't be anything else?"

She glanced around. "Not unless there's an actual witch's heart somewhere in here."

"I haven't seen anything aortal floating in a jar of formaldehyde, so let's assume not."

"Right, I don't think that's what it is either. So then, which of these many, many hearts is it? And what do we do? Push it like a button? Wait for it to speak to us? I'm at a loss here."

He looked around some more before answering her. "There are a lot of hearts in here. What about the last bit that says beware the pain of untrue love?"

"I'm guessing that's a warning against choosing the wrong heart."

"Great. So not only do we have to figure out which one is the right one, but there's a penalty for picking the wrong one?"

"I don't think that's an issue. See how some of the tails on the hearts go left, and some go right?"

He nodded.

"Witch's hearts were meant for protection, unless they weren't. From what I've read on this particular style of jewelry, a witch's heart with a tail that pointed to the right was meant for protection. A witch's heart with a tail that points to the left was meant for destruction."

He raised his brows. "So no left-pointing tails."

"I'd think not. But that's as far as I've gotten on narrowing things down."

"It's a start."

She made a face at him. "Barely."

He opened his bag of crisps. He actually like pickled onion. Or was that prawn cocktail? Now he couldn't remember, and it had been a while. He took one out, surprised by how much it smelled like feet. Maybe he wouldn't eat it after all.

Kora pushed her chair back. "I'm going to do a little recon."

"Okay. Text me if you need me."

"Will do." She got up and wandered off through the pub.

Greyson watched the men watching her. Maybe not as many as if she'd been dressed in her usual leather, but heads turned all the same. She was undeniably beautiful and, despite her outfit, looked very much like the otherworldly creature she was.

She moved slowly, making a show of admiring the old pub. Just like a tourist might.

But while the men looked, none made a move toward her, so Greyson relaxed. Not that she'd need saving from any human. With her strength and speed, she could take on a crowd and come out all right. But if there were any supernaturals in the pub, that could be different.

He hadn't detected any immediately, but there were a lot of people in here, and there was no reason to think there weren't some in the mix. A few patrons had brought their dogs in, too, which made it hard to distinguish between those scents and any that might be coming off of shifters.

Kora continued her slow trek through the pub.

He sipped his beer and started going through the people around her, face by face, looking for any telltale signs that someone was more than they seemed.

A man at the far end of the bar was particularly hairy in a way that seemed very much like a shifter. But then, beards were in, so a lot more people looked like shifters these days. Still, there was something about him that was a little more than human.

Greyson watched him closely as Kora walked past. The man's nostrils flared like a shifter taking in his surroundings. His mouth opened slightly, something else shifters and some vampires did when they wanted to read their environment more deeply. With shifters, it was like they were tasting the air.

The man turned his head slightly in Kora's direction, which hid his eyes from Greyson.

The small hairs on Greyson's neck stood at attention. His vampire senses were pinging hard, but the man had done nothing actionable yet.

This guy had to be a shifter. Or some other kind of supernatural.

Most shifters could detect vampires. Didn't mean that's what was going on, but Greyson wasn't going to take any chances now that he and Kora were separated. He focused in on the man. On his movements. On his line of sight. On his heartbeat.

His pulse was elevated. Excited.

Kora went around the corner of the bar and disappeared out of sight.

The man turned and looked directly at Greyson. For a split second, his eyes looked like they were glowing.

Greyson was instantly on alert. He kept watching the man, sure he was going to get up and go after her at any second.

A few minutes later, his phone vibrated. He glanced down to see a text from Kora.

I think I found it. Meet me in the bathroom.

When Greyson looked up, the man was gone.

At the sound of pounding, Kora yelled, "Occupied."
She glanced at her phone. No answer from Greyson yet.

"It's Greyson."

That would explain it. She opened the bathroom
door. "It's a little close in here."

He squeezed in. "That's the UK for you."

With the two of them, the sink, the toilet, and their
backpacks, there wasn't a whole lot of room for
moving around.

He looked around the small space. "You really
think the answer is in the bathroom?"

"I do. And I'll show you why I think that." Witch's
hearts were carved into the paneling that covered all
four walls. Some had tails that went left, some went
right, but it was clear they were all old. She grabbed
hold of the mirror above the sink. The oval glass was
pitted with time and hung on a tarnished chain. She
lifted it off the chain to reveal the hearts on the wall
behind it. "You see the one I mean?"

He let out a little whistle. "Yes."

She set the mirror flat on the toilet seat. "Don't break that. Seven years of bad luck is all I need."

"I won't." He touched the heart that had been hidden behind the mirror, running his fingers over the center of it where a familiar sun shape had been carved into the design. "None of the other hearts have this?"

"None that I've seen. I haven't checked the whole pub, though."

"I haven't seen any either. This has to be it. And based on that carving, what comes next seems clear." He looked at her. "I know you were supposed to return the locket, but I'm really hoping you haven't yet."

"I haven't." She reached under her shirt and produced the sun-shaped piece, now dangling from a length of new ribbon. "I had a feeling we might need it. But are you sure we should do this now? Maybe we should wait and come back after the pub has closed. Which I realize would be illegal, but—"

"No. Now. There was a shifter at the bar watching you. Doesn't mean he's someone to be worried about, but I'm not going to ignore it either. Let's do whatever we need to do and get out of here."

"Okay." She took a breath, excitement flowing through her. Carefully, she fit the locket into the sun carved in the center of the heart. It fit perfectly.

A click sounded, then the entire heart popped out a half inch from the wall.

She gasped softly. "I was not expecting that."

"Nope."

She reached for it, then stopped. "Hmm. Not sure

if I should turn it or pull it or what? I hate to do something wrong and screw it up. The fact that there was a warning about the wrong heart could mean there are booby traps set up."

A knock at the door stopped Greyson from answering.

"Oy! Hurry up in there," a voice shouted.

Greyson grimaced. "Whatever you're going to do, do it fast, or he'll break the door down."

"Right." She took hold of the heart and applied a little pressure. There was no pulling it out any farther. So she turned it. The carving pivoted about ninety degrees and stopped.

She let go. "Well, that was—"

A small, square door above the heart popped open. It was hinged on one side like a cabinet and had opened only about an inch, leaving the interior hidden.

"Huh," Greyson said. "Even with my eyesight, I didn't see there was a compartment cut into the paneling. Whoever set this up was good."

"Agreed." Kora opened the door all the way.

Three squat glass vials filled with pale green liquid sat on a narrow shelf. A sheer coating of dust covered them, but each was clearly labeled with a handwritten note that said, *Drink me and the sun will shine on you for twenty-four hours.*

The words were written in English, French, and Russian.

"What is this? *Alice in Wonderland*?" Greyson shook his head. "I'm not drinking that."

Kora shrugged. "I don't think we have a choice."

127

"What part of *the sun will shine on you for twenty-four hours* do you think sounds healthy for a vampire?"

"This whole thing was most likely set up by a vampire. They're not going to do something to harm one of their own."

"You can't possibly—"

More knocking, this time closer to pounding, interrupted him again. "Mate, get your business done already. There's a queue."

Kora grabbed all three bottles, stuck them in her backpack, then closed the cabinet and pushed the heart carving back to its flush position. "We can't do this here. Let's go to the D&B."

"Okay."

She got the sense that Greyson was still going to try to stop her, but not now.

He picked up the mirror and rehung it, then gestured toward the door. "After you."

She opened the bathroom door and slipped out.

When he followed, applause rang out from the three men in line.

Kora rolled her eyes. Not that Greyson could see her expression, but when they got outside, she gave him a look. "Great. All those guys think we were having a quickie in that bathroom."

He snickered. "I suppose they do."

"You look awfully pleased about it."

He shrugged, still smirking. "The perception that I've just been caught being intimate with a beautiful woman isn't something I'm going to feel bad about."

She laughed, surprising herself.

"What?" he asked.

"You really think I'm beautiful?"

He narrowed his eyes. "You know you're beautiful. Fishing for compliments, not so much."

"I wasn't fishing. I genuinely didn't think you thought of me that way. I just figured you thought I was more of…I don't know, a giant burden."

His smile returned. "Oh, you're a giant burden. But you're a beautiful giant burden."

She had no reply for that, no snappy comeback. She stared at him, dumbstruck. Not a feeling she was used to at all. Her need to deflect was strong. "We should get a car."

"Already called one on the way out." He looked past her. "That's probably it right there."

A silver sedan sat at the curb. The driver put the window down. "Mr. Garrett?"

Greyson nodded. "Yes."

He opened the back door for Kora, who got in and slid all the way over. Greyson climbed in beside her and closed the door. "The White Lady, please."

"Yes, sir," the driver answered as he took off.

Kora stared out the window, her thoughts still mired in Greyson's admission. She knew she was beautiful. She'd never met a vampire who wasn't. Perfection was a side effect of being turned.

But being beautiful on the outside was no guarantee of being beautiful on the inside, and that was one truth she wasn't going to hide from. She'd been ugly on the inside for so long that she'd become used to the idea that she was also unlovable.

Sure, her father and Hattie loved her, but they were family. It was practically a requirement.

But Greyson had no such obligation. And he'd been critical of her—and rightly so—for so long that she hadn't imagined he could think otherwise.

Had she changed that much? It was a good thing. But it was a little frightening, too. Being loved had its own responsibilities. Ones she wasn't sure she was capable of.

"You okay?"

She glanced at him, pushing a smile onto her face. "Just thinking."

With a glance at her backpack, he nodded.

He thought she was thinking about the vials of green liquid, but she'd actually forgotten about them. Until now.

The reminder was a welcome change from the personal scrutiny she'd been putting herself under. Much easier to question what was in those vials than if she had the skill set to be someone's girlfriend.

Because that's where her thoughts had been headed.

She almost laughed. Amazing. A handsome man said she was beautiful, and she fell into the black hole of possibilities like a desperate woman. Was she that desperate for love? She didn't think she was.

Admittedly, she was a little lonely. But that was no reason to get involved.

She sighed at herself. There she went again, assuming Greyson was even interested in getting involved. Yes, he'd kissed her. Yes, he'd said she was beautiful.

Those two things did not a relationship make.

And if she didn't cool it, she was going to do something stupid. Something she couldn't afford to do with this quest unfinished.

After she had the information about her mother, she was free to be as reckless as she wanted, but until then, she had to focus.

Besides, Greyson was still being nice, but since they'd gotten on the plane he'd been cooler. She needed to remember that.

The car slowed and pulled to a stop outside of a pretty brick row house in a line of row houses. All were trimmed in white, with wrought iron fixtures and fences.

A sign hung out front that said simply, The White Lady. Kora imagined advertising themselves as a dead-and-breakfast would get some hard looks. And with word of mouth being what it was in the vampire community, there was probably little need to advertise anyway.

They went inside, backpacks hoisted over their shoulders, and went straight to the reception desk.

The man behind the counter looked about twenty-four or twenty-five, but wore his hair in a style that hadn't been popular in a hundred years. That and his fangs let them know this was not only an establishment that served their kind, but was run by one of them, too. His name tag said Niall. "Evening, folks. What can I do to help you?"

Greyson answered the man. "I have two rooms reserved. Garrett."

Niall started tapping on the keyboard in front of him, his gaze on the screen. "Yes, there you are. I see you made your reservation online. I'm terribly sorry, but we only had one room available. You should have received an email about that?"

"I haven't checked." Greyson glanced at his phone. "I see it now."

How convenient, Kora thought. One room. Well, she wouldn't have to worry about Greyson trying anything, considering his cool attitude on the plane.

Niall smiled hopefully. "It is a double, so there are two beds. Will that suffice?"

Kora answered before Greyson could. "It'll be fine."

Greyson shot her a look, but said nothing. Probably relieved she wasn't making a fuss. Or being a *giant burden* about the whole thing.

"Wonderful," Niall said. "I'll get your keys ready. Will that be cash or credit?"

Kora walked away while Greyson dealt with the rest of it. She went across the hall to a small sitting room. A portrait of a beautiful woman hung over the fireplace.

She stared up at it, wondering who she was.

"Elizebet Charmont Cross."

Kora turned to see a well-dressed man sitting in a brown velvet chair tucked away in the corner. He had a book on his lap and a pipe in one hand.

He smiled at her. "Lovely, isn't she?"

"Very," Kora answered. She turned back to the painting, wondering what the woman's connection was to the D&B.

"This was her establishment until her passing."

Kora looked at the man, again, staring a little harder. He was obviously a vampire, but there seemed to be something a little unsettling about him. "Did you read my mind?"

He laughed and took a puff off the pipe. "No, my dear. It just seems to be the thing most people want to know when they see her portrait."

And yet, he'd answered the question she'd asked in her head.

Greyson came in. "I have the keys. Ready?"

"Ready." Kora smiled at the man. "Have a good evening."

"And you, my dear."

She followed Greyson, happy to be headed to their room and away from the vampire in the sitting room, because despite his reassurances to the contrary, she had the strangest feeling he'd done exactly what she'd thought he had.

And if he could read her mind, there would be no way to keep the quest a secret from him.

Greyson didn't know what to make of Kora's easygoing attitude. Sharing a room was okay with her? That seemed so unlike her. He unlocked the door and opened it, stepping aside so she could go in ahead of him.

When he entered and locked the door, she grabbed him and pulled him close, putting her mouth next to his ear and completely throwing him off-center.

"The man downstairs," she whispered. "I think he read my mind." She leaned back to look at him.

Greyson frowned. "What makes you think that?" he whispered back.

She continued to keep her voice low. "I was looking at the woman's portrait, wondering who she was, and he answered me."

"Could it have been coincidence?" But even as he asked that, he wondered if it was. Especially after seeing the shifter at the pub.

"Maybe. Maybe not."

Greyson took his backpack off and tossed it onto one of the beds. "I don't like it."

"Because of the shifter at the pub?"

He nodded. "I feel like we're being watched. Or at least monitored."

"Me, too." She dropped her pack on the other bed and sat down beside it. "It's making me a little jumpy."

"Do you think that burner phone of yours is being tracked?"

"Crap. Probably. But there's nothing I can do about that. And really, if the Fox wants to see where I'm going, I guess he's got the right. I am doing this quest on his behalf."

"I suppose."

She sighed, then unzipped her pack and took the three bottles out. "What are these going to lead us to?"

"You mean if they don't kill us?"

She frowned. "Why would they do that? Wouldn't be a very helpful clue if they did."

"You have a lot of faith in whoever set this up."

"Isn't the purpose of this trail to actually find the thing it leads to? So why not have faith in them?"

"I suppose. I'm surprised you of all people are so trusting, though."

She looked down at the bottles in her hands. "Maybe because I want the reward so much."

He sat on the bed opposite her and spoke quietly. "And if the pot of gold that's at the end of this rainbow really is the source of Rasputin's power? What then?"

"Doesn't matter what it is. I'm turning it over to get my answers."

"But how do you know the person you'd be giving it to is a person who should have such a thing? That's a lot of power to put in one person's hands."

She shrugged. "Rasputin was only one person."

"And he created an entire line of vampires. And made quite a name for himself, too."

She shrugged, but there wasn't much conviction behind it. "I need to know what happened to my mother. This thing that I'm trying to find is just a means to that end. Vampires are already powerful. What else could this thing really do? Make them fly? Rasputin couldn't do that. Predict the future? That was his real gift, right? So what if someone gains that ability? Rasputin never changed anything with it."

"But someone might be able to."

"Maybe." She glanced at the bottles again. "Look, I don't want to be here any longer than we have to be. I'm going to down one of these and see what happens."

"Not alone." He'd already made that decision on the ride here. "We're doing it together, or you're not doing it at all."

"Are you sure? Isn't that taking a risk?"

"You said these things were harmless—"

"I didn't say that exactly. But I don't think they are. Wouldn't make sense."

He held his hand out. "Then give me one, and let's do this."

"Door's locked?"

"Yes."

She put one vial in his palm, then set the third one down, keeping one for herself. She pulled out the wax-sealed cork from hers and held the bottle in the air. "Bottoms up."

"Sláinte."

At the same time, they tipped the vials back and downed the contents.

Greyson nearly gagged at the stale grassy taste that finished with an undercurrent of bad seafood. "That was awful."

Kora nodded, tongue out. "Really awful."

His vision wavered like heat waves were rising off the floor. "Is your sight going funny?"

She nodded, putting a hand up as if trying to touch something in front of her. "And I'm starting to see—"

"Stones?" He saw them, too. Faint outlines that showed up best in his peripheral vision. When he tried to focus on them, they disappeared.

"Getting sharper now," she mumbled.

His were, too.

Then the vision unfurled in full color and clarity, like a movie. It wavered for a moment. Those weren't stones. Words came into view.

He read them out, but kept his voice soft. *"Arrête! C'est ici l'empire de la mort!"*

The vision disappeared, leaving him and Kora staring at each other.

Excitement glittered in her eyes. "I know that place."

"So do I."

In unison, they mouthed the words, "The Paris Catacombs."

She grabbed the remaining bottle. "No one else can use this." She went straight to the sink in the bathroom, uncorked the bottle, and dumped out the contents.

He followed her, closing the door and turning on the shower to mute their conversation against the possibility of prying vampire ears. "We should leave now. Unless you want to rest first?"

"No, let's go. I'm ready. We can rest there if we need to. I can't travel during the day anyway, so we should make full use of the dark while we have it."

"You don't think that vial might have just given you the power to daywalk?"

"No. I don't think that's what the sun shining on you means. Call it a hunch."

"Okay. But I don't think we should leave by the front door. I don't want your mind-reading friend to know. Just in case."

"I'm good with that. Are you going to call ahead to let the pilot know?"

He hesitated. "If we're being watched, I think we should leave the plane right where it is. We take off, and they're going to know we're on to the next clue."

"Okay. But the plane is the fastest way. And they won't know where we're going."

He nodded. "True. Do you want to risk it?"

"For the time factor, I think we should." She thought for a moment. "What about having the pilot file a false flight plan? Have him put down that we're headed back to Georgia."

Greyson seemed to mull that over. "I don't know the man, but he works for the Ellinghams. All things considered, I think he'd do it. Especially if I tell him we have eyes on us."

"Then that's our plan." She glanced at the empty vial in her hand. "I'm taking all three bottles with us. I'll ditch them in a random bin on the street."

Greyson pulled out his phone. "I'll let the pilot know we're on our way."

Kora nodded. "To the necropolis we go."

A little over two hours later, they were in Paris. It was yet another city Greyson had spent time in many, many years ago, but hadn't been back to in a while. He should have been, but time had gotten away from him, and he'd been too busy with other pursuits.

Besides, things here were well looked after by others paid to do just that.

He wasn't surprised to see that the city had changed, but he was pleased to see how much it had stayed the same.

He and Kora had ditched their student apparel on the plane and gone back to clothing they both considered more standard attire. Their student looks would have worked, but they were entering the catacombs after hours. Best to blend into the shadows a little more.

Which was why they were both now in head-to-toe black.

They'd also decided to settle in for a few moments at a sidewalk café that was conveniently open late. They had coffees in front of them and an awning above them to shield them from the slight but steady drizzle. They had no great use for the coffee, but it was a chance to try to see if they were being watched.

Greyson kept replaying the way the shifter at the Dragon's Hoard had looked at him, and it seemed intentional every time.

"Anything?" Greyson asked.

"Nothing." Kora's gaze was focused in the opposite direction. "The rain is working for us. You?"

"A woman walking a very reluctant dog." He sipped his coffee. "I don't think she's an issue."

"How much longer do you want to wait?"

"Not long."

With a short nod, she drank a little of her coffee, then put her hands on the table and gave him an expectant look.

"Okay." He got up, opened the cheap umbrella he'd borrowed from a hotel lobby, and together they took off.

Staying under the umbrella was good cover, too. They could have been any couple out for a stroll on a drizzly Paris evening.

"You're sure about our way in?" she asked, leaning in.

"Yes." He leaned back, keeping the distance between

them the same. "Unless something's happened to it in the last fifty years."

She frowned at him. Or maybe it was because of his actions. He wasn't sure and couldn't care. Not if he was going to treat her as a job to be done. "You realize that's entirely possible."

"I do. But change happens more often above this city than below it. We'll be fine." That was his hope, anyway. The main entrance to the catacombs, the one used by tourists, would be locked at this hour.

And breaking in would draw too much attention, even on a night like this.

He followed the map in his head until they came to a manhole cover a few yards down a side street. He handed her the umbrella. "Give me some cover."

She positioned herself between the street's busy end and the manhole cover, using the generous umbrella as a shield.

Greyson used brute strength to pry the metal free. It was well stuck and likely hadn't been opened in a good number of years. He liked that. It meant this way into the catacombs had probably been left untouched.

When the cover was loose, he eased it to one side with care, to make as little noise as possible. Then he gestured to the open hole. "After you."

"Thanks." She set the umbrella down, grabbed hold of the sides of the hole, and lowered herself.

Greyson followed, but held on to the edge of the hole long enough to pull the cover back over it. Enough so that it wasn't instantly obvious it had been tampered with.

Then he dropped to the ground beside Kora.

She had her flashlight on and was looking around at the walls of hewn stone. "Old sewer?"

"Yes. The smell kind of gives it away."

She laughed softly. "Funny, but that smell always makes me think of this city."

"How long did you live here?"

"I grew up here. But after that, off and on for nearly a century."

"Maybe we should have used your entrance. Why didn't you push for it more?"

She shrugged. "You haven't led me wrong yet."

Her confidence in him was so unusual, he wanted to feel her forehead to see if she'd become feverish. But he couldn't touch her. Not anymore. "Thank you."

He turned his flashlight on and checked the right side of the tunnel about three feet down. He grinned. "Yep, this is it."

"Let me guess. You were a young vampire filled with the passion and gravity of the newly turned." She shook her head at the graffiti revealed by the circle of light. "*Le sang est la vie et la vie est la mort.* Blood is life and life is death. How very deep of you."

He shrugged. "I wasn't that newly turned. But I was kind of hung up on the whole idea of immortality. You know how it goes."

"Not really." She smiled like she owned the world. "I was born a vampire."

"Oh. Right. I forgot about that. Well, take my word for it. Those of us who are turned usually spend a few years deep in thought about what immortality really means. It's heady stuff."

"I'm sure." She turned toward the other side. "Which way do we go to get to this secret entrance?"

"Not that way. Follow me."

She did, and while he found his way toward the illegal entrance into the catacombs, he pondered what she'd said. She'd been born a vampire. One who owed half her bloodline to her reaper father, but the vampire blood canceled out most of that.

She'd never been human. That might explain some of her past behavior, but it also made him wonder how much she was really capable of change.

And though it pained him, he felt that his decision to keep his distance from her was the right one.

Even if his heart didn't fully agree.

To Kora, it felt like they'd walked in silence for fifteen or twenty minutes, and she was lost from all the turns they'd taken. They'd also descended a good twenty feet.

Much like the catacombs, all the old passageways that ran beneath the city of Paris were a maze.

Greyson grunted in disappointment, and she could see why.

About three feet off the ground, a slightly oblong opening had been bricked up. And it had been done a long time ago, judging by the look of it.

"Hold this." He handed her his flashlight.

She took it.

He put his hands on the brick patch and shoved, his eyes lighting with the effort.

The bricks caved in with a thunderous noise, but they were too far underground for anyone to have heard. She hoped.

He took his flashlight back. "Let me go through

and make sure none of the other passageways have been bricked up."

"Okay."

He climbed in and, a moment later, stuck his head back out. "All good."

"Excellent." She joined him on the other side.

This wasn't a main area of the catacombs, but one of the secondary limestone tunnels that led to them. "We have a ways to go yet, don't we?"

"We do. Especially if you want to start at the inscription."

"I think we should. It's what the vision showed us. It's all we have to go on."

"Agreed. All right, let's move."

"You know the way from here?"

"I do. Probably another thirty minutes of walking. Unless you want to go faster."

"I'm all for that. So long as you can guide us without running us into a wall of bones."

A little half smile bent his mouth. "I can. I spent way too much time here in my past. Just keep your flashlight on, and we'll be fine."

"Done."

With the increase in speed, they reached the main entrance of the catacombs in minutes. When they stopped, they stood before the arch with the inscription they'd seen, thanks to the potion in the vials.

Arrête! C'est ici l'empire de la mort! Which meant, Stop! This is the empire of death!

But there was no stopping them now.

Kora stared at the words illuminated by her flashlight. "I wish I had a clue what to do next."

"Hang on," Greyson said.

He moved off to one side, the beam of his flashlight bouncing across the steps that brought tourists down from the street above.

His beam focused on something she couldn't make out. The soft scrape of metal against stone followed, then electric lights flickered on throughout the catacombs.

She laughed as she turned her flashlight off. "I guess you did spend a lot of time down here."

"Yep." He brushed his hands off. "So where to from here?"

"I don't know. I guess we go into the catacombs and hope we find the reason we're here."

He glanced at the arch in front of them. "Let's each take a side. We won't go too far, but we'll cover a little more ground that way."

"All right."

They went through the arch, Greyson going right and Kora going left.

She carefully scanned the walls of bones as she passed them, not knowing what she was looking for, but hoping she'd understand the clue if and when she saw it.

But with foot after foot of wall, nothing appeared. Her frustration level was rising. Maybe she and Greyson needed to talk this through some more. It felt like she was missing something.

She went back toward the entrance, and as she

crossed into Greyson's side, a gentle warmth spread through her chest.

The sensation was so odd, it stopped her in her tracks. She put her hand to her body. She could feel the warmth through the thin silk T-shirt she wore. How was that possible? What would cause such a — the locket.

She was still wearing the locket on a length of ribbon she'd strung it on. Having it on her person had just seemed like a good idea. The locket rested on her sternum, right where the warmth was.

She lifted it from under her T-shirt.

It was warm and glowing softly.

"Greyson," she whispered.

He was too far ahead for her to see, and in the catacombs, sound wasn't always reliable. She went farther in the direction he'd gone, but he appeared around a bend a few seconds later.

"Did you find something?"

"Sort of." She held the locket out.

His brow furrowed. "I don't get it."

"The locket."

"Right. But that's not new. You've had that since Nocturne Falls."

"Can't you see how it's glowing?"

"No."

"Huh." Then something behind him caught her eye. She stepped sideways to get a better look. "Wow."

"What?" He turned to look in the same direction.

"That skull. Third row up. It's got a sun on it."

He gave her a rather dubious look. "Where?"

She walked over to it and crouched down. "Right here."

The locket got warmer.

Her eyes widened. "I think I know what the saying on the vial meant about the sun shining on us."

She stood up and took the locket off so she could hold it out to him. "Feel this."

He clasped it between his fingers. "What am I feeling for?"

"How warm it is."

"Right, but it was just next to your skin, so—" He nodded in understanding. "But you're not naturally any warmer than I am."

He glanced down at the skull she'd just been crouched next to. "And now that I'm touching the locket, I can see the sun you're talking about." He let go of the locket. "Now I can't."

She grinned. "This locket is the sun that's shining on us."

"Then that skull must hold the next clue."

"Or..." She looked around the corner where he'd come from. "Nope. There's another sun farther down. I think they're just markers leading us to the clue."

"Then, by all means, let's follow them."

She slipped the locket around her neck again and decided to test his new demeanor toward her. "Maybe if you hold my hand, that will be connection enough to the locket so you can see them, too."

He shrugged and stuck his hands in his pockets. "I trust you."

So he was really committed to keeping her at a distance. Well. She wasn't a quitter. "But I'm not sure I trust myself. What if I miss one?"

"You won't. You've found two already."

This wasn't the time or place to argue with him, and she didn't want to alienate him further, so she let it go.

But as she turned away to head down the passageway, her pleasant expression disappeared. She was hurt. It bothered her how much. She'd never really cared what anyone thought about her before, and now that she did, he was pulling away for reasons she couldn't understand.

She had to talk to Hattie and see if Lucien was behind this, but Kora was starting to wonder more and more if Greyson just hadn't decided on his own that she was too much trouble.

Especially after his comment about her being a burden.

She did her best to quell the oncoming crankiness her line of thought was creating and tried to focus on finding the next sun. After all, the suns were leading her ever closer to the truth about her mother, and that should make her happy.

But at the moment, all she could think about was that if her mother had been a little more loving or a little more caring or just a little more motherly, Kora wouldn't be in these dank, chilly, musty catacombs to begin with.

Then it hit her. Caring about what had happened to her mother was just like caring about Greyson. She was bearing the burden of the emotion, while they were basically uninvolved.

Was that her new path in life? To experience unrequited affection? If so, it sucked royally.

A new sun appeared a few yards ahead. It was on the bulbous end of what might have been a kneecap.

She pointed it out to Greyson. "Another one."

He nodded, but said nothing.

She kept moving forward. For a long while, they went straight ahead, but nothing new appeared.

Then she found another sun, and it led them into a space she knew well. Which meant Greyson had to know it, too. She looked back at him.

"The Crypt of the Sepulchral Lamp," he said softly.

Two thick columns supported the roof of the space, which was lined with skulls and femurs. At the center of the room was a square pedestal made of mortared stone blocks holding a round oil lamp once used by workers to illuminate their efforts. "But there's no sun in here that I can see."

"Walk all the way around. There has to be something, right?"

"I hope so." She did what he suggested, following the wall of bones around, but at the halfway point, she shook her head. "Nothing yet."

"Keep looking. Or give me the locket if you want, and I'll try."

She turned toward him, considering that idea, and found the next sun. "I see it. It's on the lamp pedestal. And it's a lot bigger than the others. Our next clue must be in this room. But where?"

He walked around to the same side of the pedestal as her and held out his hand. "May I?"

She took the locket off and gave it to him. The sun disappeared.

"That is a big one." He crouched down to look at it straight on. "I have an idea." He got up and handed the locket back. "See if anything shows up."

"What are you going to do?"

"Apply the kind of effort only a vampire can." He took hold of the pedestal from behind and tipped it back, grunting a little with the effort.

She gasped as the bottom came into view. "Well done, Greyson."

"What's there?"

"I'm not really sure."

Kora motioned for him to come over. "Have a look."

He carefully laid the pedestal on its side, then came around to her side again. The shape was recognizable and painted in black so he didn't think touching the locket was required to see it. "It's a bull up on its rear legs."

She nodded. "But what does that mean?"

"I have no idea." He pulled out his cell phone and snapped some pictures. "But we can search the image and find out."

"Hang on. I think there's something else under there." She went closer to look and picked something out of the dirt. "It's a little ring set with some gems. Six altogether. Only two are the same. Looks old. I have no idea if it's part of the clue or not, but it's awfully coincidental that there was a piece of jewelry under this pedestal."

"I think so, too."

She slipped the ring on her finger as she turned to him. "I'm taking it. Better to have it than not, just in case."

He looked at his phone. "We'll have to get to cover soon. Sun will be up before you know it."

She closed her eyes for a moment and looked slightly sick.

"You okay?"

She nodded and opened her eyes. "I'll be fine." Then she put a hand on his arm and leaned in to check the time on his phone, then muttered a soft curse. "We should probably make our way out *now*."

"Agreed." Her touch, even through the sleeve of his jacket, set small fires inside him.

She took her hand back. "Did you already get us rooms somewhere?"

"No. But I've got it covered."

She didn't protest or ask for more information, so he took that to mean she still trusted him.

He righted the pedestal, then she kicked some loose stones, bone fragments, and dirt around the base to make it look untouched.

When she was done, she put the locket around her neck again, then glanced at him. "Ready?"

"Back the way we came in?"

She nodded. "And fast."

They were so deep in the catacombs that returning to Greyson's secret entrance took nearly ten minutes, even at the speed they were traveling. By the time they made it back to street level, the sky was beginning to lighten.

Greyson understood Kora's panicked look. She was probably feeling the familiar prickle of the coming sunrise on her skin. It was an early warning, and as far as he knew, all vampires felt it. Even those who were half reaper. For him, it barely registered, because the sun wasn't an issue.

"Hurry," she whispered. Her voice held the desperate edge of panic that was so unlike her, he imagined she was cringing inside.

Greyson wanted to pull her close in a comforting embrace. Instead, he slid the manhole cover back into its spot. "We're only five minutes away."

"Good."

He started down the street opposite the way they'd entered. "Come on."

She kept pace with him, wringing her hands together once but quickly pulling them apart again.

He led them a couple of blocks away, then walked up the steps of an average-looking apartment building that might best be described as old but clean. Exactly as it was meant to appear.

She stayed close to him as he produced a key and unlocked the door. "You know someone here?"

"I did." He pushed the door open and went in.

She followed him up five flights of steps. The building was exceptionally quiet. On the fifth floor, he unlocked another door and led them into a beautiful apartment.

It was furnished with the kind of taste and elegance that seemed uniquely Parisian. Opulent and restrained at the same time.

Kora looked around. "Hattie would love this place. Who lives here?"

"No one." He dropped the key on a small baroque side table. "But I own it."

Her mouth came open in surprise. "This place is yours?"

He nodded, but her surprise produced no happiness in him. "It was left to me by my sire. This was her apartment." The bittersweet memories that filled him brought a nostalgic smile to his mouth. "She would have liked you very much, I think."

Kora didn't seem to know what to say to that.

Greyson changed the subject to spare her. "The windows are all UV tinted. The whole building is. Only vampires live here."

"That's pretty cool." She was still looking around. "I wonder why I never knew about this place when I lived in the city."

"Because I keep it quiet. And I only rent to those who agree to do the same."

Her mouth came open again. "Wait a minute. You mean you own this whole building?"

"Yes. Catherine willed it to me through the Vampire Council." Sweet, generous Catherine.

Willing it through the Vampire Council was about the only way such things could happen when someone had been alive for centuries and had no way of providing a human will.

"She must have loved you very much."

The bittersweet feeling returned. "She did. And I her." He took a breath he didn't need, but filling his lungs with the scent of this place was an indulgence he rarely got to partake of. "I never expected her to be gone as soon as she was."

"It must be hard for you to be here. I assume it's been a while?"

"It has been. But I'm fine. The memories here are overwhelmingly good."

There was sympathy in her smile. He couldn't recall ever seeing that from her before. "I'm glad."

It was kind of her to say, but he was done talking about his past. "We should feed. There's a butcher shop not far from here that's been supplying the tenants of this building for as long as it's been here. I'll run out and get us something."

"Okay. Do you want to text me the pictures of that bull? I can work on the image search while you're gone."

He took his phone out and sent her the pictures. "Done. There's Wi-Fi. Connect to Cath1600. Password is Immortal67, capital I. I'll be back as soon as I can."

"See you in a bit, then."

He started for the door. "Lock up behind me. And make yourself at home. Whatever you need."

"Thank you, Greyson."

He glanced at her before he slipped out. She was remarkably beautiful. "You're welcome."

Then he shut the door and went down the steps. He heard the lock being turned before he reached the fourth floor.

He wasn't just leaving to get them sustenance. He wanted to be sure they weren't being watched.

As he exited the building, he took a long look in both directions. The sky was bright with the rising sun. He squinted into it. Seemed brighter after time underground. The street was empty, but this had always been a quiet neighborhood, which worked well for those who rented from him.

He turned up his jacket collar and started toward the butcher, but added a few blocks to his route just to see if he could pick up any tails.

The butcher shop was just two blocks ahead, and he was still alone. He'd been sure they were being watched in Dublin, but leaving the way they had must have done the trick.

That was all well and good, but he wasn't dropping his guard. Not when Kora was in the mix.

He went to the shop's back door and knocked. It was very early, but the butcher had always started his day around this time.

A couple long minutes later, an older woman in a long white coat and apron opened the door. Not who he'd expected. She looked at him blankly, then hesitant recognition filled her eyes. "You are the vampire?"

She spoke French, so he answered her the same way. "I am. You know me?"

She nodded. "You used to come here when I was a child. But not for many years. Of course, you look the same. I do not."

Then recognition struck him as well. "Margot?"

"*Oui*." She smiled timidly. "You are...Garson?"

"Greyson. Garrett." He shook his head. He had been gone a long time. She had barely been the height of the shop's counters when he'd last seen her. "Is Hector still here?"

"My father is retired. He and my mother moved to the coast of Spain." Her smile took on new strength. "I run the shop now."

"Very good. Then you know why I am here?"

"Yes. Your tenants all come." She glanced at the sky. "Not usually at this time."

He shrugged. "I am one of the rare immune."

She moved out of the way. "Come in."

He entered. "Thank you."

"How much do you need?"

"Enough for two. Your best." He stayed by the door, not wanting to be in her way.

She went straight to the massive refrigeration units that lined the shop's back walls. Through a small window in the white-tiled room, he could see the shop front. The cases were dark, as she wasn't yet open for business.

A slab of meat lay on the central cutting block, an enormous cleaver resting nearby.

A few moments later, she brought him a bleached muslin shopping bag. Inside were two brown paper-wrapped glass jars. Not everything had changed since he'd been here last. "On your account?"

"*Oui, s'il vous plaît.*"

She smiled. "You're welcome, Greyson Garrett."

With a nod, he took his leave. He wound the straps of the bag around his hand. The glass jars clinked softly against each other, the paper muting the sound.

On the way back, he kept the same watchful gaze on his surroundings as he had going to the shop, but this time he took the most direct route to the apartment. He'd been gone long enough.

As he turned the corner toward the building, the sight of a man standing near the door set his internal alarms ringing. Greyson slipped back behind the corner and watched for a moment.

The man was just standing there, hands in his jacket pockets. He made no attempt to hide himself. Instead, he looked very much like he was waiting for someone.

But who? Greyson wasn't aware of any of his tenants being daywalkers, so the chances that this man was waiting for any of them were slim.

Could he just be meeting someone there?

Then why stand on the small landing in front of the doors? Why not stand on the street?

Only one answer came to mind. The man was waiting for someone. And that someone was Greyson.

He inhaled and picked up the scent of wolf. A shifter. Not the same one from the Dragon's Hoard, though.

Kora was waiting. Whatever the man was up to, Greyson figured it was better just to find out.

He went around the corner and straight to the building. When he was a few feet away, he called out in French, "Who are you waiting for?"

The man answered in French. "You, I believe."

Greyson stopped at the bottom of the steps and switched to English. "Why?"

The man hesitated before answering in the same language. "To warn you. What you are looking for? It should not be found."

Greyson chose his next words carefully. "I don't know what you're talking about."

The man's eyes narrowed. He slowly descended the steps to stand on the street in front of Greyson. "The power you seek will destroy more than it saves. It could even start a war."

"Again, I don't know what you mean."

The man's resolute expression was unchanged, but his eyes flared with a wolfen glow. "You have been warned. Do not make us do so again."

"Who's this 'us' you speak of?"

After a moment's hesitation, he said, "The Brotherhood." Then he turned and walked away.

Greyson watched him for a moment, then unlocked the door and went inside. He watched the man through the glass until he was no longer visible, then Greyson sent a quick text to Birdie, asking her for information on the Brotherhood. If anyone knew, it would be her. Or she could find out. The woman was magic that way.

With the text sent, he went up the five flights to Catherine's apartment, all the while trying to decide what to tell Kora.

Or maybe not to tell Kora at all.

17

At the sound of the door being unlocked, Kora turned toward it excitedly. Only as Greyson entered did she realize it could have very well been someone else. But she was too wound up to pay attention to safety.

She couldn't let herself do that again.

"Everything all right?" he asked.

She nodded enthusiastically. "I think I figured out the bull."

He was carrying a bag. He put it on the table in front of the sofa. "Tell me."

She pulled up the photos she'd found on her phone. "It could be one of two places. I think. Or it might not be either of these." Frustration tightened the muscles in her jaw. "Do you know how many places have a bull as a symbol? A lot."

"How did you narrow it down, then?"

"First, by year. If they weren't around when Rasputin was, I eliminated them. Next, I tried to think like a vampire who needed to hide something in a very secure spot. Not that hard to do, really."

"Okay. Let me see what you have."

She turned her screen so he could see it. "This is a bullfighting museum in Portugal. It was originally a school for bullfighters. See the emblem on the front of the building?"

He nodded. "A bull on its back legs. That's pretty close. But I don't know."

"Well, what's also interesting about this place is their cook was supposedly Russian. The years are right for it to have been the Romanov maid who escaped."

His brows lifted. "That feels like a strong lead."

"I think so, too."

"Show me the other one."

She tapped her screen a few more times to bring up the next picture. "Okay, this is the Castillo del Toro. The castle of the bull. It's been around since the 1800s and was built by the Bragado family. That name has something to do with bulls, too. I looked it up." She turned the phone his way again. "And look at their family crest."

"A rampant bull. That looks exactly like the drawing underneath the pedestal. This is in Portugal too?"

"No, this is in Spain. Near Toledo. It's a historical site now. No one's lived there for a long time."

"Spain, huh? Someone I know just retired there." He shrugged. "Not that it means anything."

"Unless it's the universe trying to point us in that direction."

He gave her a funny look. "Since when do you believe in signs like that?"

"I don't. Not really. But this is a hard decision to make."

He dragged a hand through his hair. "Both places are old enough. Both have a lot of hiding places. One might have had a Russian cook."

She tapped her phone off as she nodded. "I know. How are we going to decide?"

He held his hands up. "I don't want to influence you. It's your quest. Your decision. But it doesn't have to be made now. Now all we need to do is get some rest. I'll text the pilot and tell him we'll give him an update this evening."

She nodded, but disappointment surged through her. How was she going to decide? "Okay. I could use the rest. I can feel the sun. Even in this apartment. It's sapping my energy."

He pointed to the bag on the table. "Feed before you sleep. It's cold, but it will help."

"Thanks for doing that."

"No problem. I'll be in the room on the right if you need me. Sleep well."

"You, too."

He lifted a brown paper-wrapped package from the bag and disappeared into the bedroom he'd indicated, shutting the door behind him.

She took the other package, a jar by the feel and heft of it, and found her way to the second bedroom. The very feminine space was decorated in rose, cream, and gold. Had this been Catherine's room?

On a whim, Kora opened the wardrobe. Exquisite gowns of all colors and description filled it, all of them from bygone eras. She ran her hand along the shoulders. Silk, satin, feathers, beads, sequins, velvet… had she the time and energy, she would have looked more thoroughly.

She closed the wardrobe and took her dinner to the bed. She set the jar on the nightstand, then went to the windows and closed the drapes, shutting herself off from the day.

At last, she sat on the bed, took the lid off the jar, and satisfied her cravings. She was exhausted, but her mind was going too fast to sleep just yet.

Spain or Portugal? How was she going to decide?

She lifted the jar to her mouth to finish what was left, and light from the crystal chandelier sparked off the ring on her finger.

After draining the jar's contents, she put it down to study the ring. Was this thing connected to the hunt they were on? It had to be, didn't it? She didn't buy that it just happened to be under the pedestal along with the bull drawing. So what did it mean? What was the point of it? Was it like the locket in that it would help her see what couldn't be seen otherwise?

She got her phone out again and started searching for gemstone bands, trying to find something that looked similar in hopes it might give her a clue. She searched relentlessly until her head drooped.

Sleep tugged at her, trying to take over. She lay down and let it.

Her slumber lasted until the chirping of her phone

woke her. Groggy, but functioning as best she could, she grabbed the phone to see what was so urgent.

A text message from the Fox. *Are you making progress?*

That woke her up a little more. She sat up in bed, yawning and stretching. The prickle of the sun on her skin was gone. Twilight was well upon them. She could feel it just like she'd felt the rising sun.

She stared at the message, trying to decide how to provide an answer that was positive but didn't give too much hope. After all, she and Greyson didn't even know what country they were headed to. She typed a single word.

Some.

Then she went to the windows and pulled the curtains back, but held on to them as she leaned against the window frame and looked outside. She hoped that answer was enough for the Fox, because she wasn't eager to say more. Sure, they'd made some progress, but they were at a crossroads now.

Spain or Portugal? It wasn't that big of a deal, the countries were right next to each other, but a wrong choice was still going to delay finding the treasure. And sleep hadn't helped to make that decision. Nor did they have any idea what to do when they got to the next location.

With a sigh, she wondered if Greyson was up. Maybe he'd had an epiphany in a dream. She turned away from the window, but the curtain came with her. The little gemstone ring had snagged on the fabric.

She carefully freed the curtain, then ran her fingertip over the band's surface to see if a prong had bent. Antique jewelry needed extra care, and she probably shouldn't be wearing the thing. The prongs felt fine, but she took the ring off and decided to loop it onto the ribbon holding the locket and keep it around her neck instead. If only she knew what significance it might hold toward finding the next clue.

She turned on the bedside lamp and studied the ring under the bright light. Nothing about it had changed. She looked at the stones. Such a random assortment. Coral, amethyst, another coral, then a deep orangey-brown stone that she thought was some kind of garnet or possibly topaz, followed by an opal, then finally what she'd thought was emerald, but under the bright light, she noticed that the green wasn't right. The last stone had to be tourmaline.

It wasn't a combination of stones she would have put together, but they had to mean something.

Were they birthstones? If so, did they represent people? Six stones, six children? There had been only five Romanov children. Unless this was some kind of clue that there had been a sixth.

No. That was too much of a rabbit hole. Too much information for one ring and a drawing of a bull.

So, what, then? Maybe they were still birthstones, but the months they represented meant something. She looked up. There was a small desk in the bedroom. She dug through the drawers until she found a pad of paper and a pencil.

Then she went to work. Her knowledge of gems wasn't so extensive that she knew every birthstone, but she had the internet for that.

Coral wasn't a traditional or even modern birthstone, so at best all she could find was that it was an alternate for October.

That alone made her rethink the birthstone idea. It was too much of a stretch. If this ring meant anything, it had to be something easier to figure out.

Something that a person of any era might grasp.

But how easy could it be if she was racking her brain and coming up with nothing?

A knock on the open bedroom door brought her head up.

Greyson stood there. "I was going to ask how you slept, but you look busy. Anything I can help with?"

She held the ring up. "Just trying to figure this thing out. If it means anything at all."

He stayed near the door. "It must. Why else would it have been under the pedestal?"

"That's what I think, too." She let out a groan of frustration. "There are too many possibilities. I keep going down rabbit holes that lead nowhere."

"When I'm in a situation like that, I write down all my random thoughts to get them out of my head and make space for new ones."

She held up the pad of paper and pencil. "I was going to write down the month that each gem represents as a birthstone—"

"Good idea." He walked toward the bed, but stopped a few feet away.

"Except that coral, which is in the band twice, has never really been used as a birthstone." She gestured to the end of the bed. "Sit. Two brains are better than one."

He did as she asked, bending one leg in front of him so he could sit facing her. "Then birthstones are out."

"I think so."

He held out his hand. "May I?"

She offered him the ring. "Sure.

He shook his head. "The paper and pencil."

"Oh. Yeah, of course." She gave those to him. "What are you thinking?"

"You know a lot about gems, right?"

"A decent bit."

"Well, you know more than I do. So let's go down the list of what's in the ring and see what we can come up with for each stone."

"Okay."

"What gems are there? Tell them to me in order."

She held the band between her two fingers. "Coral, amethyst, coral, garnet—I think, but I'm not sure what kind exactly and it could be topaz—then opal, and tourmaline."

He wrote as she spoke, then looked at the list, eyes full of intense concentration. Then he shifted his gaze to her and frowned. "I really thought this would help."

"Here." She held the ring out to him. "You have a look at it."

He put the pad down to take the ring, then turned it in his fingers, holding it up to the light and peering at it with great intent. "What's the little symbol inside the band? Looks like a fly."

She groaned. "I was so focused on the gems, I didn't even look inside the band. Let me see."

He handed the ring to her. She leaned back on the bed to look at the band under the light again. "Definitely looks like a fly, but not quite."

"You know," he said, "Catherine gave me a pair of cufflinks once. Each one had two square red garnets set into it. She said the garnets were to represent my initials. GG."

Kora let out a little gasp and sat up. "That's it."

"What's it?"

"The gems are letters. The word is our clue."

"How can you be so sure?"

"This isn't a fly on the band, it's a bee. A honeybee. Napoleon used the honeybee as a symbol of his reign, and he loved acrostic jewelry. The gems are letters. That has to be it."

Greyson grabbed the pad of paper. "C-A-C-G-O-T? That's not a word. Neither is C-A-C-T-O-T if it's a topaz."

"Then we have a letter wrong. Hang on. It's the garnet, I know it is. Give me a second." She picked up her phone and ran a search on garnet color names. She scrolled through a list. "It's hessonite. It has to be. The color is right. What would that spell if the G was an H?"

"*Cachot.*" He looked at her. "The French word for dungeon. A bullfighting school wouldn't have a dungeon, but a castle would."

"You're absolutely right." The sheer excitement of arriving at the answer made her want to kiss him again. Somehow, she refrained. "We're going to Spain. Thank you for figuring that out."

"Me?" He laughed. "That was all you."

She grinned. And kissed him anyway.

Greyson's practical sense screamed at him to pull away. But that noise was quickly silenced as his desire won out. He leaned into Kora's unexpected kiss, reveling in her happiness and the satisfaction of having worked as a team to figure the clue out.

But the incomparable pleasure of her mouth on his was what kept him connected to her. Kept him wanting more. Why had he thought this was a bad idea?

Because of her father. And the million dollars he'd promised.

But Greyson had never agreed to the deal. And he realized now that he never would. He couldn't. Lucien had been good to him. And Greyson considered the man a friend. But Kora was becoming something so much more. Something worth the risk of angering Lucien.

At least he thought they *could* become so much more. He wanted the chance to explore that. As crazy as it sounded.

Lucien would have nothing to worry about when it came to Kora's safety, though. He had to know that. Greyson would die for her, if need be. That desire to protect her was the same reason he wasn't telling her about the Brotherhood just yet. She would worry. And worry could make a person careless.

She pulled back from the kiss, laughing a little. "Thanks for not turning away."

"Why would I do that?"

She shrugged. "You've been a little cold since we got on the plane in Nocturne Falls. Well, not cold, exactly. But cool, I guess. Like you wanted distance from me. But maybe that was my imagination."

So she'd noticed.

He didn't want to tell her about the conversation with her father, and when he didn't immediately offer an explanation, she sat back like he'd just proven something to her.

"It wasn't my imagination."

Greyson sighed a little. "I was trying to treat this like any other job I might do. I didn't want my feelings to cloud my judgment. Or interfere with how I might react."

She nodded, but didn't look completely satisfied with that answer. "You think caring about me might make you less effective as a protector?"

"No, not that. But it might make me more…lenient. I might accept a bad decision I wouldn't otherwise."

Her eyes tapered down. "And of course, my father gave you specific instructions about how this was all supposed to go, right?"

Greyson wasn't about to go down that road. He shrugged. "Your father just wants you safe. Any father would want that."

"I suppose." But her expression said she wasn't quite buying his answer. "Shouldn't you let the pilot know our game plan?"

"I should, yes. Then I'm going to shower." He got up. "I can be ready to go in fifteen minutes. You?"

"Same."

"Good." He went toward the door, then stopped. "If you want a change of clothing, I'm sure Catherine's things would fit you. Although they're probably all too out of date to suit you."

Her smile was easy and kind. "That's a generous offer, but I can wait until I'm on the plane."

He nodded and left. He'd never brought another woman to this apartment. Never considered it. This was too much of a shrine to Catherine. Of his life with her. Too much a reminder of the past. And what might have been.

He went back to his bedroom. Even staring out the windows here reminded him of those days. What would Catherine think of her city today?

Would they even still be here?

He thought they would. Catherine had loved Paris more than any other place in the world. And he'd loved her more than any other woman.

But her affection for him hadn't been quite the same. She'd often treated him...not unkindly...but more like a child. Which, he supposed, she had a right to do, seeing as how she'd sired him.

173

That hadn't kept him from falling madly in love with her. He knew that was why her death had struck such a blow. She hadn't been just his sire. He'd thought she was his future. He'd planned his life around her.

Then, just like that, she was gone at the hands of a necromancer.

He shook his head. This city made him sentimental. He didn't like that. Not when there was work to be done. He pulled his phone out and texted the pilot with their plans, then he got into a very hot shower and did his best to scrub away the past.

They were on the plane an hour later, sitting next to each other in the excessive comfort of the Ellinghams' jet and making plans for when they arrived in Spain.

"We'll go right to the castle," Kora said.

"Which means we'll have to enter it illegally."

She shrugged. "I don't think that can be helped. I can't go during daylight hours, and really, do we want to be searching for our next clue while there are tourists milling about?"

"You're assuming they let tourists into the dungeon."

"Hmm." She gave that some thought. "Did we check to see that this place has a dungeon, or are we just assuming that because it's a castle?"

He refrained from letting loose the curse that was sitting on his tongue. "Good point." He pulled up the castle's website on his phone. Read a little. Then sighed. "The castle had a dungeon, but it hasn't been open to the public in fifty years. No one is sure where the entrance is anymore, since it was bricked off so long ago."

She frowned. "I guess that's good and bad."

"How is it good?"

"No one's been down there in a while, so the clue we're searching for should be untouched."

"Okay, I agree that's good. But getting into the dungeon isn't going to be easy. I'm really hoping we can manage it without attracting a lot of attention. It might mean taking out a portion of a wall."

"So? You did that in the sewer without any problem."

"But that was old mortar, weak with damp. A bricked-up access to a dungeon inside a castle? That's not going to be the same thing at all."

"We'll figure it out when we get there."

"I imagine we will." He hoped they'd get to figure it out alone, but he had to wonder if the shifter he'd met on the steps would return. After that warning, Greyson believed the Brotherhood were serious. Whatever lay at the end of this treasure hunt, someone wanted it to stay hidden.

The silence remained between them for a while. Kora was typing away on her phone, but he couldn't see the screen and had no idea what she was doing.

Then his phone vibrated with an incoming message. He checked the screen. Lucien.

You haven't checked in. Is everything okay?

Before answering, Greyson turned his phone away so Kora wouldn't see the screen. *Yes. Sleeping, then traveling again.*

Where to?

Nowhere dangerous. All is well.

I'm paying you to answer me.

That would be true if I'd agreed to your offer. Which I didn't. Greyson knew then that he had to tell Lucien the truth. *I care about Kora. She's not a client to me. Or a job. She's a friend. I will absolutely get her home safe.*

By whose standards?

Mine. He hesitated, then with a reckless smile on his face, added, *So there might be kissing.*

I'm going to assume that's a joke.

You can assume what you want, but I'm dead serious. Greyson laughed to himself. "No pun intended."

Kora looked up. "What?"

"Nothing. Just texting with a friend." He put his phone away. Nothing Lucien could say was going to change his mind. A million dollars would be amazing. But not as amazing as a chance at a future he'd never expected. "I'm going up to the cockpit for a minute. Do you need anything?"

"No, I'm good." Then she unexpectedly put her hand on his arm. "Thanks for all this. I don't think I could have gotten this far without you."

"I think you would have. Might have taken you longer, but you would have managed."

"I appreciate your confidence in me. I'm not sure I agree, though."

He smiled at her. "Kora, you don't give yourself enough credit. Even when you were...not the responsible adult you are now, you were still a very capable woman."

"Capable of getting myself into trouble."

He chuckled. "True. But even in those situations, your intelligence and resourcefulness were evident."

Her smile was bright and instant. "Thank you. That might be one of the nicest things anyone's ever said to me. Makes me really sorry for all the trouble I caused you. I'm especially sorry about Rome."

"We both made it out alive. That's what matters." He picked up her hand and brushed his mouth across her knuckles. "We're going to make it out alive this time, too. And when we get back to Nocturne Falls, maybe we could try an actual date. Just to see if we're any good at that."

Her lips parted. "Are you asking me out?"

"I am."

She bit her bottom lip, fangs tantalizingly on display. "My father is not going to like that."

Greyson planted a real kiss on her knuckles. "I can deal with that if you can."

She faltered for a moment. "I only just made things right with him. I'm not sure I want to upset him. But I would love to go on a date with you."

He stood, releasing her hand reluctantly. "You don't have to decide now. You can tell me when we get home. There's a lot of ground left to travel until we set foot in Georgia again."

She grabbed his hand and pulled him down toward her, planting her mouth on his in a hard, fast kiss that felt like a very definitive answer.

She let him go and grinned. "I don't need to wait. I might have done a lot of growing up lately, but my decision-making skills haven't changed. I know what I want."

"All right, then." A little buzzed from her kiss, he pointed toward the cockpit. "I'll just go see if we're still on time to land."

"You do that." She went back to her phone.

He walked the rest of the way to the cockpit with a grin on his face that felt permanent. He and Kora were going to go on a date.

Lucien was going to hate that, no questions asked.

But Greyson wasn't sure when he'd been happier.

Not in a million years would Kora ever have imagined that she'd feel so giddy about going on a date with a man, especially one she'd essentially considered her nemesis until just a few days ago.

Now she was pretty jazzed about spending time with him in a romantic way. And kissing him some more.

Crazy how life could do a complete one-eighty without you ever seeing it coming.

Still smiling with the kind of deep satisfaction Waffles often displayed after destroying his favorite catnip mouse, Kora sent Hattie a quick text. *Hey there. How are you? Thinking about you. Love you.*

She put her phone away in her belt bag, now firmly on her hip. Hattie wasn't the best texter, and there was no telling when she'd actually answer. And Kora had lost track of what time it was in Nocturne Falls. Hattie might be in the middle of gardening. Or asleep.

Kora closed her eyes. Not to sleep, but to lose herself in thought. For a moment, those thoughts were about the castle and the dungeon and how they were going to find the next clue. But her mind went to Greyson pretty quickly.

He was about as perfect a partner as she could hope for. He was kinder than she remembered. More patient, too. But maybe that was because of how she'd changed. Maybe she was easier to be around now.

Whatever the reason, he was being pretty wonderful so far. He took care of her in a way that didn't make her feel helpless. She appreciated that.

She also loved the glimpse into his past that she'd gotten. To think he owned that entire apartment building in Paris. All thanks to Catherine, of course, but what a woman she must have been.

Her decision to turn Greyson made him even more desirable, in Kora's estimation. Catherine obviously had a discerning eye. When she'd looked at Greyson, she'd clearly seen a man she wanted to spend centuries with. The thought was deeply intriguing, and for a moment, Kora lamented that Catherine wasn't around to speak to.

But then, if Catherine had still been here, Greyson wouldn't be a part of Kora's life. He'd probably never have come to Nocturne Falls. Never found a need to distract himself by doing jobs for her father.

In a way, Catherine's death had paved the way for this very moment.

Kora laughed. Such a reaper thought to have, that death was a kind of gift. For all the ways she was her mother's child, so much of herself was cut from the same cloth as her father.

Her phone vibrated, bringing her out of her head. She glanced at the screen. Hattie had replied.

So good to hear from you. Love you, too. How are things?

Good. Did I wake you?

No, just finished dinner. Going out for a walk with Mae Ellen next door.

Kora smiled. It was so nice that Hattie had friends now. *Have fun.*

Are you sure everything is all right?

Yes, positive. Why?

Your father seems upset.

That was curious. *Why?*

I don't know.

Kora was suddenly dying to find out. *Use your magic. Get Dad to talk. Then tell me what's going on!* She ended with a winky face emoji and a heart.

Hattie responded with, *Will do!* And added three hearts.

Kora tucked her phone next to her and settled in. If anyone could pry information out of Lucien, it was Hattie. The next text should be very interesting.

Lit on three sides, the Castillo del Toro rose out of the darkness like a monument to the past. An imposing structure with its sloping walls, fortifications and battlements, the stone edifice looked impenetrable. Which, Greyson understood, was exactly the point. And exactly the kind of place to hide something you wanted to stay hidden.

Kora stood at Greyson's side. "We're never getting in there—"

"It's not going to be easy, but we'll figure it out."

"You didn't let me finish." She nudged him good-naturedly. "We're never getting in there without breaking in. We'll have to pick the lock and hope for the best. What kind of security system do you think they have?"

"I'd say a very good one based on some of the artifacts that are supposed to be on display. And we're not going in through the main door. We're also not picking any locks. That way, we won't set off any alarms. Hopefully."

"No?"

"No."

"Then how are we getting in?"

"I have a plan. Based on some research I did earlier."

"Do tell." She crossed her arms and stared up at him with amused curiosity.

He wanted to kiss her again. He decided he would, just as soon as the next clue was in hand. "I'm going to scale the parapet on the left side. Supposedly, there's a window there that's never been fixed since it was broken by a visiting royal in 1912. They think fixing it'll bring bad luck or something. Anyway, I'll go through that window and make my way down to the second floor, where I'm sure I can find an unalarmed door or window to open for you."

"What if that window's been fixed?"

Yes, he definitely wanted to kiss her. If only to get the smirk off her pretty face. "It hasn't been. But even if it has, there will be something else. I'll find a way."

"And where am I in all this?"

"Keeping guard. We haven't done any recon. Just because we don't see any kind of security patrol doesn't mean there isn't one."

"So do we have a signal? Some kind of special whistle. Or a birdcall. You know, in case something comes up. How am I supposed to warn you?"

He gave her a skeptical look. "Our phones will do just fine."

She coughed suddenly, and he could have sworn

he heard the word *boring*. So much sass. Forget the kissing. She needed a good biting. Or spanking. He was up for either.

He stifled his urges until such time as he could appropriately act on them. "Try not to get into trouble until I can get you inside, okay?"

"Yes, Greyson, dear."

He shook his head, but smiled. "Be safe. I'll move as quickly as I can. I'll text you when I'm in."

"I'll be here. Waiting patiently."

"I doubt that." With a wink, he took off at full speed for the dark side of the castle. When he reached the wall, he stayed there for a moment, listening.

He didn't think he'd been detected. Human eyes weren't always capable of picking up vampire movements at such speed. Especially in the dark. He didn't hear anything.

He listened harder, focusing on the castle's interior. The thick stone walls made it difficult to arrow in on any sounds, but he thought he detected something faint. It was a repetitive sound. Like a heartbeat.

They might have company inside. Would make sense to have at least one overnight guard. Greyson and Kora would just have to do their best to be quiet and stay out of the man's patrol path.

He gave it a few more seconds, but there were no other sounds. Content with that, he moved away from the wall about six feet to give himself some space, then took two big steps and leaped to the second level.

He bent his knees as he landed, absorbing as much of the sound as he could. He repeated what he'd done below: found some shadow for cover, then listened for any sign that he'd been heard.

Satisfied that all was clear, he made his way to the parapet with the broken window. If it had been repaired, it was about to be broken again. He wasn't climbing all the way up there just to come back down again.

He stayed on the dark side of the tower and ascended with careful precision, using the nooks and crannies of the stone block construction as his ladder. He wasn't particularly fond of heights, but he kept his eye on the prize. The walkway at the top.

Falling wouldn't kill him, but it wouldn't be pretty either. Kora would have to get him to safety in a bucket. And the recovery would be long and painful.

He dug his fingers a little deeper into the next crevice, using every ounce of his extraordinary vampire strength to cling like Spider-Man to the tower's sheer wall. He moved with as much haste as he felt was safe. He did not need to be discovered like this.

At last, he made the walkway, hurling himself over the battlement to land on the stone ground. He lay there for two seconds, appreciating his own hard work, admiring the stars, and thanking the universe for not letting him become a vampire pancake on the ground below.

Then he righted himself and went to find the broken window.

It was, most happily, still broken.

He carefully hoisted himself through it and dropped onto the steps that wound up to the walkway's entrance.

A quick listen now that he was inside revealed the heartbeat he'd thought he'd heard earlier. And a second one.

Two guards. He and Kora would have to be twice as careful.

But vampire stealth was a very real thing, and he descended the steps with all the quiet of the undead.

On the second floor, he did a quick round to ascertain where the guards were. First floor and stationary. As much as he wanted to go down and see if they were sleeping, he didn't. He and Kora could handle that together. First, he had to find a way to get her inside.

Like she was reading his mind, his phone vibrated with a message from her.

What's going on? Are you in?

Your patience is remarkable, he texted back. *Looking for a way to get you in now.*

He found that way in a small room with narrow windows. None of them had alarm sensors, maybe because of the size of the windows. But Kora could fit. She was tall but slim.

Although there was her chest to deal with. A thought that derailed him for a moment.

Second floor, he texted. *Look for three narrow Gothic windows, one open. I'm there waiting for you.*

On my way.

Then, not more than fifteen seconds later. *Are you kidding? I don't think a three-year-old could get through there.*

You'll fit. All you have to do is jump to the second story, then use the bottom of the open window to pull yourself up.

A moment went by, then he heard a dull thump, followed by a soft grunt.

"A little help?"

Two hands gripped the windowsill. And that was about all the width there was. He went over to give her an assist, leaning out to see her. "I may have overestimated the size of the window."

She shot him a look. "You think? I'm going to have to come in sideways. I need help for that."

"You got it." He took hold of her right arm just below the wrist and lifted her until she could slide her right foot through.

"Don't let me go."

"I won't." And he meant it. Kora would come to no harm on his watch.

She wriggled through with the grace of a limbo dancer, finally hopping down to stand beside him. "I'd much prefer to walk out of here, if that's an option."

"If we can find a way out through the dungeon, it should be. But we have company."

"Guards?"

He nodded. "Two on the first floor. They weren't moving, so either they're asleep or playing cards or staring at the ceiling. Not making enough noise to be doing anything else."

"Still, we'd better be quiet."

"Agreed. Thankfully, the priceless antiquities are all on display on the ground floor, so I can't imagine they do much patrolling up here."

"We have to go down there, though, to access the dungeon."

"I know. But we don't know *how* to access the dungeon."

"Ah." She smiled and held up a finger. "But we do. I put Birdie on it. She was able to find a set of plans for this castle. As best she can tell in comparing those plans to the most current set, the passageway that was bricked off is through the armory."

He was impressed with her resourcefulness, but then, there wasn't much Birdie couldn't get done. "Do you know where the armory is?"

"Not a clue. But Birdie also said there was a princess here, once upon a time, whose beloved was imprisoned in the dungeon, and she had a secret passageway constructed to visit him while her father was off at war. Or something like that. Anyway, that can be found in the library."

Greyson frowned. "The library is where the antiquities are displayed."

Her brows lifted. "I guess we'd really better hope those guards are sound sleepers."

Having Greyson lift her through the window had made Kora's insides slightly fluttery. It wasn't a reaction she'd expected. Sure, she liked the guy and was pretty jazzed that they were going on a real date when they got back to Nocturne Falls, but she was a vampire-reaper hybrid, for crying out loud.

Not a teenage girl who'd spent her afternoon writing *Mrs. Greyson Garrett* on the back cover of her notebook three thousand times.

What was going on with her? This kind of emotional softness was very confusing. On one hand, she imagined it was all part of her maturation process. On the other hand, it made her feel weak.

And she didn't like weak.

Weak could get a vampire killed. These new feelings were doubly hard to take when Kora had lived most of her life believing that her mother's death was caused by weakness. Finding this treasure and getting the truth couldn't come soon enough.

Greyson insisted on going first down the wide stairs to the first floor. She let him, since her own thoughts had taken part of her concentration.

He went to check on the guards and came back a moment later. "Two, asleep as I suspected. We should be fine, but they are right at the entrance to the library."

"I can creep as good as the next guy."

"I have no doubt." He gave her a wry smile. "All right, let's go. If they wake up, we—"

"Knock them out?"

He frowned. "Use our speed to get out of their sight line."

"Party pooper." But she smiled to show him she was kidding. "When we get into the library, you take the right side, I'll take the left."

"Deal."

They went into stealth mode, moving past the guards with as little sound as possible. The guards continued to snooze.

Once inside the library, they had to remain silent, but that was harder to do as they searched for the secret entrance to the dungeon. There was nothing to hide behind either. In a room that had once held shelves and shelves of books, it was now a wide-open space filled with waist-high display cases showing off the treasures of past eras and long-gone nobility.

The walls were all they were concerned with, however. The wood panels were the perfect height and width to provide entrance to a secret passage.

With the guards just feet away, knocking on the

panels to see which one had empty space behind it was out of the question.

Kora watched Greyson. He was holding his hands in front of the panel seams. Feeling for a draft, no doubt.

Smart. But she could accomplish that more effectively with a simple tool. She dug the lighter out of her belt bag, flicked it to life, and used the flame to look for escaping air.

Greyson turned at the rasp of the flint, then nodded his approval.

Few vampires were fans of fire, but she hadn't grown up with that fear, since she'd been primarily raised by her father. Carrying the lighter was something she'd started doing after setting fire to a department store (with matches found in the employee breakroom) had proved to be the perfect amount of distraction for her to escape a sticky situation.

Of course, that wasn't the kind of situation she imagined she'd ever be in again, now that she was on the straight and narrow.

But old habits die hard, and the lighter was once again proving useful.

Greyson was pushing on a panel as if hoping to spring a hidden latch. When nothing happened, he moved on to the next one.

She returned to her own work, testing the air around the panel seams and watching for the flame's telltale flicker.

One of the guards let out a loud, choking snore. She froze, glancing at Greyson with eyes wide.

He held up a finger and mouthed the word, "Wait."

After a few moments, the guard's snoring returned to the same cadence, but her nerves stayed tightly wound. It was silly to feel that way. The human guards were no match for her and Greyson. The humans were slower, their sight was impaired by the relative darkness, and they didn't have a vampire's strength.

And yet, the thought of being found out twisted Kora's belly into knots.

With a shake of her head, she went back to work, moving the lighter slowly past the seams. It was slow going by necessity. Moving the lighter too fast would cause the flame to quiver and make her think she'd found something.

Every once in a while, she'd glance over at Greyson. From the set of his jaw, he looked frustrated. She understood. She was, too. They'd been at this for nearly twenty minutes and had nothing to show for it.

But even frustrated, he was handsome. And very hard to take her eyes off of. Besides the frustration, was he feeling the same thing she was? Disappointment?

Because she'd expected to saunter in and find the passageway instantly. Why she'd thought it would happen like that, she wasn't sure, but the longer they were in here, the more hope she lost.

They might have to get a room and come back tomorrow night. Or go back to the plane. But the idea of sharing a room with him had appeal for reasons better left unexplored at the moment.

She stopped watching Greyson and went back to her own wall. She started on the side of the next panel.

The flame flickered.

She went as still as stone. Easy to do when you had no pulse and no need to breathe.

The flickering continued, bending the flame nearly in half. She moved the lighter down the seam. The flame danced and wavered, even when she held the lighter still.

In a nearly inaudible whisper, she called out, "Greyson."

He joined her a second later. He smiled at her and nodded, the wordless equivalent of *good job*.

She moved out of the way, and he put his hands on the panel, pushing like he'd done with the others.

A soft snick rewarded his efforts, and the panel protruded a few centimeters on one side.

He got his fingers under the edge and opened it.

The squeal of rusted metal shattered the silence. Both guards came to life with the sounds of being woken. Voices followed.

Then footsteps.

Greyson yanked the panel all the way open. "Go," he whispered.

Kora dashed in. He followed and closed the panel behind them.

Darkness descended. The pitch-black kind, devoid of even the tiniest bit of light. Even vampire eyes needed a speck of illumination so they could see.

Kora reached out for Greyson and found him next to her. The passageway was narrow and short, so they were both stooped down. Her hand closed around his arm. He put his hand over hers.

They stayed still and silent.

The footsteps came closer as the guards entered the library. Light suddenly leaked through three sides of the panel they'd come through.

Greyson put his finger to his lips, then motioned that they should stay where they were. She nodded. The passageway was stone block on all sides. About as utilitarian as it got. It sloped downward, then turned. Here and there along the way were piles of rags, old papers, and broken crates, making Kora wonder if the passage had been used for storage at one time.

As soon as the guards were gone, they'd head down the slope and into the dungeon that had to lay beyond. Probably using her lighter to guide them.

The guards' conversation was minimal, and even though it was in Spanish, not one of Kora's best languages, she sussed out that they were chalking the noise up to a ghost named Catalina.

Birdie had mentioned her, too. Kora made a mental note to keep an eye out for the woman in case they ran into her. If anyone knew the castle, it would be the ghost who inhabited it.

The men finally went back to their post, turning the lights off and leaving Greyson and Kora in utter darkness again.

She spoke softly, hoping the passageway didn't have any echo effect. "There's a turn about ten yards down."

"I saw," Greyson answered. "Should be safe to use your lighter once we get past that. I don't want to risk the light shining through the panel seams."

"Okay."

He patted her hand, which was still on his arm. "I'll go first. Keep hold of me."

His movements were evident by his brushing against her and the sounds of his boot soles scraping the stone under their feet. Together, they carefully descended the incline.

Kora kept one hand on Greyson and one hand on the wall. When they made the turn, they stopped.

She got her lighter out and flicked it to life. It was as bright as the sun after such complete blackness, making them both squint for a second.

The passage ahead went only a few more feet before it opened up and turned into steps that led farther down. At the top of the steps was a gated landing and a torch held by a metal ring bolted to the wall.

Greyson went through and picked up the torch. "Good thing you have that lighter."

"You think it's okay to light that thing?"

He nodded. "We're far enough away from the panel now." He looked up at the gate. It was only about ten feet high. "We'll have to climb this. The guard might not see the light, but they might hear the noise of us breaking through this much metal."

"Or…" She used her free hand to dig into her waist bag and pull out her lock-picking kit. "We could use this."

194

"You and your bag of tricks." But he held his hand out.

She tossed the kit to him, then walked the rest of the way down and took the torch. "This thing might go up pretty fast. No telling how old it is."

"If I have to pick the lock with only the flame from the lighter, that's fine. But once we get down into the dungeon, we'll need something to see by. I'm thinking the lighter might not be enough then. Depends on how large a space it is."

She held the flame closer to the lock while he knelt and got to work. "Maybe there will be rushes on the floor or something else we can burn for light."

"Let's hope. We have no idea what we're looking for, so it could take us a while."

The lock released, and he stood. He eased the gate open enough for her to get through. It creaked, but not too loudly. "After you."

"Thanks." She went down a few steps and held the flame to the torch. It sputtered, then caught. She closed the lighter and put it away. The torch gave off more than enough light. It spilled over the steps and into the cavernous space below.

Greyson joined her, and they made their way down. The floor was mostly dirt. Some stone in places, and here and there, the remains of rushes, the straw used to cover the dirt, were visible.

Metal rings protruded from the walls. Some had chains still attached.

Kora shuddered. "This place is creepy."

"We were just in the catacombs."

"Yeah, that was like Disney compared to this." She grimaced as they reached the bottom of the steps. "Let's find whatever we need to find and get out of here."

"I'm all for that." Greyson stopped, then did a slow circle. "There are a lot of smaller rooms. Searching this place is going to take a while. Do you have any idea what we might be looking for?"

"None. Sorry. Maybe something that doesn't belong?"

"Or maybe something very familiar." He put his hand on the torch and guided her around in his direction, pointing toward one of the many arched doorways. "What does that look like to you?"

She stared at the stones, her mouth coming open. "It's a sun."

He nodded. "I say we go that way."

Greyson waited while Kora examined the sun symbol etched onto the stone arch, holding the torch for her so she could clear away the grime.

She nodded at him from her crouched position. "It's the same as what we saw in the pub and the catacombs. I don't know why I wasn't expecting it. I should have been. Good thing you saw it."

"You would have found it."

She stood, brushing her hands off. "Probably. But I'm glad it didn't take that long."

He used the torch to gesture toward the passage. Cells were visible beyond. "Through here, then?"

"Yes. I hope the next sun is a little more obvious."

But it wasn't. In fact, the next one took longer to find. It was scratched onto the metal of a cell door, near the top corner and almost invisible due to cobwebs.

Greyson cleared the webs away with his hand. "It's a match. So what do you think? Inside the cell? Or farther down?"

"Inside. Even if just to eliminate the chance our next clue is in there. If there's nothing, we go farther down this passage."

"Agreed. Hold this." He handed her the torch and tried to open the door. "I don't think it's locked, but settling has caused the walls to shift slightly, and that's basically crushed any clearance."

"You're going to have to muscle it open."

"Exactly, but it might be loud."

She shrugged. "We're too far down to be heard now. I hope. We don't have a choice."

"Here goes." He wrenched the cell door off its hinges. The noise echoed through the space, making them both cringe.

Kora glanced upward. "Hopefully, the guards will think it's just Catalina again."

"That's the ghost the guards were talking about, right? My Spanish isn't great, but I picked up on that word."

She nodded. "Same here. Birdie sent me a little snippet about her. She was a very *interesting* woman who apparently died in this dungeon."

They went into the cell and started looking for the next sun sign.

"Lovely," he said. "Why was she incarcerated in the first place?"

Before Kora could answer, another voice spoke. "What do you want, vampires? Why do you disturb me?"

They turned to see a translucent woman in a tattered black lace gown blocking the door they'd just come through. She hovered a few feet off the ground. Her eyes gleamed like dying embers, while an ethereal wind tugged at her hair and dress.

Kora stepped forward, impressing Greyson with her bravery. But then, her grandmother had been a ghost for years, so maybe that helped. "Senorita Catalina. I'm Kora Dupree. It's a pleasure to meet you."

Catalina's burning eyes narrowed, but the wind around her calmed slightly. "You think it's a pleasure to meet me?"

Kora nodded. "You're the mistress of this grand castle, aren't you?"

Catalina seemed to take that in and, after a moment, accept it as a compliment. She lifted her chin slightly. "I am the mistress of this castle. Why are you here?" She pointed at Greyson. "And who is that?"

"This is my servant. Greyson." Kora put her hand on his arm and squeezed. A signal to go along with her story, he assumed. But why it mattered that he was her servant, he wasn't sure. "Like me, he's a vampire. I turned him. He was an orphan when I found him. He means you no harm."

Greyson had so many questions his tongue was burning. Still, he remained silent and let Kora do whatever it was she was doing. After all, she'd read up on this ghost, so she knew more than he did about how to handle her.

The fire in Catalina's eyes died. "You must be a kind woman to rescue an orphan."

Kora shrugged off the compliment. "We all need to do our part."

"Yes," Catalina muttered. "We must."

The edge to her voice told Greyson there was a whole lot going on here that Kora was going to have to explain later.

Kora smiled. "As to why we are here in your beautiful home, I am seeking something that's been hidden here. When I find it and return it to its rightful owner, they have promised to tell me the truth about my mother's death." Kora swallowed, and Greyson wasn't sure if it was genuine emotion or part of the act.

Either way, Catalina was riveted. "Your mother is dead?"

"Yes," Kora said. "My father raised me. But I have been plagued all my life by not knowing what happened to her."

Catalina clasped her hands together. "What do you seek? Perhaps I can help you."

Kora reached under the neck of her shirt and lifted the locket free. "This is the only clue I have. There are sun symbols that match it scratched into the stone and metal here in this dungeon, but I don't know how many there are, or where they lead. Have you seen them? Do you know if there are more than just the two I've found?"

Catalina's smile made her look creepier, but Greyson wasn't going to complain. Help was help. "I know what you are here to find. She was also a vampire."

"She?"

"The woman who made those marks. Follow me."

She floated through the doorway and farther down the passage. Kora shot Greyson a look, and they went after Catalina. There were a few torches still in their sconces on the way, so Greyson touched them with the flames from the one in his hand and brought them to life. The light revealed that some of the cells on both sides also contained bones.

Kora was right. This place was far creepier than the catacombs.

Catalina stopped at the end of the passage. There, the dungeon opened up into a small chapel area. Perhaps the prisoners had been allowed to pray? Greyson had never seen such a thing, but the Spanish were a very religious people.

Kora and Greyson stayed outside the threshold, but he held the torch up so they could see better.

Two rough-hewn benches sat side by side before an altar, the centerpiece of which was a beautiful statue of the Holy Mother on a platform that raised her several feet. Squat candles gone gray with grime and soot lined a narrow wooden table before the statue.

Catalina floated backward into the space, keeping her eyes on Kora and Greyson. "This is sacred ground. Holy, even. I have heard vampires may not tread upon such. And yet, the woman was in here."

"And she was a vampire?" Kora asked.

"Yes." Catalina hovered near the statue of Mary. "She prayed here. And made an offering."

Kora visibly went on alert, her frame straightening. "What kind of offering?"

Catalina nodded at the top of the pedestal the statue stood on. "See for yourself. Which item do you think she left?"

Kora and Greyson looked at what had been left, but it was Kora who spoke. "Matryoshka. Of course."

Little wooden carvings of animals, some crude, some skillful, sat there along with a few seashells, an almost completely decayed bunch of flowers, a frayed silk neckcloth, and the item Kora had called out, the item that had most likely been left by the woman in question—a Russian nesting doll.

Greyson nodded. "Offerings from the prisoners. And the woman who designed this scavenger hunt."

"Catalina," Kora began, "can you bring me that doll? Please?"

Catalina shook her head and held her hands out. "I am sorry, I cannot. I am unable to affect the mortal world."

She didn't look sorry. In fact, Greyson thought the ghost was enjoying this. Like it was a game.

As if to prove her point about the mortal world, Catalina slid through the Mary statue like a breeze passing through a screen door.

"I see." Kora sighed and looked at Greyson. "I have to go in there."

"On hallowed ground?" He shifted the torch to his other hand. Walking on hallowed or sacred ground wasn't a thing vampires did.

Kora nodded. "I know, but I'm half reaper. That should buy me some time."

Catalina moved closer with sudden concern, the fire in her eyes bright again. "You cannot just take an offering. You must leave something in return."

Kora quickly slid the acrostic ring off the ribbon around her neck and held the piece up. "Will this do?"

Catalina inspected it, then nodded, seemingly appeased. "Very well."

Kora nodded. "Good. I just hope we don't need this again."

Greyson touched Kora to get her attention. "You sure you want to do this?"

"I don't see that I have a choice. I'll be fine. At the speed I can move, I'll be in there two, maybe three seconds. Not long enough to fully burst into flames." She smiled as if she thought that might soften the meaning of her words, but there was fear in her eyes. She knew what she was risking.

Greyson leaned the torch against the stone wall and pulled his jacket off. "You burst into flames and I'll put them out. We're in this together."

"Thanks." Some of the fear faded away. "But hey, if the vampire who set this up was in there, maybe the space isn't as hallowed as we think."

Catalina made a noise, but Greyson chose to ignore it. "Maybe. But I don't like this. It could be some kind of trap."

"And we could be overthinking it."

He put his hand on her arm. "Please, go as quickly as you can. Then let's get out of here."

"I will."

He tightened his grip on her arm and pulled her close, kissing her quickly. "Hurry."

Her smile finally reached her eyes. "I'll be right back."

Kora gripped the acrostic ring in her hand, ready to drop it in place of the matryoshka dolls. She hoped with everything in her that being half reaper was enough to keep her from bursting into flames.

And if it wasn't, she hoped she was fast enough to get out of the chapel before she went full inferno.

She dashed into the space and came to an abrupt halt. Not because she wanted to, but because her speed just disappeared. On top of that, she felt very odd. And everything around her went dim. Had the torch gone out?

"What's wrong? Why did you stop?" Panic widened Greyson's eyes.

"I don't know, I just couldn't—" She put her hand to her heart and gasped. "My heart is beating." She stared at him with the same fearful expression he was giving her. "My *heart* is *beating*. Am I about to die?"

The torch in Greyson's hand sputtered but didn't go dark.

"Wait," Kora said. "I'm breathing, too."

Catalina laughed. "Silly vampire. You're not about to die. But you *have* become human."

"Human?" Kora glanced down at her body,

although she wasn't sure what she expected to see. Then she looked at Greyson again. "Do I look different?"

He nodded warily. "Yes, a little."

"How so?"

"Less…you. I don't know. A little rougher around the edges maybe."

She went from panic to anger. "How is this possible, Catalina? I have never been human. I was born a supernatural, the child of a vampire and a reaper."

Catalina shrugged, lifting herself off the ground a few more inches. "It is a spell. Ask the witch who made the offering."

"Witch? You said she was a vampire." Red edged Kora's vision. She'd trusted Catalina only because Hattie had been a ghost, but that was Kora's mistake. Hattie hadn't started out insane. Catalina had.

"Hey," Greyson shouted. "Get the dolls and get out. This torch is about to die, and I don't want to spend another second down here."

Kora shook her head. "What if I stay human?"

"Then you stay human. It won't change my feelings for you. Just means I'll have to turn you back into a vampire. Now hurry up. The longer you're in there, the more likely this thing is to stick."

As if becoming human hadn't given her enough pause, now Greyson had admitted he had feelings for her. She suddenly felt like crying and laughing all at the same time. "Oh no."

"What?" Greyson asked. His torch went out.

She was glad for the darkness to hide her face. "I think I'm feeling human emotions."

"Kora. Get the dolls and get out. Now. I need another torch." He tossed the extinguished one to the side and motioned for her to come to him.

Motivated by his tone, she grabbed the dolls, dropped the ring in their place, and went to meet him at the chapel's entrance.

But she stopped right before stepping over the threshold to look back at Catalina. "Is it safe for me to leave? Am I going to stay human?"

Catalina went slightly more transparent. "I do not know. No one has entered this room since the offering was made."

"I have been nothing but respectful to you, Catalina. I hope you are being honest with me."

The ghost's eyes flared red. "Do you suggest I am lying?"

Kora shook her head. "I am suggesting you might have reason to want to keep us here. But I hope you are not that selfish."

Catalina's spirit quieted. "I would not lie."

"No," Greyson muttered. "But she might not tell the whole truth." He held out his hand. "Come to me, Kora. Whatever happens, we'll get through it."

With a final glance at the ghost, Kora took his hand and stepped out of the chapel.

"I think I'm all righ—" She wheezed as her heart stopped beating, and the breath left her body. Then everything went wobbly and, finally, black.

Greyson saw Kora's eyes roll back and anticipated what was about to happen. He caught her in his arms before she hit the dirt floor, snatching the matryoshka dolls, too, to keep them safe.

After what she'd risked, he wasn't going to let the next clue be ruined.

As he lifted her, he shot an angry glance at Catalina, but kept his mouth shut. He wasn't sure what the ghost was capable of, despite the show she'd put on about not being able to influence the mortal world.

He shifted Kora so that he could grab a fresh torch, one of several he'd lit on their way in, and started back toward the stairs that had brought them down here.

He was about to exit the passageway when Catalina appeared before him. "Where are you taking her?"

"To safety." Why he was even talking to this specter, he wasn't sure.

"I can keep her safe here."

"No." When Catalina didn't move, Greyson walked through her.

She shrieked as her form disintegrated in whirls of vapor. "How dare you?"

He was done talking. He slipped the torch into the closest holder, then marched forward, Kora boneless in his arms.

Catalina blocked his way again, the wind that surrounded her whipping her hair and skirts in a wild frenzy. She pointed at him as he approached. "You cannot leave."

A ghost had yet to wield any kind of power over him, and he'd had his share of run-ins with them. When it came to undead supernaturals, vampires were much higher up the food chain.

For a second time, he walked through her.

Kora shifted in his arms. "What happened?"

"You turned human, then passed out when you became supernatural again. The nesting doll is in your lap."

"I'm not human anymore?" Her one hand went to her chest, while the other found the dolls. "No heartbeat. But I'm talking to you, so I'm obviously not dead. Okay, that was weird and scary, and I don't ever want to repeat that."

"I don't think you'll have to."

"You can put me down now. I'm sure I can walk."

Catalina shrieked at Greyson, "You cannot leave, Vampire."

Kora peeked around his arm to look behind them. "Oh boy."

"Yeah." They were only yards from the steps now, so Greyson set Kora on her feet. "You sure you're okay?"

She nodded as she tucked the dolls into her belt bag. "I feel a little bit like I'm hungover, but otherwise, good."

"Okay. Because Catalina's created a new issue for us."

Kora nodded. "All that racket. The only good part is she can't leave the dungeon. That's at least according to everything I've read about her."

"That's great, but if the guards haven't heard all her wailing, then they're deaf. There's no way they don't know something's going on."

"Don't you think they're used to her noise?"

"No, I don't. I think, until our visit, she's only ever been a fairy tale to them. Something to tease each other about."

A big, bright grin lit up Kora's face.

"What are you smiling about all of a sudden?"

"I know how we're getting out of here."

Kora prided herself on her appearance. It was a fault, she knew that, but she couldn't help it. She liked to be pulled together. More than that, she liked to be stylish and as flawless as possible. Being half vampire, half reaper made her a rare and unique creature, and she liked to express that through what she wore. From her hair to her makeup to her jewelry, everything had to be on point.

Which made her current getup something else entirely.

Greyson held her lighter up, the flame providing all the illumination she needed. "You look dreadful."

"That's the point." She rubbed her fingers on the burned end of their last torch, getting them good and sooty. Then she swiped her fingers under her eyes and slashed them down the hollows of her cheeks.

"Good thing there's a fully equipped bathroom on the plane."

"That's for sure." She wiped her hands on one of secret passageway's rags, then draped that rag over herself with the rest of them. "Okay, this is as good as it's going to get. What do you think?"

Greyson cocked one eyebrow, his smirk undeniably amused. "You look hideous."

"Thanks." This was the only time he'd get away with that answer. "Have you found their heartbeats?"

He nodded. "I'd judge they're not far beyond the library. And, bad news, there's a third."

"So they called in reinforcements."

"Seems like it. You'd better sell this hard."

"That's my plan. And you know yours."

"I do."

"Then let's get this party started. Sun will be up in about an hour, and by then, I want to be on that plane." The phantom itch of the sun's rise was already present on her skin, but she was fighting hard to ignore it.

"Me, too."

She went first, back to the door that was really a panel in the library. She crouched to avoid hitting her head on the low ceiling, but was careful not to shake loose any of her costume. She listened closely at the panel. Faint voices reached her, but they were definitely not in the library.

She pushed the panel open and stepped through. She had to remind herself not to smile. Catalina most likely wouldn't, and anyway, to be all happy and grinning wouldn't make for a very frightening ghost.

She stuck her arms out a little, mostly to show off the rags covering her. She passed by a mirror and caught a glimpse of herself, happy to see she looked as much of a fright as she'd hoped.

The voices were coming from the left.

She started with a deep, guttural moaning, then went into the one Spanish word that she knew would make sense in this situation. "Alejandro. Oh, Alejandro."

The voices stopped.

With a shuffling gate borrowed from one of her favorite zombie movies, she turned the corner toward where she believed the guards to be. Behind her, she sensed Greyson had also come through the panel.

A chubby guard with a moustache saw her first due to where he was standing. His mouth came open, and the walkie-talkie in his hand dropped to the floor with a crack. He started mumbling in rapid Spanish.

When his colleagues didn't pay attention, he lifted his hand and pointed, shouting, "*Fantasma!* Catalina! *Catalina!*"

Kora kept playing her part, shuffling toward them, moaning, and calling out for Catalina's long-lost son.

The men acted exactly as she'd hoped they would. Once they saw what their fellow guard was all worked up about, they, too, got on the freaked-out bandwagon.

Which was her cue to take it up a notch.

Until then, she'd kept her gaze neutral and vacant. Now, she fixed it on them and turned on the vampire glow.

It was a little tricky to do that without also extending her fangs, but since there was no evidence that Catalina had been a vampire, the fangs wouldn't have made sense.

She raised her hands a little more and changed direction to head directly for the men.

In perfect response, they took off running. She dropped her arms, but kept up the moaning, increasing her volume a little until she heard a door slam.

Then she waited a few seconds before whispering, "Heartbeats?"

"All outside, as best as I can tell. And all of them pretty rapid," Greyson answered from somewhere behind her. "Nicely done."

She grinned and started pulling the rags off. "Thanks. Hattie would be mortified, I'm sure. Now let's get out of here while the coast is clear."

They did, and Greyson, in typical form, had a car already waiting for them a block away. They got in, he gave the driver directions for the airfield where the

Ellinghams' plane was waiting, then they settled in for the ride.

Sunrise was now less than fifty minutes away, and the trip to the airfield would take a little more than forty minutes. Kora didn't like how close that was going to make things, but she did her best to stay calm.

After all, they'd come this far without major incident.

Still, she had a hard time keeping her eyes off the horizon.

Greyson slid down in the seat a little, exhaling in either relief or exhaustion.

She glanced at him. "Tired?"

"A little." He nodded. "I texted the pilot that we're on our way. He's fueled up and ready to go, but we have no destination yet."

She unclenched one hand to pat her belt bag. "Judging by what we found, I'm guessing somewhere in Russia. I'm hoping we learn more once we dig into these."

He nodded. "Not now?"

"On the plane." She didn't know the driver, and while she didn't find him particularly untrustworthy, she had no reason to trust him either. Not with something so important. Plus, he kept giving her strange looks.

"Okay." Greyson closed his eyes. "I guess that will be after you wash all that soot off your face."

She groaned, then laughed. "No, that can wait until we have our next destination worked out." No wonder the driver was looking at her like she was a lunatic.

Greyson took her hand. "We'll make it before sunrise."

"Is it that obvious?"

"A little."

They made it to the plane as the sky was turning pink and gold, a beautiful sight, Kora imagined, if the end result of watching the sunrise wasn't death. Even so, she could appreciate it for its beauty, which was enhanced by seeing it through the plane's UV-filtering windows.

As eager as she was for a shower and to change into clothing that hadn't been covered with rags and grime, they had no idea where they were headed until they figured out the next clue.

And until that was accomplished, the plane was just sitting there.

So she got the dolls out of her bag and took them to the lounge area. She sat to work on them, and Greyson joined her. She held up the first doll. She hadn't paid much attention to it when she'd been snagging it from the chapel, but now that she looked at it closer, it wasn't a typical matryoshka doll.

She turned it around to see the whole thing. "This woman looks familiar. Does she look like anyone to you?"

"Not anyone that immediately comes to mind. But she doesn't look like the kind of character normally painted on a nesting doll. Her clothes are a lot fancier, for one thing."

"They are." She unscrewed that doll and took out the one inside it, then put the first one back together again. She repeated the process until she had six dolls on the table in front of her. The sixth one was a little boy.

She shook her head. "This one has to be Alexei."

"Who's that?"

"The youngest child and only son of the Romanovs."

Greyson's eyes widened a little. "And the rest of them?"

Kora put her finger on the first and largest. "The Tsarina Alexandra, mother of the five children."

"Is that it, then?"

Kora picked up the sixth one and gave it a little shake. It rattled. "One more to go."

The seventh one wasn't anyone at all. It was decorated ornately, almost like a Fabergé egg, which made perfect sense considering who the dolls represented. Fabergé eggs only existed because of the Romanovs, who had commissioned them. Kora turned the last doll in her fingers before putting it in line with the others. "I believe this one represents the tsar himself."

Greyson picked up the seventh one. "I'd buy that. The top is a crown, most definitely." He held it out to her. "But the bottom looks like the cathedral in Saint Petersburg. Or the basilica in Moscow. I'm not familiar enough with them to know the difference. Or what they have to do with the Tsar Nicholas II."

She took the last doll. "The top might represent him, but the bottom part is most likely our next clue.

And I'm hoping, since it seems like we're headed to Russia, that it's also our final clue. We just need to know for sure if we're headed to Moscow or Saint Petersburg."

Greyson took out his phone and started tapping away. Then he turned the screen toward her. "I'd say we're headed for Saint Petersburg."

She looked at the photo of the cathedral he'd pulled up, then the image on the doll. "I'd say you're right." She grinned. "And now I'm headed for a shower."

Greyson showered after Kora. Their time in the dungeon had left them both pretty grimy, but especially Kora, who had outdone herself in her role as the resident ghost. He smiled when he thought about her draping herself in refuse and putting on such a show.

It certainly wasn't the Kora he'd once known. And her willingness to do such a thing had only deepened his affection for her.

Now he was settled in for the remainder of the trip, which would be about five hours. They'd have to stay on the plane after they landed until sundown for Kora's sake. He shook his head in empathy for her, glancing toward where she was in the small galley, getting something to drink.

He hadn't lived his life by the sun's rule for many, many years. Catherine might have turned him, but it was his Roma heritage, and the kindness of a great-aunt, that had made his life as a vampire so livable.

His great-aunt, Lavinia, had created the small

magical pouch he wore around his neck. That pouch, and the magic she'd imbued into it, allowed him to walk in the sun.

Lavinia had refused to create one for Catherine, so he'd used it only sparingly at first. Once she'd died, he'd put it on and never taken it off again.

Lavinia had asked for nothing in exchange for her gift. All the same, he'd offered to turn her. To give her life eternal. It was all he'd had to offer then. But she'd refused with a kind smile and the excuse that she was too old to live forever.

No amount of arguing on his part could change her mind either.

She'd made her living telling fortunes and making herbal remedies. Greyson had never really considered her a witch, despite her skills, but she was far from an ordinary human.

When she'd passed, he'd built a mausoleum for her of the finest Connemara marble. His financial situation had changed a great deal by then, and giving her such a gift, even posthumously, pleased him. Even now, the memory made him smile. Lavinia would have thought the mausoleum ostentatious and fussed that it was far too much. But to him, it was the perfect tribute to a woman who had changed his life in the most unbelievable way.

Kora brought her coffee over and sat down. After her shower, she'd put on black leggings and a black T-shirt. They'd be sleeping soon, so he imagined those were basically her pajamas. Or at least the ones she was willing to let him see her in.

"That smells good."

She sipped her coffee, looking over the cup's rim at him. "I would have made you a cup."

"Thanks, but I'm not in the mood." Although a small glass of whiskey sounded pretty good. "Say, I keep meaning to ask. What was with that stuff you told Catalina about me being an orphan and all that?"

"Oh, that." She laughed softly. "The info that Birdie sent me had a few paragraphs about Catalina. Apparently, when she was alive, she came to the castle every couple of months with a different child, an orphan off the streets, and claimed that it was the castle lord's child. Saying that he was the father and refused to acknowledge either of them. And she was always dressed in a wedding gown."

"But when we saw her, she was in black lace."

"That's what Spanish brides used to wear. Something about showing their devotion until death." She held her cup with both hands wrapped around it like she was enjoying the warmth. "Anyway, I figured telling her you were an orphan would buy us some sympathy points."

"And telling her I was your servant?"

"She's not fond of men. Not after the lord of the castle finally imprisoned her in the dungeon to shut her up. The real kicker is he visited her numerous times while she was incarcerated. Enough that she did eventually bear his child, a little boy named—"

"Alejandro."

"Which is why I used that name."

"What happened to him?"

"The lord of the castle sent him off to boarding school, and she never saw him again. Legend has it she died of a broken heart."

"Wow. Sad." Greyson frowned. "She might have been crazy, but I feel for her."

"Me, too," Kora said. She stared into her cup.

"You're thinking about your mother, aren't you?"

She nodded. "Hard not to when faced with something like that. A crazy woman cared more about her child than my mother cared about me."

"But despite her, you turned into an amazing woman. You should give yourself credit. And Lucien and Hattie, too."

She lifted her head, meeting his gaze again. "I do, absolutely. Without their patience and understanding, I'm not sure where I would be."

"Probably not driving a Ferrari."

She smirked. "I might still be driving a Ferrari."

"Maybe a stolen one."

She snorted. "True." Then she sighed and glanced out the window, squinting against the brilliance of the sun. "This has to be the last clue, don't you think? The one that will lead us to whatever treasure we're supposed to find."

"Considering that we're headed to Russia, where this all began, I'd say yes."

"Good. Because I'm ready for this to be over." She looked at him. "It's funny, because I've always loved adventure and the next unknown thing. But now all I can think about is getting home to Waffles and my life. Back to work and my routine. So weird. I never thought I'd be the kind of person who enjoys the mundane."

"You're half reaper, half vampire. I don't think anything about your life can be considered mundane."

She shrugged. "I go to work, I take care of Waffles, I visit with my family on occasion. I'm not exactly living on the edge."

"So? If you're happy, what else matters?"

She took another sip of her coffee, letting a few moments pass before she answered. "Nothing. But...it would be nice to have someone else to spend time with."

He smiled. "I agree. I'd like to be that someone else."

She smiled back. "I'd like that, too. I don't want to rush into anything. But I'm all for hanging out and seeing where things go."

"That sounds perfect to me. I'm in no hurry to jump back into a serious relationship." So long as whatever relationship they *were* in included kissing.

She finished her coffee, then got up. "I know I need to do some research on the cathedral, but I'm going to get some sleep first. I'm not used to being awake during daylight, and it's making me foggy."

"Okay. See you in a bit."

He caught her hand as she went past and pressed it to his cheek, then kissed it before releasing her. "Rest well."

"Thanks." She smiled at him before heading to the plane's bedroom.

He didn't intend to stay up much longer either,

but doing a little research wasn't a bad idea. He should have done more on the castle, but he'd been distracted by thoughts of Kora and her father—and the werewolf's warning.

That reminded him that Birdie hadn't responded yet to his request for info about the Brotherhood. He should send her a little nudge via text.

But instead, he sat quietly for a while longer, just looking out the window and thinking about everything that had happened so far. He started to drift off, giving in to the tug of sleep and the exhaustion of the trip.

Then his phone vibrated, snapping him back to reality. He checked the screen, fully expecting it to be the info from Birdie.

We know you've found the next clue.

A chill swept through him, followed by anger. He didn't recognize the number, but he knew who the text was from. How they'd gotten his number wasn't that much of a mystery. Anything was possible with the right connections and enough money.

He texted back, *What are you so afraid of?*

A little time passed with no answer, and he wondered if his response had shocked them. Maybe they hadn't expected him to respond at all. But then they answered.

A power shift. A war. Human casualties.

The words gave Greyson pause. He couldn't imagine that whatever awaited them at the end of this treasure hunt was that valuable. Money wasn't usually enough of a factor for supernaturals. Most had more than they could spend. So what kind of power did this treasure hold? Was it really Rasputin's source of power? If so, who had the most to gain—and the most to lose—from such a thing? He had to ask them more questions. *What is it you think we're hunting?*

If you don't know, it's better that way.

Maybe a different question would get him a better answer. *Who are you afraid will use this power?*

Another long pause. *The one you and your friend are working for. And more like her.*

Her? You mean my friend?

No. The woman she's working for. Stop your search before it's too late.

Did this group know who Kora was working for? This Fox? It sounded like they did and they thought the Fox was a woman, something Kora didn't even seem to know. Greyson looked up. Or did she? Could Kora have kept that information from him for some reason? But why? What did it matter to him what gender the Fox was?

He sent Birdie a text, reminding her he was waiting on her answer.

She got back to him almost immediately with an apology and the info he'd been asking for. He read it, but his mind was on Kora.

He didn't want to think she'd deliberately held information back. But the Kora he'd once known absolutely would have. How much had Kora really changed? Enough that she was now honest about everything?

He closed his eyes. He wanted to believe that the

woman he was falling for had truly changed. He did believe that. And yet, it was hard not to have doubts after their history.

The struggle inside him raged on. Nothing would stop him from protecting her, but he realized that letting himself have feelings for her wasn't a smart move. Not until this whole thing was over.

Or really, maybe never. Not if there was a part of him that wasn't sure he could trust her. Because what kind of foundation would that be for a relationship?

Kora's head hadn't been on the pillow for more than five minutes when her phone lit up. It was still on silent, but the screen showed an incoming call. She picked it up to see who it was.

Hattie.

She smiled and answered. "Hi, Mémé. How are you?"

"Oh, honey, I'm just fine. It's so good to hear your voice. How are you? Are you all right? Are you safe? Are you getting enough rest? You know travel can be very tiring."

Kora laughed. "I'm doing just fine, and I'm lying down right now."

"Did I wake you? I'm sorry. I didn't know if it would be a good time to call or not, but I thought I'd take the chance. Are you alone?" Then Hattie laughed. "If you're in bed and you're not alone, maybe don't tell me, okay? I know you're all grown up, but there are some things I'm not quite ready for."

Kora snickered. "I'm alone, and no, you didn't wake me. Everything all right at home? How's Waffles?"

"He misses you, I can tell, but he's doing just fine. My lands, that cat sure does fill up his litter box."

Kora's face was starting to hurt from smiling. "I'm glad he's all right. What else is new? Did you find out why Dad was so cranky?"

Hattie sucked in a breath. "I did, and that's what I'm calling about."

"Oh?" Kora sat up a little. "What's going on?"

"Apparently, Greyson isn't responding to his texts, and your father is mad because of all the money he's paying him to keep you safe and—"

A chill went through Kora. "Dad is paying Greyson?"

"Yes. Your father didn't say how much, but I got the feeling it was a rather large sum."

Kora's smile was gone. So much for not being a client. "What else did you find out?"

"Your father muttered something about him not laying a hand on you."

"What does that mean?"

"I'm not sure, honey, but based on some of your father's other ramblings, I think he thinks Greyson might be, how should I put this, romantically interested in you? And your father isn't happy about that. Which is part of why he's giving Greyson so much money. I think. Don't take any of that as gospel, because you know how cryptic and uncooperative your father can be when it comes to details and information."

"Right." But all Kora could see was red. She wasn't sure who she was madder at—her father or Greyson. Both of them deserved a good smack. Her father for trying to run her life and make decisions for her, and Greyson for being a party to it and for being so weak as to give up any shot with her for cash. Especially when she knew how solid he was financially. And what was all that business about a date when they got back? Was that because by then this *job* would be over?

The nerve of them both.

"Listen, honey, you should get some rest. Where are you headed?"

"I probably shouldn't say. Just to be safe."

Hattie gasped. "Are you not safe? I thought you were. Do you need your father to come there? Or meet you somewhere? Or—"

"It was just an expression. I'm perfectly safe, I promise."

Too bad she couldn't say the same for Greyson.

Kora was dressed in a tight, low-cut black lace dress that revealed more skin than it covered. Greyson smiled. She looked unbelievably sexy. And she was his. That much he knew. Just like he knew that she was a ghost, but it didn't matter.

"Greyson."

Her tone didn't match the smile on her face, though. Was she mad at him? Had he forgotten to feed the cat? What was his name? Pancakes?

"*Greyson*, wake up."

He blinked, losing the hazy enjoyment of his dream to the clear actuality of Kora staring down at him, eyes aglow with anger. "What? I'm up. What's wrong?"

"How much money is my father paying you to take care of me? Hmm?" She crossed her arms. "What is that worth to you?"

Greyson blinked again, still not completely free from the clutches of sleep. "I, um, he said a million doll—"

"A million dollars?" Her fangs were visible now. "Are you serious?"

The last time he'd heard a shriek like that, it had come from Catalina. He was well and truly awake now. He sat up, running a hand through his hair. "That's what he offered, but I—"

"You've got to be kidding me." She shook her head and stomped off down the aisle toward the front of the plane. "Of course you took it. Who wouldn't? Well, maybe someone who didn't need the money." She turned at the cockpit door, glaring at him as she came back around in his direction.

He stood up, feeling like that might give him a better chance of defending himself. "I didn't take the money."

She stopped in midstomp and less than twelve inches from him. "You didn't?"

"No." She was incredibly sexy when she was worked up.

"Why not?"

"For one thing, I don't need it. For another, I didn't want your father dictating what happened during this trip. And I didn't like the stipulations that came with the money."

"What kind of stipulations? And why didn't you tell me the truth when I asked you what my father said to you?"

"I didn't lie to you. I just kept some info to myself."

"What did he say? I want to know. What were these stipulations?"

Greyson frowned. Was he really going to tell her all this? He wasn't sure he had any other option. Besides, she was an adult, and she deserved to know. Lucien might never forgive him, though. Greyson shrugged. "Stipulations. Things that could be done, things that couldn't be done."

Kora narrowed her eyes and tilted her head. "I know the definition of stipulations. What were they specifically?"

Oy. She was stubborn. "I had to keep my hands off you." Which was something he really didn't want to do right now. In fact, he wanted to grab her and kiss her and show her exactly what he wasn't supposed to be doing.

"Keep your hands off me? My father said that? In what capacity? I mean, if you're saving me from falling off a cliff, then—"

Greyson took her by the shoulders and kissed her with all the desire built up from his dream and all the deep-seated need to do exactly what he'd been told not to.

For the briefest of moments, he wondered what Lucien would think. Then Greyson realized he didn't care. He also realized that even if Kora wasn't the most trustworthy person in the world, she wouldn't double-cross him.

He couldn't bring himself to believe that she would, not when she was pliant and willing in his hands. Not when she was kissing him back with the same intensity that he was kissing her. His hands slid lower to her hips and pulled her closer. There was nothing pretend about the small sounds of pleasure trilling out of her.

Two things were certain. They cared about each other. And Kora had changed. A lot. There was no way she was going to muck all this up by lying to him.

And so, as the kiss came to an end, he knew there was more he had to tell her. Reluctantly, he let her go.

She was silent for a moment, lips parted. She blinked once or twice, as if getting her bearings again. "My, uh, father doesn't want you kissing me?"

Greyson shook his head. "He doesn't want me to distract you from your new life and your new responsibilities."

"He, uh, said something about that." She nodded slowly like she was underwater. Then a little smile danced across her face. "That was very distracting. But in a good way."

He allowed himself a slight grin, then indulged himself further and pulled her into his arms, holding her against him for purely selfish reasons. He liked the feel of her this close. The softness of her body, the way they fit so well together. "I think you already know I like you a lot, Kora. I don't want to jinx this, but we are really good together."

"I like you, too. And I agree. It's crazy that we were once so at odds with one another, and yet now, I feel like…" She leaned back to stare at his chest, absentmindedly playing with a button on his shirt. "Like we could be best friends. Like there aren't many other people I'd rather be spending time with."

"That's a very good way to start a relationship."

"It is."

"But what's not good is keeping secrets."

She looked up at him with sudden confusion. "I'm not keeping any secrets."

"But I am." He sighed. "Not a secret, exactly, but there was an incident at the apartment in Paris that I didn't tell you about."

"An incident?" Concern marred her pretty face. "What happened? Was it the man from the pub? Or the vampire from the D&B?"

"Neither. A shifter I'd never seen before. He was waiting for me on the apartment steps when I returned with our meal. He tried to warn me off pursuing this treasure. Said the power we were after would destroy more than it saved. That it could even start a war."

"That's not good."

"No, it's not. And there's more. This group, they call themselves the Brotherhood, just texted me with another warning. But in that text, they revealed that they believe the person who sent you on this quest is a woman. Did you know that?"

She shook her head and sat down in the closest seat, which happened to be across from the one he'd been in. "No. I figured he was a man. She was. Whichever."

"Why?"

She shrugged, looking a little like the air had come out of her balloon. "I don't know. Just what I thought. So this Brotherhood, who are they? How do they know what I'm after?"

He sat opposite her. "I texted Birdie to see what she could find out. All she could tell me was that they're an ancient order of werewolves who fancy themselves the protectors of all werewolf kind. Sort of a Knights Templar with fur."

A half grin bent her mouth for a mere second. "But the Knights Templar were all about protecting the Holy Grail. What's the Holy Grail for the Brotherhood, then? This thing we're chasing?"

"Maybe."

She frowned. "What would werewolves see as something that needs to be protected?"

"What would they think could cause a war because of a power shift?"

They both sat in silence then, thinking.

Greyson steepled his fingers in front of him, but it was Kora who spoke first. "Has to be something that benefits vampires, don't you think?"

"Definitely."

She leaned forward. "Let's say it is the source of Rasputin's power, but he sent it off to be hidden away...or like Ivan told us, it was stolen by this Romanov maid that he'd turned into a vampire who just also happened to be a witch. It has to be something pretty amazing to cause all that drama."

Greyson nodded. "Right. But what power would the shifters of the world be most afraid of vampires getting?"

Kora pursed her lips. "There the big one, of course. The power to daywalk."

"That would be big. But there are already some

vampires like myself with that ability and no shifter has come after me. Or the Ellinghams, and they're well-known for being out and about in broad daylight."

Kora's gaze tapered down. "What about the power of shifting? What if vampires could shift?"

Greyson sat up straighter. "Why is it that a lot of old vampire movies show the vampire turning into a bat?"

She lifted one shoulder. "Because once upon a time, there were vampires that could?"

"They say fiction is based in truth."

She sighed. "All this for something that gives vampires the ability to become bats? I can't say that really blows my skirt up, but I guess it would for some people. Do you think it's such a great power?"

"I've never been anything but who I am, but I suppose there are those who would like the ability to become something much smaller that's able to disappear quickly."

She smiled suddenly. "Yeah, when you put it that way, the old me would have been into it." She laughed. "Okay, I can see how this could cause problems. But hey, if that Brotherhood wants to step in, they can deal with the Fox. I'm just the messenger here."

Greyson nodded. But he had a feeling the Brotherhood wasn't going to be so understanding.

The pilot's voice crackled over the PA system. "We'll be touching down in half an hour. Sun will be up for another six hours after that."

Kora got up. "In that case, I'm heading back to the bedroom for some shut-eye. You want to share the bed?"

Did he ever. "I don't think that's a good idea. Not after that kiss. Not if you really intend to sleep."

She giggled. *Giggled.* And with a shy smile, she patted him on the shoulder. "See you in a few, then. Sweet dreams."

"You, too." Of course, he already knew what he'd be dreaming about. The same thing he was when she'd woken him.

Her.

Russia was cold enough that Kora added a black turtleneck, leather jacket, and boots to the leggings she was already wearing before getting off the plane.

Greyson had changed, too. He was in black tactical pants and a black wool pullover with gray patches on the elbows. They both looked very chic, but also a little like they were up to something.

Which they were.

The car Greyson had hired took them from Pulkovo Airport into the center of Saint Petersburg. Their ultimate destination, the cathedral, or the Church of the Savior on Spilled Blood, was easy to see. With its five onion domes decorated brightly in jeweler's enamel, it stood out from the rest of the staid, monochromatic Saint Petersburg skyline like a carnival tent.

But Greyson had the driver drop them off a few blocks away, at a small tavern, where they went in and sat as if that had been their destination. They ordered glasses of vodka that they sipped. With a vampire's metabolism, it took a great deal of alcohol to reach a level close to inebriation. The shots might as well have been water.

But the drinks were part of a show designed to help them blend in and disappear amongst the other tourists, most of whom seemed to be European.

While they sat there, they both watched the crowd around them for any sign that they'd been followed. They sniffed the air, testing for traces of shifters. More specifically, wolf. But after her run-in with the creepy vampire at the D&B, Kora had to wonder if the Brotherhood didn't have some other supernaturals working for them.

Anything was possible in this day and age.

Greyson kept his head and his voice down. "I don't see anyone."

She picked her glass up, then put it back down again just to look occupied. "Neither do I."

"Then let's go."

He'd already paid at the bar, so they got up and left. Eyes wide open, senses on alert, but with all the nonchalance of tourists out to stroll the city and see the sights.

Kora hooked her arm through his as they stepped outside. When he looked at her, she smiled up at him, playing the part of his adoring girlfriend. At least she hoped he understood that's what she was doing.

He seemed to as he put his hand over hers, and they walked through the cobblestone streets with deliberate aimlessness. Not easy to do when they were absolutely headed toward a specific destination.

But the wandering was important. It was one more way to be sure they weren't being tailed.

She snorted. Tailed. Considering the Brotherhood was a bunch of hyped-up shifters, that was funny.

Greyson gave her a questioning look, but she shook it off.

They continued on, looking very much like a couple in love taking in the sights. That was the goal, anyway. Not once did either of them get the feeling they were being watched or followed.

Maybe this Brotherhood wasn't as keen as they'd made themselves out to be. But it wasn't really the Brotherhood Kora was thinking about. Was the Fox a woman? If so, who? Could she be the witch who'd originally hidden the treasure? If she was also a vampire, there was every reason to think she'd still be around.

But why would that woman do such a thing? Was it some kind of test? And if so, for what? And beyond all questions about the treasure, how did this woman know what had happened to Kora's mother?

Or maybe the Brotherhood was just making it up that the Fox was female.

The questions were enough to make Kora's head hurt, but she supposed she'd know soon enough when she turned over the treasure and got the answers she sought.

After a few more minutes of wandering, they finally approached the cathedral. At this late hour, it was closed, of course, but well lit. And just like all the tourists around them, they stopped and took pictures.

The church had been built as a monument to Tsar Alexander II, who had been assassinated on the very spot. And what a monument it was. Not an inch was left undecorated in some way.

They kept taking pictures while speaking softly.

Greyson held his phone up, snapping away. "It's better lit than I expected. And there are a lot more people here."

She nodded. "We might have to wait until the streets empty out a little more. Even if that means into the wee hours of the night."

"But the longer we wait, the more chance we have of being found."

"You think the Brotherhood are actually on to us? We've been very careful."

"They might be. I was careful in Paris, too." He looked at her. "Do you really want to risk it when you're this close to finding the thing you need?"

"No. But we can't exactly waltz in with all these people here or with the place lit up like a Christmas tree."

"That, we can't. Not without bringing a whole lot of unwanted attention to ourselves." He glanced at the river that ran alongside. "We might have to go in from the water."

"Which means finding a boat. The walls of that canal are straight up and down."

He sighed.

She nudged him. "I guess being able to turn into a bat sounds like a pretty good idea right about now."

He snorted. "That would make things easier."

"Let's walk all the way around and see if we can find the best access point. Actually, you look. I'll keep an eye out for anyone watching us. Then I might have a plan."

His brows lifted, but he said nothing, just started to walk. They made their way around. She didn't see anyone looking at them for more than a moment and then only in the most disinterested way.

But twice, she could have sworn she felt eyes on her.

As they rounded the building, Greyson smiled. "Scaffolding. Perfect."

She glanced over. The back side of the cathedral was under renovation, according to a sign written in Russian and English. "That's excellent."

"Now we just need a distraction."

They stopped by the iron fence that separated the curved street from the gardens that sat next to the church. She peered through the bars of the fence. The park beyond was pretty vast. It was as perfect as the scaffolding.

Her gaze shifted back to him for a moment. "I can handle that."

He leaned on the fence beside her, his interest still exclusively on the church. "What are you going to do?"

She held on to the fence, but looked at him. "Small boom. Nothing to worry about. Then all the cover you could ask for."

"A small boom is nothing to worry about? I like the cover part, but how exactly are you going to make this happen?"

She glanced down at her belt bag, then back at him and smiled brightly.

He shook his head. "I don't want to know."

She decided to tell him anyway. Better to be prepared than scared, that was her motto. "Magic. A spell that cost me three uncut diamonds."

"I said I didn't want to know." Then he sighed. "But now I'm curious. Who'd you get it from?"

"An Egyptian witch in Turkey. Yezmani. Nice woman. Not a lot of teeth, but very cordial and a grand master of Bedouin magic."

A muscle under his eye twitched. "What is this spell going to do?"

"A little noise to draw attention, then a sandstorm will sweep through this area, giving us about three minutes of cover. Really helps, too, that we don't need to breathe. This spell has always kind of been my get-out-of-jail-free card."

"And I appreciate you using it now, but..." His brows bent. "A sandstorm. In Saint Petersburg."

"You have a better idea?"

He frowned. "No."

"Great! Then just give me a minute to read through the enchantment a few times, and we're good to go."

He hitched his thumb toward the church. "Shouldn't we go stand by the scaffolding so we can duck under tarps as soon as this starts up?"

"You can, but I need to be by the gardens here. This spell only works if it's within spitting distance of ten cubits of sand or dirt." She tipped her head toward the gardens. "That's way more than ten cubits."

"I'm not leaving you here alone." Then he snorted. "I'll tell you one thing, hanging out with you is never dull."

She winked at him. "You're welcome."

"In all seriousness, that's a pretty hefty spell you're about to use up. You sure you want to do that for this situation?"

He'd given up a million dollars so he could keep kissing her. She nodded. "Yes."

"Okay. I'm ready to run when you are."

She pulled a yellowed piece of parchment from her bag and read through the words in her head a few times. As she read them, the Arabic pronunciations came back to her. When she felt comfortable with them, she steadied herself and spoke them out loud.

For two long seconds, nothing happened.

Then a crack formed in a patch of bare ground on the other side of the fence. A low rumbling followed, like a steam engine off in the distance. Or thunder. Or an earthquake.

The sound grew, intensifying in breadth and depth so that people had no choice but to stop and look for the source.

Confusion covered the face of every person around Kora and Greyson.

Then, as a great billowing cloud of swirling dust spilled out of the heart of the garden, panic took over. People ran, screaming and yelling in too many languages to count.

The cloud spilled over the fence. Sirens cried out in the distance, and the stars overhead started to disappear in the dust.

Greyson grabbed Kora's hand. "Let's go."

Together, they raced through the curtains of sand toward the church. It wasn't far, and they were fast, but they were still covered head to toe in grime by the time they reached the scaffolding. And the sand was pervasive. Even without having to breathe, Kora could feel the grit in her mouth, nose, and ears.

But they had work to do, so they ignored the dirt and started to climb. The tarps covering the scaffolding gave them a little protection from the storm, but as the seconds ticked by, that protection vanished as the sand pushed through every crack and crevice.

"We need an open window," Greyson said, eyes squinted against the onslaught of particles. He was a level above her, scanning the building. "Or at least one we can—there!" He pointed up and to the right.

"I see it." She pulled herself onto the same platform. "That should work."

"It's going to be a tight fit."

"I'll go first." The howl of the winds started to die down.

"You realize getting out is going to be a completely different story."

"I know." She shrugged. "And I don't have any magic for that."

"We'll figure it out. We'd better get in there before our cover is gone."

"Right." She jumped onto the next platform and went to the window.

As he joined her, she gave him an odd look.

"What?"

"It just occurred to me that we're about to enter a church. Hallowed ground. I mean, if I become human again before I land, I'm going to end up with a pair of broken ankles, but you could be a pile of ash before you hit the ground."

He shook his head. "Not in this case. I did some research on the plane. First, this might be called a church, but it was built as a memorial for the assassinated tsar, and secondly, after the last restoration, it was never reconsecrated. I don't believe it qualifies as sacred ground anymore. If it ever did."

"You feel sure enough about that to jump through this window?"

"Mostly. But I figure if you land and you're human, then I know not to follow you." He frowned. "Which also means I won't be able to rescue you."

"If I land as a human and break my ankles, just call the cops. They'll get me out, and you can rescue me once I'm outside the cathedral walls."

"Deal."

Kora took hold of the sides of the window. It was a long drop.

She really hoped she was still a vampire when she touched down.

Greyson had thought long and hard about the possibility that stepping inside the church, or jumping into it through the upper window, could be very detrimental to his health.

As a precaution, he'd checked the European Vampire Council's website to see what the church's status was. It had been listed as a noninflammatory site, which was great. But the building was under renovation, so the chance existed, however small, that the space had been consecrated again recently.

For that reason, he was cautiously optimistic, but not a hundred percent sure he wasn't going to burst into flames and then disintegrate to ash before he hit the floor. Fortunately, Kora was the willing canary in the coal mine.

Kora slipped her feet through the window, teetered on the edge as she got her arms in, then let go.

Please don't let her get hurt. He braced himself as he

waited for the verdict, listening for anything that sounded like a bad landing.

"You were right," she called up. "It's not hallowed ground. I'm still vampire."

He exhaled the breath he'd been holding, an old human habit few vampires ever lost. "Glad to hear it. On my way."

He shimmied through the window, tight as it was, and dropped.

He landed softly, with bent knees and the catlike grace of their kind. Kora was a few feet away, toward the center of the space, staring up. He could see why. "Wow."

She continued to gaze at the cathedral's incredible interior. "Have you ever seen anything like it?"

"Never." The massive crystal chandeliers weren't lit, but the light spilling in from outside illuminated the place nicely, making the tiny glass tiles of the mosaic-covered walls gleam like jewels. "The pictures online don't do it justice."

"No, they don't. It's like standing inside a jewelry box," Kora said.

"I was just thinking something very similar." Much like the outside, every inch of space was decorated, but unlike the outside, the cathedrals walls were much more intricate because of the mosaics. And what wasn't mosaics was marble. Color was everywhere, as were touches of gold. The floor was a gorgeous pattern of inlaid semiprecious stone that went a few feet up the wall.

"You know what else is interesting?" Kora asked.

"What's that?" His nose wrinkled at the faint but pervasive smell of incense. This might not be a true church, but it smelled like one.

"There are suns everywhere."

As soon as she said that, he saw them. In the halos around the heads of the saints depicted in the murals, as part of the decorative patterns, in the floor tiling, carved into the stone, everywhere. "How are we supposed to know which one is meant for us?"

"Good question." She turned to face him. "I think the last clue we found has to be our guide. It should point us in the direction we're supposed to go. All the other ones have."

"True. Okay, the dolls, then. The Romanovs were all represented as themselves, except for Tsar Nicholas, who was represented by a depiction of this building and his coronation crown. The building led us here, obviously, so how does the crown help us in this space?"

She bit her bottom lip, turning slowly to look at everything again. "This entire place exists because of the assassination of Tsar Alexander. Tsar Nicholas was also assassinated, along with the rest of his family."

She stopped turning, her gaze fixed on something straight ahead. "The shrine. I read about it in my research."

Greyson nodded. "So did I. It marks the exact spot where Tsar Alexander was killed."

They looked at each other. Kora stopped biting her lip. "We start there."

Together, they walked over to the four stone pillars that surrounded the cobblestones where Tsar Alexander had been attacked. In truth, he'd died elsewhere, but the bomb that had wounded him had detonated on this exact spot, according to history.

The pillars were capped with an enormous canopy in the same colors as the inlaid stone floor. An ornate, knee-high gate closed off the columns at the front. Out from the gate, a stone wall ran around the perimeter of the pillars at the same height. On the outside of the gate, a red carpet ran back a few feet to where Kora and Greyson were standing. They were stopped from going closer by a simple gold rope strung on thin brass stanchions.

Clearly meant to block overly curious tourists, not vampires in the midst of a treasure hunt.

Kora stepped over the little rope to get closer, but stopped at the ornate gate. Greyson joined her, and the two of them stood there, studying every inch of the shrine.

Outside, the sirens prompted by the sandstorm had faded away, and he imagined things were returning to normal, although he expected the dust storm would probably make the news.

Kora sighed. "Do you see anything?"

"Halos around the heads of the icons on the four corners. Also, the round flowers at the top of the canopy. Those could be suns."

"They could be. But in every other clue, the suns were distinctly the same as the locket. Why would they be different now?"

"Good point." He tipped his head, trying to see under the canopy. "Do you really think the suns would be visible to the general public?"

"They were in the pub and the dungeon. Well, if the general public was allowed down in the dungeon, they could see them."

"But they aren't that way in the catacombs."

"So they might not be here either."

"I'm going in." She stepped over the gate and onto the cobblestones.

He followed.

She tilted her head back and stared into the depths of the carved canopy above them. "The lack of light and the dark paint aren't helping. Do you see anything?"

"Not really. Which is odd, because our eyes should be picking up something."

Kora glanced at him. "Maybe there's a deliberate reason for that."

"Magical protection?"

"Could be." She turned her gaze back to the canopy. "Nothing's out of the question at this point. Especially if the Romanov maid was a vampire and a witch."

"Then maybe you need to get closer."

She snorted. "I'm not suddenly going to grow a few more feet."

"Yes, you are." He crouched down. "Sit on my shoulders."

"Okay." With a little snicker, she climbed on. "Don't drop me."

"Not in a million years." There was no way he'd ever let her fall. He took hold of her legs to secure her as he stood. "How's that?"

"I'm definitely closer. Now for a little light." She reached into her belt bag, took her lighter out, and fired it up. The small flame seemed like a bonfire in the enclosed space. She gasped. "Greyson."

He looked up as best he could.

There in the center of the canopy, sunk into the stone or whatever the roof was made of, was a sun symbol that perfectly matched the locket.

Just like they'd thought. He moved closer to the center to put her directly under it. "Can you reach it?"

"No." She wiggled her fingers at it, but there was still a few feet of air above her. "Too far."

"Then stand."

"You're sure?"

"I'm already covered in dirt. What's a few footprints?" He let go of her left leg to reach a hand up. "Here, use my hand to steady yourself. Just be careful with that lighter."

"I can put it away." She clicked the lighter shut, throwing them into shadow again.

"I can hold it. Then you'll still have light."

"I'd rather you hang on to me."

That made two of them. "Okay."

"Besides, once I get to my feet, I can feel for what I need. And I have to get the locket out anyway. I'm assuming it will be the key, like it was in Dublin." She took his hand. "Here goes."

Carefully, she repositioned herself. First, she lifted

a knee, then with a hand on his head, she brought her other foot straight up onto his shoulder. He held perfectly still, moving only to put his hands securely on her feet to hold her.

A little more movement, and her hand came off his head. "Okay, I'm up. And I can reach."

He dare not move to see what she was doing, in case shifting would throw off her balance, so he kept his focus on the ground under his feet. Even so, he could hear the sounds of her pulling the locket from underneath her turtleneck, then fitting it in place.

"It's in. Fits perfectly. But I don't know what to do now. It doesn't push in or turn, and nothing clicked or moved or—"

Light flared up around Greyson's feet. "The cobblestones," he said. "Look."

The area of stones within the shrine looked as though they'd been marked with phosphorescent paint. The design was a sun, of course, its rays spiraling out from the round orb, much like the locket.

Kora made a little noise of surprise. "Oh wow. You can see that even without holding on to the locket?"

"Yes, but we are connected. That might have something to do with it."

"True. Coming down."

She jumped, landing next to him. The sun glowing on the stones disappeared. "Can you still see it?"

"No. It's gone now. You?"

"I can still see it." The locket was in her hand, the ribbon wrapped around her fingers. "Put your hand on my arm and see if it reappears."

He touched her. "It's back."

"It has to mean we look under the stones. Don't you think?"

"Yes." Greyson crouched down and pulled out a switchblade, releasing the knife with a little click. He slipped the blade into a crevice and worked it to loosen the stones where the glowing symbol had been.

Kora crouched beside him and flicked on the lighter. "Is this okay? Or should I just keep a hand on you so you can see the sun sign?"

"Either is fine." He looked up at her. "Thanks."

She smiled. "Thank you. I couldn't have done all this without you."

"I don't know about that." He scraped away at the compacted dirt holding everything in place. Ages had passed since these stones had been put in place. But then again, that wasn't necessarily true if they'd been lifted to hide something underneath.

"I do." Her voice was softer and more introspective now. "I owe you a lot, Greyson."

He pried the first stone free. "I don't feel like you owe me anything." He went to work on the next one. "In fact, this whole trip has been a lot of fun. Not the part where we were threatened by the Brotherhood, but the rest of it."

She laughed softly. "I'm so grateful that you came. And are having fun. But I definitely feel like I owe you. And that's not even taking into consideration the money that you turned down from my father."

The second stone popped loose. He picked it up and was about to respond, when the dull, dark glint of something odd caught his eye. He brushed the dirt away. "Hey, look."

"What is it?"

He stuck two fingers through the iron ring he'd just exposed and tugged. The movement loosened a few more stones and revealed two edges of an iron box. "I'd say it's whatever we came to find."

"Yank it free," Kora urged. She'd been about to spill more of her heart out, more than just how grateful she was for Greyson's help on this crazy trip, but also about how she'd come to realize that it was possible to be a strong woman and rely on a good man at the same time. How he was that good man and how thankful she was that she'd gotten to know him as more than just a guy who worked for her father.

Greyson had proved himself to be a wonderful, caring individual with a surprisingly tender side. He was sharp and witty and resourceful. He was, Kora thought, very much like a male version of herself.

Except with money.

The metal box scraped the remaining cobblestones as Greyson strong-armed it out of its resting spot. It was about six-by-six square, a little patinaed with age, and locked.

Greyson handed it to Kora. "This is your adventure. You open it."

She handed him the lighter. "You really think the source of Rasputin's power is in here?"

"I have no idea. But I hope whatever's in there is the thing you need to get the truth about your mother."

"Me, too." She shook the box lightly. No sound. But there was some heft to the thing. "I guess brute strength is the way to go since we don't have a key, and I don't feel like picking the lock."

"Go for it."

She got a firm grip on the top and bottom halves of the box and applied upward pressure until the hinges creaked and the lock popped. She looked at Greyson. "This is tripping my nerves like crazy. Wild, huh?"

"But the reward that awaits you is what matters."

"Right. So let's see what we've got." She opened the box.

Nestled inside was a remnant of animal pelt bound up with red silk cord.

Greyson leaned in for a better look. "Looks like ermine."

"A favorite of the Romanovs, if I recall." She took the bundle out of the box and began to unwrap it. "There's something heavy in here. Egg shaped."

"Fabergé?"

"That's a very real possibility. We'll see in a sec." She tugged the remaining bit of cord free, then unwound the pelt carefully. At last, she tumbled the contents into her hand.

A large, partially faceted stone lay in her palm. It was slightly larger than a quail's egg and, in the flickering flame of the lighter, shone with a deep blood red that seemed fathomless.

"Ruby?" Greyson asked.

Kora held it up between two fingers and looked at it with the lighter behind it. "I don't think so."

"You can tell by looking at it?"

"No, that's almost impossible. But my gut says this is spinel." She squinted at the stone. "I feel like I've seen this stone before. But how would that be possible?"

"I'm not sure."

She kept studying it, the nagging feeling that she ought to recognize it gnawing at her. "It's not exactly faceted in the traditional way. It almost looks...I don't know, as if it's been partially left in its natural state and just polished."

"Does holding it make you feel any different?"

She cut her eyes at him. "You mean do I have the sudden urge to turn into a bat? No."

He shrugged one shoulder. "Just asking."

"Well, whatever it does, it doesn't matter. We need to get out of here, and I need to contact the Fox to let him—or her—know I have the item."

"Agreed. But we should cover our tracks."

She looked at the hole in the floor. "Right. That's kind of noticeable." She tucked the red jewel into her belt bag, then worked on getting the metal box back into the space it had occupied.

With that in place, they returned the cobblestones to their spots, which was a little like working a puzzle, then they smoothed the dirt into the cracks and stood back to admire their work.

"It's not perfect." Greyson brushed off his hands. "But the good thing is no one ever really gets this close."

"Yeah." She shook her head. It was pretty easy to see the stones had been disturbed. "Actually, the really good thing is that no one knows we were here."

"Hang on." Greyson crouched down again and used the edge of his fist to pound a few of the stones flatter. He stood again. "Better?"

"You know, I think it is. Now let's get out of here." As they left the shrine and headed back toward the main part of the cathedral, she glanced at the window they'd come through. "How are we going to do that? Think we can jump up to the window and pull ourselves out?"

"Yes. I know I can. Can you? If not, I might be able to find some rope or—"

"No, I can make it." She looked at the window a little more. How high was that? Twenty feet? "I think I can."

"Why don't you try first?"

A soft shuffling sound behind them made them both whip around. A bearded man in a black cassock, brimless black cap, and white collar stood in the center of the cathedral. They'd been surprised by a priest.

He blinked at them, then said something in Russian.

Kora shook her head. "Sorry, we only speak English. We got stuck in here when the cathedral closed. Can you let us out?"

The priest frowned. "You should not be in here."

Kora smiled and tried to look apologetic. His English was good, despite the heavy accent. "I know. I'm so sorry. We'll be on our way." She pointed behind him. "Is that door open?"

Greyson put his hand on Kora's arm to stop her. "Look in the shadows."

Her gaze shifted deeper into the darkness at the back of the cathedral.

Two more priests emerged.

She took a step back toward Greyson, putting her in direct contact with his left side.

He kept his hand on her arm and spoke very softly. "Inhale."

An odd request, but she did as he asked. And realized a second later that the smell of incense had been replaced with the musky, earthy aroma of wolves.

The Brotherhood had found them.

"The window," Greyson said in a tone that clearly wasn't to be argued with. "Now."

The next few seconds happened in a blur of time that was both lightning quick and molasses slow.

She bolted for the window, her leap fueled by adrenaline as the snarls of wolves filled the cathedral. She caught the sill with her fingertips, but hit the wall hard. She hung on as lights flashed before her eyes.

More snarling echoed up from the chamber below her. Then the metallic snick of a blade being brandished.

She pulled herself up and through the window. Low growls rumbled through the air. Then a yelp.

Then Greyson was at the window, hauling himself out. "We need to run."

The sleeve of his sweater was torn at the shoulder, revealing three deep, bloody scratches. A single, smaller one cut across his jaw.

"You're hurt," she said.

"I'm fine. We need to move. I only slowed them down."

They swung through the scaffolding like acrobats, skating from platform to platform with speed and ease until their feet were on cobblestones again. They slipped through the tarps on the ground level and mixed in with the tourists, though Greyson's injuries got them a few looks.

They kept going until they were several streets away, then found a taxi.

Greyson directed the man to take them to the airport. "Pulkovo."

Kora frowned at him. "Won't they expect that?"

"Maybe. But we're safer on the plane than anywhere else. Plus, we can get out of here. Have you made your contact yet?"

"No, but I'll do that now." She pulled out the burner phone and sent a text.

I have what you want. Exchange point?

"Done." She looked at his scrapes again. "Are you sure you're all right? Those should be healing already."

He glanced at his arm. "You're right. They should be."

Suddenly, his eyes seemed to lose focus, and a curse slipped from his lips.

Alarm bells went off in her head. "What?"

He shook his head slowly as his eyes started to roll back in his head. "Their claws...tipped with... something."

He went silent and still and a tiny bit gray.

"Greyson." She grabbed his uninjured arm and gave him a little shake. Nothing. He was out cold.

Now it was her turn to swear. The Brotherhood had drugged him or poisoned him or something. Whatever they'd done, it was clear he'd been compromised.

Her phone buzzed. She grabbed it and checked the response.

Well done. Where are you?

Saint Petersburg. There was no point in being secretive about anything now.

Interesting. I will meet you in Rome. Text me when you arrive. Don't be long.

Greyson wouldn't be happy about going to Rome. Actually, there were officials in Rome who wouldn't be happy about her showing up there. But what choice did she have? *Will do.*

She checked out the back window to see if they were being followed. Traffic was thicker than she would have expected for the time of night, but she didn't see any cars that looked suspicious. Still, she didn't want to take any chances.

She dug into Greyson's pocket and found his cash. He had a lot on him, but all she needed was a single hundred-dollar bill.

She leaned forward and held the banknote up so

the driver could see it in the rearview mirror. "Faster. Understand?"

His eyes flicked from the money to her face, and a big smile bent his mouth. "Da. Fast is good. Da?"

She nodded. "Da."

Then she got snapped back against Greyson when the driver stepped on the gas. She laughed softly. Money always worked.

She stayed snuggled up against Greyson, placing her hand on his chest. He probably wouldn't be out for long. Vampire metabolisms were hard to subdue. Of course, she didn't know what the Brotherhood had used on him.

What was their goal? Knock them both out, then what? Take the jewel? Kill them?

That was a terrifying thought.

But it was the kind of thought that got her thinking even more. If the Brotherhood was willing to kill to stop this jewel from falling into the hands of the Fox, that was pretty hardcore.

Who was the Fox?

And what could this thing do that made everyone want it so badly?

Greyson's body ached, and his head felt like it was wrapped in cotton wool. He groaned as he accidentally rolled over onto his injured arm, then realized he had no idea where he was. It was dark. And very quiet. Except for a dull hum. Had he been captured? If he had, the bed was exceptionally soft for a prison cell. But, no. That wasn't right. He'd been with—

Kora opened a door and let a blinding blast of light into the room. "Was that you? I thought I heard a noise. How do you feel? Are you awake?"

"I am now," he groused as he blinked at the light. "We're on the plane?"

"Yep." She shut the door and turned on the room light, which was softer.

"Headed where?"

She made a little face. "Rome."

He grunted. "Are you even allowed back in that city?"

She came over and sat on the edge of the bed. "I

wasn't going to ask permission. But forget all that for a minute. How are you feeling? You look a little pale. Paler than is standard."

"A little weak and foggy." And his arm was killing him, but that would pass. "What did the Brotherhood do?"

"Scratched you up in the fight, remember? I'm pretty sure their claws were laced with sedatives. My guess is they planned on knocking us out and possibly staking us."

That woke him up. "Wow."

"Exactly."

He thought back. "I remember the fight. And getting out through the window. Then...we got in a car?"

"Right. We got a taxi. That's about when you passed out." She put her hand to his face, turning his jaw slightly. "Your handsome face seems to be healing up nicely. That's good. Let me see your arm."

"It still hurts." He'd admit that much. He brought it across his chest to show her. Surprisingly, he liked the attention. Liked her being concerned about him and his well-being. It was sweet. And something he could easily get used to. Too easily, maybe.

"Hmm. I'm not sure those scratches look better. For some reason, they're healing slowly. Maybe it's whatever drugs the Brotherhood used. Look how raised and red the marks are."

He glanced down. Three thick, jagged welts had scabbed over across his bicep. "Probably more than just sedatives on their claws. Could have been some poison, too. My arm is a little hot there." Actually, it was on fire and throbbing, but he didn't want to worry her.

"Well, something's irritating your skin, but obviously your system is working to get rid of it. Which is more reason for you to feed. It'll help."

"I will in a bit." He put his arm back at his side, tired of talking about his injury when there was more info to be gathered from her about what was happening next. "Why are we headed to Rome?"

"To meet the Fox."

"The big exchange, huh?"

Kora nodded. "At last. I want you to go with me."

"Weren't you told to come alone?"

"Yes, but it would be foolish to walk into a meeting with a stranger and not have backup."

"Agreed." Greyson was impressed. Kora really had changed. Not long ago, she would have insisted on doing a thing like that on her own.

"Plus, I'm sure the Fox will have people with her, don't you think?"

"I'd imagine so. Are you worried she won't give you the information you want, though? I mean, since you're breaking the agreement by bringing me along?"

Kora shrugged. "I have the jewel. I'm in the catbird's seat, so to speak."

"Very true." He yawned away the last of his grogginess.

She dipped her head for a moment, breaking eye contact. "I was worried about you."

"Thanks. I was worried about both of us for a minute there. Three against two is pretty decent odds when you're talking werewolves and vampires, but you never know. Sure, we're faster, stronger, and obviously superior creatures, but they had the upper hand in that situation."

She laughed at his bravado. "Thank you for protecting me. Maybe when my father hears about it, he'll give you some of that million dollars after all."

Greyson took her hand in his and laid them both against his chest. "I didn't do it for the money."

"I know. And I appreciate that." She held his gaze for a second. "There's about forty-five minutes left before we land if you want to shower and change."

"I do." Especially since she obviously had, based on how nice she smelled and how clean she looked in her new outfit of black leather leggings, boots, and a slouchy dark red sweater. "I still have sand in areas that really shouldn't."

She snorted as she got up. "I don't need to know that."

"Why not? It's your fault."

Grinning, she headed for the door. "I'll pour you some breakfast when you get out of the shower."

"Thanks. Hey."

She turned. "What?"

"How did I get on the plane?"

She grinned. "I carried you."

"I was afraid of that."

"Really?" She tipped her head. "That's what you were afraid of? Not that I might violate your personal space while you were unconscious?" She wiggled her fingers at him while leering mischievously. "You have no idea where my hands might have been. You're a strange man, Mr. Garrett."

With a wicked smirk, she left the room, leaving him to wonder if she really had violated his personal space. If she had, it sucked that he couldn't remember it.

He showered, probably using up all of the plane's hot water, but he needed it. Running through that sandstorm had coated every inch of him with grit. He washed the welts on his arm, too, not liking how rough and bumpy they felt. He hadn't thought vampires could get infections, but there was no other way to describe what was going on with his arm, not with the redness, the heat, and the throbbing.

If it wasn't better by the time they got back, he was going to have to see someone. Preferably someone who understood poisons, because that had to be what the Brotherhood had used on him.

He got out, dried off, then dressed in the last clean clothes he had: dark jeans and a charcoal sweater. He put on his lug-sole boots and went out to the cabin.

Kora was in the lounge area where the seats were positioned around a low table. She was charging her phone and looking at the jewel they'd found in the cathedral. The matryoshka dolls had been put back together and now sat at the end of the table.

As promised, breakfast awaited him in a tall glass.

He sat catty-corner to her and drank half of it in one draught. As soon as the liquid hit his system, energy coursed through him. "Having new thoughts?"

She shook her head. "No, the same ones, actually. Wondering what this thing does that has everyone after it. Oh, and I figured out why it looks so familiar. It's identical to the red spinel that sits atop the Imperial Crown of Russia."

"How about that? Whatever power this stone has, it must be something pretty amazing."

"I agree. I don't think it's the power to shape-shift, although I could be wrong."

"You think that because you've tried, right?"

She snickered. "Yes. Well, wouldn't you?"

"Totally." He emptied the glass.

"It still could be that, and I just don't know how to make it work, but would that be enough to get the wolves all worked up? I mean…I guess it would be if it was kind of a general shapeshifting power. I'm sure the werewolf community wouldn't want vampires to suddenly be able to become wolves, too."

He leaned back in the seat, crossing one ankle over the opposite leg. "That would be enough to get them riled up, for sure."

She glanced at him. "Then what happens if I turn this over to the Fox, and war really does break out? I don't want to be responsible for that kind of rift in the supernatural world. Things are pretty smooth right now. And have been for a while. Can you imagine returning to the days of chaos?"

He uncrossed his legs, unsettled by such a thought. "No. And as much as I'd like to think we're past that, the Brotherhood was pretty adamant that things would go south if that stone fell into the wrong hands."

"So what do I do?"

He thought for a moment. "Is there any way the Fox wants it so she can put it into storage? You know, safekeeping so that the power in that thing isn't abused?"

"Anything's possible, but without knowing who the Fox is, how can I say what her intent is?"

"Right. And without knowing more about the Brotherhood, or what that thing actually does, we can't rightly assume anyone's motive."

She sighed. "Which brings me back to what do I do?"

He put his elbows on his knees. "I don't think I can tell you what to do. This is your decision to make. You're the one who did the work. The one with something to lose."

"Greyson, I want your advice. What would you do?"

He steepled his fingers under his chin. "I would meet the Fox, ask some questions, maybe get a demonstration of this stone's power, then I would go with my gut and my heart and make the decision that feels the most right."

She stared into the stone, her expression a mix of uncertainty and frustration. "I can do that." She looked at him again. "And if I don't like the answers I get, or what this thing does, then you're going to have to help me get out of there alive, because if I don't turn this stone over to the Fox, my gut is already telling me it's not going to be pretty."

He reached out and squeezed her knee. "You never have to worry about me having your back."

267

"Thanks." Her smile was thin and unconvincing. "But listen. I mean this in all sincerity. As much as I want your help, I don't want you putting your life on the line for me again. I got myself into this. I don't want you hurt again because of me. Or worse."

"Kora—"

"I'm serious, Greyson. You've already done so much for me. I couldn't live with myself if something happened to you and it was my fault. I know how heavy guilt is. It's suffocating." She clenched her fist around the stone. "Please promise me that if it's a life-or-death situation, you won't sacrifice yourself for me."

The very idea made his heart hurt. "I can't promise you that."

She closed her eyes for a second. "If you die because of me..." She swallowed. "I can't bear that weight for eternity." She met his gaze again. "And I won't. Do you understand?"

He nodded. What he understood was that he had to get them both out alive. No ifs, ands, or buts.

Rome in the evening was as beautiful and crowded as Kora remembered, but there was no time for sightseeing on this trip, not any more than she could do from the table of the sidewalk café where she and Greyson were currently parked. It had become their procedure. Find a spot to people watch in order to see if anyone was watching them.

So far, nothing out of the ordinary. But she was itching to move.

She wanted to be done here as quickly as possible, and not just because she didn't want the authorities to find out she was in town.

And sure, she wanted to avoid another run-in with the Brotherhood, but she also wanted to get back to Nocturne Falls. Back to her family, back to her life, and back to Waffles.

Her gaze moved to Greyson, who was watching the crowd strolling past.

Another part of her really wanted to see what

would happen between the two of them once everything went back to normal. It was easy to be attracted to someone who was saving your life and living on the edge with you in this kind of minute-to-minute adventure they were on.

How would they feel about each other when the big excitement was a movie night on the couch?

She grinned. That actually sounded pretty good to her. Partially because it wasn't something she'd ever really done and partially because spending an evening tucked up against Greyson had its own appeal.

But would he still be interested in her when she wasn't a leather-clad warrior woman? Time would tell. Then again, he'd been pretty gone over the elf princess, and she'd run a toy shop.

At least Kora managed Greyson's favorite night spot. They could always hang out there.

Her phone vibrated. Hopefully with the Fox's answer to Kora's text that they'd arrived. She checked the screen. It was. The Fox had sent an address, along with a simple response.

I'll be waiting.

Kora stared at the text for a moment. It was all about to come to an end. She'd finally have the information she'd always wanted.

"Is that what we've been waiting for?"

She looked up and nodded. "Yes. I need to plug the address into the GPS, and then we can go. Have you seen anything?"

His eyes went back to the people going past. "Nothing worth noting."

"Good." She copied the address out of the text, then pasted it into her maps app. "We're twenty minutes away."

"By foot or by car?"

"Either. Apparently, with traffic it's a wash."

"I'd rather walk."

"Me, too."

They paid and left, ever mindful of their surroundings. Greyson took her hand.

She looked at him in surprise.

He smiled. "We're just two tourists on a romantic trip to Rome."

If only that were true. She smiled back. "Got it."

He held his expression, but his eyes turned darker. "I wish I didn't feel like we were being watched."

"I thought that earlier, but you said you didn't see anything suspicious, so…" She shrugged.

"And I still don't. But I can't shake the feeling there are eyes on us."

"We are two supernaturally attractive people, if I do say so myself. Maybe it's just normal eyes. Not creepy-wolf-shifters-who-want-to-stake-us eyes."

"Maybe. But based on how things have gone so far, that wouldn't be my guess."

"Right." She scanned the passing crowd, but if they were being watched, it wouldn't be by someone in front of them.

She made a show of stretching her neck and shoulders, using the movements to check the buildings around them, but she saw no one partially hidden by a curtain, no one on a balcony, no one on a rooftop who looked suspicious.

As they walked, the area became more residential, and the tourist traffic lightened. There were still some people out walking and taking in the grand villas, peeking through the gated entrances, and snapping selfies for social media, but the foreigners were easy to spot.

Greyson and Kora turned a corner, and he suddenly pulled her into a doorway.

"Shh," he whispered.

She nodded. They were waiting for whoever might be following them to make the turn as well.

Footsteps echoed off the walled estates and down the street. Shuffling footsteps. Almost…animalistic.

Greyson put his arms around her and kissed her. She gasped in shock. That wasn't what she'd been expecting in the moment.

But she welcomed the distraction, melting into him with every fiber of her being. Even if this was part of their cover, she was all about it.

The footsteps went past.

Greyson broke the kiss, turning them both to see the owner of the footsteps.

A little old man and his sheepdog out for a walk.

They both relaxed, but only a little. There was every chance they were still being watched.

Greyson shook his head as he looked at her again. "How much farther?"

She lit up her phone's screen. "Not much." She showed him the map. "Straight on, then a right and two more blocks."

"If it's one of these homes, your Fox has done all right for herself." He checked the street in both directions before stepping out onto the sidewalk again.

"Then maybe I should ask for a little money in addition to the information."

"Couldn't hurt to try." He offered her his arm—his uninjured one—and they set off again.

Their final destination brought them to a walled estate with a gated entrance much like all the others on the street. Beyond the gate was an elaborate garden with olive and lemon trees and white stone pathways that all seemed to spiral out from a gorgeous marble fountain. A ceramic plaque on the side read Palazzo Volpini.

The GPS announced that they had arrived.

Kora closed the app and tucked the phone away. "I guess we should just go in. She said she'd be waiting."

Greyson tried the gate. It wasn't locked. He pushed it open cautiously. "Better than standing out on the street."

"True." She went in.

With one more look over his shoulder, he entered as well. He shut the gate, but they were both aware there was nothing keeping anyone else out either.

They headed through the garden, past the low Moroccan-inspired fountain in the center and on to the main house. That brought them to a portico and another gate, except it was really a door. Two, to be exact. High, arched wrought iron backed with glass.

And they were locked.

Kora pushed the small bell off to the side, then they stood waiting.

Two statues flanked the entrance, maidens carrying vessels. Maybe of wine, maybe of water, Kora had no idea. But they looked like very old marble, just like some of the urns in the garden.

There were designs painted around the entrance, too. Terra-cotta and turquoise, faded by time and the Roman climate. Probably painted around the same time as the two statues had been carved. Everything about this home spoke to its age and the wealth of its owner.

A man came to the door. He wore the black livery of household staff, and although he clearly wasn't young, he also had the unmistakable vibrancy that only one thing could provide.

The immortality of being a vampire.

He opened the door. "You must be Kora."

"I am."

He looked at Greyson, then back at Kora. "Your guest may remain here."

"No. He comes with me, or I don't come in at all."

The manservant didn't look upset. He just nodded. "I'll let the signorina know of your wishes."

He closed the door and left them outside.

"Signorina. So it is a woman." Kora looked at Greyson and snorted. "She'd better be okay with you coming in, because I am not going inside without you."

"What if she says no?"

"She won't. She wants the jewel too much, I'm sure."

He nodded. "I guess we'll see."

The manservant returned a few minutes later. "She is not pleased, but she will allow it."

Kora shot Greyson a look before walking into the house. "That's very generous of her, considering what we've been through." She frowned at the manservant. "No one could have done alone what we did."

He nodded. "Yes, miss. Right this way."

They followed him through the enormity that was the palazzo. Past rooms painted with frescoes. Past rooms filled with enough statuary to be mistaken for museum galleries. Past rooms appointed with the kind of opulent, ornate furnishings that only a long-standing Roman estate could get away with.

This wasn't a house, it was an ode to extravagant living and old money. Exactly the kind of place where an ancient, wealthy vampire would live. And Kora had no doubt that was who they were about to meet.

The manservant led them through a set of burled-wood doors and into a sitting room with an intricately tiled floor and olive-green wallpaper with a scrollwork design. Gold leaf and more burled wood showed up in the furniture, but the ceiling was painted with a mural of satyrs and nymphs cavorting. "The signorina will be with you in *una momento*."

"Thank you," Greyson said. As the manservant left and shut the doors behind him, Greyson's brows lifted. "This is some house."

Kora nodded. "You can say that again." She kept her voice down. "I'm definitely asking for expenses."

"At least."

Three or four minutes passed before the doors opened again.

Kora turned to meet the woman who had sent her on this wild chase. And stared straight into a face she'd never expected to see again. She went hot and cold, stiff and weak, sick and elated all at once.

How was this possible?

The woman smiled. "Hello, Kora."

Her throat frozen with disbelief, Kora finally found her voice. "Mom?"

Pavlina held out her hand. "Now that you have the answer you were promised, I'd like the treasure that's due in exchange."

Greyson had never met Pavlina, never seen a picture of her, never even heard her described, but there was no denying the resemblance she and Kora shared. The slight upturn at the corners of the eyes, the same elfin smile. A certain something around the mouth. Even their jawlines were similar.

Except that while Pavlina looked rather unmoved, Kora looked like she was about to throw up. Or cry. Or punch something. She could use a moment to gather herself, he thought.

He stuck his hand out. "Pavlina?"

She turned toward him, and the hand she'd been holding out for the stone went into his. "Ah, yes. And you must be Greyson." She shook his hand, her grip firm and cool. The movement made him grit his teeth because of the pain in his arm, but he managed not to react more than that.

If Pavlina noticed, she didn't let on. "I understand you've been very helpful to my daughter. For that,

I'm grateful. But you must understand I am less than pleased to have an employee of my former husband's in my home."

"I'm not currently working for Lucien, nor have I recently."

Her smile was thin and placating. "Well, that's something, then, isn't it?"

"How?" Kora spat the word like it was all she could manage. She still looked dumbstruck, which Greyson found completely understandable. "Why?"

Pavlina glanced at her daughter again. "I'm sure you have many questions, Kora. I will answer what I can, but you must tell me if you truly have what I sent you to find."

"I do."

"Excellent news. Most excellent. Why don't we sit?" Pavlina gestured to the grouping of silk upholstered armchairs positioned by the fireplace, which didn't look as though it had been used in centuries. The rug under the chairs was probably equally as old.

Kora sank into a chair, seemingly grateful not to have to support her own weight any longer. Greyson's heart went out to her. What a gut punch this had to be.

To find out that the mother you thought was dead was still alive and living what appeared to be a rather extravagant life and hadn't reached out to you in, what, seventy-five years? A hundred? Nor did Pavlina seem particularly excited to see Kora. No wonder she was in a state of shock.

He didn't know how to protect her in this situation. Or how to fix it. There was no life experience that prepared you for this kind of business. So he did the only thing he could think of. He made small talk. At the very least, it would buy Kora some time to compose herself. At best, he might learn something that would explain why Pavlina thought abandoning her daughter had been the right move.

"Have you lived here long, Pavlina? This estate is beautiful."

"Thank you." Her smile seemed more genuine now. "I've lived here quite a while, but I don't live here alone. The southern wing houses quite a few others."

That was an odd answer that only created more questions. "Others? Other vampires?"

"Yes." Her expression turned serious. "We are the Prosvita. Perhaps you've heard of us?"

He had, but he played dumb, preferring to see what she might tell him about the splinter group of Russian vampires who claimed they would someday rule the world, as was their birthright. Crazies, as far as he was concerned. "No, I'm sorry. What is the Prosvita?"

"We are the Enlightened Ones. The elite vampire children of Rasputin and the heirs to his power, which has lain dormant since it was hidden a century ago."

Wheels turned in Greyson's brain. "You're a descendant of Rasputin?"

"I am." She looked at Kora. "As is my daughter. All the Prosvita are. It's a requirement for membership."

And the jewel they'd unearthed was supposed

to be the source of Rasputin's power. No wonder the Prosvita wanted it. They thought it was their inheritance, so to speak. "Why is the Brotherhood after the jewel?"

Pavlina's eyes gleamed with sudden emotion. "Did the Brotherhood come after you? Do they know what Kora found? That she brought it here?"

"Yes, they came after us. Several times." There was no point in lying. He didn't like Pavlina enough to spare her from the truth anyway. "If you mean do they know that Kora found the source of Rasputin's power, then yes, they know what we were after and that we found it. I don't think they know we brought it here. We were careful not to be followed."

Pavlina was quiet for a moment, but before she could speak, Kora did.

"I want answers." Kora's shocked expression was gone, replaced by an unyielding look of determination. "Why did you disappear on me and Dad?"

Pavlina turned toward her daughter. "Because the Prosvita had work for me. And sometimes that work was dangerous. It was safer to stay away. Besides, your father was perfectly capable of raising you, a fact he enjoyed proving to me over and over again. Eventually, my work won out."

That answer did nothing to quell the growing anger in Kora's eyes. "So you just abandoned your child for some organization. Did it ever occur to you that I might need you more than a bunch of vampires?"

"Kora, be reasonable. The Prosvita are much more than that. You have no idea what we're working toward. What the jewel you found will enable our people to do."

"Then tell me."

Pavlina slanted her eyes at Greyson. "He is not one of us."

Kora lifted her chin. "He's with me, and that should be good enough."

"It's not," Pavlina shot back. "What our father, Rasputin, has provided for us will make us the envy of all other vampires. We will be their superiors. I will not speak of this further in front of him."

Kora was clearly fed up. She shifted her gaze to Greyson. "I guess this is where she explains how we're going to be able to turn into bats."

Pavlina snorted and rolled her eyes. "As if such pettiness would drive us all these years. No, what I speak of will change the lives of all who bear Rasputin's blood in their veins. It will lift us to our rightful place. And because of your efforts in finding the stone we have been searching for, because you are my daughter, I offer you a place here with us, Kora."

"You want me to join you." Kora shook her head. "Was this all some kind of test?"

Pavlina seemed confused that Kora wasn't jumping at the offer. "Not a test, no. The stone has been missing for nearly a century. All we had was the half of the locket to go on. None of us could make sense of the small portion of the inscription we had. What you did was above and beyond any test."

To put it mildly, Kora was miffed. "But now, after all these years, now that I've done something you deem worthy, you want me with you."

Pavlina didn't seem to grasp Kora's bitterness or the irony of the situation. "Your rightful place is here with me. You are my child."

"*Was* your child. I'm an adult now. My own person." Kora stood, practically vibrating with anger. "But you know what? None of that matters. I'm done. I can't believe you're alive. And yet, I find myself not really caring." She nodded at Greyson. "I'm ready to go."

Pavlina jumped to her feet. "You will not leave without turning over Rasputin's Stone. It belongs with us. With his children."

"No can do, Mommy Dearest. For one thing, it's not on me. For another, if I'm a descendant of Rasputin, then it belongs with me just as much as it does you. But the bottom line is we're going to negotiate new terms. You want that stone? Fine. I want to be paid for my time. Scratch that, I *need* to be paid. For my time, effort, and expenses. Greyson's, too, since he only came along at my bequest. Ten million in gold, diamonds, or cash. Your choice, because I'm easy like that."

Pavlina opened her mouth to respond, but the doors to the sitting room burst wide before she could say a word.

The manservant from before came flying in, eyes glowing with urgency. "Signorina, there are wolves in the garden and more at the gate."

Greyson and Kora looked at each other and simultaneously spoke the same words. "The Brotherhood."

Pavlina pointed at Greyson, her fangs bared. "You led them here."

"I did nothing of the kind," he snapped back. "Kora, we need to get out of here."

She nodded, but Pavlina snatched her arm. "Give me the stone."

Kora pulled free of her mother's grip. "I told you I don't have it with me. We'll discuss payment and the exchange later, if we're all still alive."

She grabbed for Kora again, but missed. "You cannot leave." Then she shouted at the manservant. "Aldo, alert the others."

"Yes, signorina." He left as quickly as he'd entered.

Again, she pleaded with Kora. "You cannot go. They will follow you and take the stone. Better to stay here and fight with us. The odds are in our favor. We are more than fifty strong."

Kora looked at Greyson. He frowned. "I hate to admit she might be right, but that's a lot of vampire power."

"Fine," Kora said. "We'll stay and fight, but this business with the stone is not resolved."

"No, it is not," Pavlina said. "Follow me."

She led them through the estate and upstairs. On the way, they passed numerous other vampires getting ready for the onslaught. Once, through a window that looked out onto the garden, Greyson swore he saw the glow of eyes.

But even without that, the scent of wolf was strong. There was no denying they were surrounded. What he couldn't understand was how the Brotherhood had found them. He and Kora had been so careful.

He went around a corner after Kora and her mother, bumping his arm against the wall as he did. The contact made him wince. His arm was no better. In fact, it might be a little worse. He put his hand to the wound. Heat seeped through the fabric of his shirt, and the welts felt like they'd swollen.

Whether it was poison or infection, he was starting to feel the effects of it on his system. His reaction time was a fraction off, and his other senses were not as sharp. He was going to need medical help soon.

But he'd be fine until the Brotherhood was dealt with.

He hoped.

Kora didn't want to fight. She also didn't want anyone to die, but more than that, she wanted all of this to be over. The Fox was her mother. And her mother was still very much the woman Kora had recently come to understand her to be.

Selfish. Uncaring. Concerned only with her own interests and what was best for Pavlina. She wasn't any more interested in being a mother to Kora than she ever had been.

The pain of that realization seared through Kora like a hot blade.

There was no way on this green earth that Kora was going to give her Rasputin's Stone. The woman didn't deserve it. Not even for ten million dollars. No amount of money or jewels or gold would make Kora hand it over.

She still wanted very much to know what power it held, but what did it matter? She knew enough. If Pavlina and the Prosvita thought it was going to turn the Rasputin vampires into superior creatures, Kora understood the trouble that would create.

No wonder the Brotherhood had said it would start a war.

The room Pavlina took them to was large enough to be a ballroom. It overlooked the garden with a small balcony, but on the other side, the estate backed up to a narrow span of ground and then the exterior wall. Beyond that was a sidewalk and a road.

For all its palatial expanse, the palazzo was still in Rome, and Rome was every inch a city.

The room was dark, giving them the benefit of some cover, although the wolves had excellent eyesight as well.

Kora sidled up to the edge of the doors that opened onto the balcony. She looked into the gardens, trying to spot the wolves.

Greyson went to the windows on the opposite side. "There are several on the street. I'm sure we're completely surrounded."

Pavlina paced the floor, wringing her hands. "Come away from the windows. They'll spot you."

Kora frowned. "They already know we're in here." She went back to searching the garden. As her eyes adjusted to the darkness outside, shapes began to form. She counted quickly. "At least twelve. No, make that fourteen. Fifteen. At least that many."

Pavlina made a sound of disgust. "Foolish creatures. They will die in their attempt to stop us. But I suppose some of them might prefer that to servanthood."

Kora detected what sounded like madness in her mother's voice. "What on earth are you talking about, Pavlina?"

Pavlina stopped pacing. "When we take over, the wolves will become subject to us again. All shifters will. They are lesser creatures."

Greyson made a rude noise. "The wolves were right. You are going to start a war."

Pavlina's lip curled. "Perhaps, but it will be a short one, I assure you. And we will win."

"What makes you so certain? Shifters outnumber vampires in vast amounts. You think all you have to worry about are the wolves?" He walked toward her. "Every supernatural that can transform into another creature will join with them."

She only looked more defiant. "Our strike will be swift. And unexpected. They will have no choice but to bend to our will."

Greyson's eyes narrowed. "You are hell-bent on destruction, aren't you?"

Kora shook her head. "I wish I'd known it was you who'd hired me. And how insane you truly are. Why did you call yourself the Fox, anyway?"

Pavlina shrugged. "It's a loose translation of the name of this estate, after the man who built it. Edwardo Volpini. So I went with it."

Greyson met Kora's gaze with sympathy. "I'm not dying here. Not for her. And neither are you."

Kora nodded. "I know what I need to do. But it's going to take a few uninterrupted minutes." She hoped he understood what she was asking him to do.

He smiled. "I'll give you all the time I can."

Pavlina took a step toward Kora. "What are you going to—"

Greyson blocked her path. "Take another step toward her, and we're going to have a problem."

"Thanks," Kora said.

Then she opened the doors to the balcony and stepped out to face the wolves.

More pairs of gleaming, glowing wolf eyes looked up from the garden than Kora could count. She'd never faced that many angry shifters before. And certainly not a group that most likely wanted her dead.

Intimidating, to say the least.

But she was half vampire, half reaper, and she was not about to let this moment in time get the best of her.

She cleared her throat. "I wish to speak to the leader of the Brotherhood."

Behind her, Pavlina cursed. "What are you doing, you fool girl?" Then, "Let go of me."

"No," came Greyson's immediate response. "Not until Kora's done what she needs to do."

That bolstered Kora's resolve. "Well? Which one of you is in charge? Don't tell me you came here without a leader."

Another moment passed, then a woman with short gray hair and a Roman nose stepped into the clearing near the fountain. "I am Vittoria Ricci, and I am the captain of the Rome Brotherhood."

Kora wanted to make a comment about how it should be the Personhood, then, but knew that wouldn't get her anywhere. "Nice to meet you, Vittoria. I'm Kora Dupree."

Vittoria's expression didn't change. "We know who you are. What do you want?"

"To put a peaceable end to all this."

Vittoria snorted. "Is that so?"

"Yes, it is." Kora glared at the woman, hoping to make her see that she was being serious. "Why do you want the stone?"

"Because it's too much power for one small group to possess. Do you have the stone?"

Kora ignored the question. "What is this power?"

More noise behind her. She looked over her shoulder to see that Greyson had his arms wrapped around a struggling, snarling Pavlina.

Pavlina attempted to lunge forward when she made eye contact with Kora. "The wolves are full of lies. Don't listen to them. They only want the stone for their own uses. They want to destroy all vampires."

"They haven't said anything yet." Kora focused her attention on the garden again.

"We don't want to destroy anyone," Vittoria snapped. "We have no feud with peaceable vampires. The Prosvita are not peaceable. They mean to rule the supernatural world."

Kora couldn't argue that, since Pavlina had said as much. "Please, Vittoria. What power does this stone hold?"

"You went after the stone without knowing its value?"

"I did, because its value to me was the exchange of information promised upon its delivery." She glanced at her mother before looking at Vittoria again. "But that information proved to be less than satisfactory, and now I find myself thrust in the middle of this...unfortunate situation without knowing why."

Vittoria held her hand out. "Give me the stone, and I'll tell you anything you want to know."

Kora tilted her head with disbelief. "Do you really think I would agree to that? Your people tried to kill my partner and me. The Brotherhood lost any chance to be trusted in Saint Petersburg."

Vittoria dropped her hand. "They wouldn't have killed you."

"Really?" Kora raised her brows. "Because they sure tried."

Greyson snorted. "Ask them what kind of poison they laced their claws with."

Kora nodded, trying not to let her worry for him show. She hated that he'd been hurt. "Good point." She turned back to Vittoria. "If they didn't mean to kill us, what kind of poison were they using on their claws?"

She shook her head. "Just a little laudanum to slow you down."

"She's lying," Greyson muttered. "My arm's on fire. Laudanum wouldn't do that."

Kora stared down at Vittoria. "What else? This is your last chance to tell the truth."

Vittoria frowned. "They also imbedded a tracker in the male who was with you."

"A tracker?" Greyson snarled. "No wonder my arm hurts so bad."

Pavlina hissed. "I told you that you brought the Brotherhood here."

"Yeah," Greyson said. "You did. But that changes nothing."

Kora held her hands out. "Tell me what the stone does."

"First, tell me if you have it," Vittoria responded.

Kora nodded, resting her hands on the balcony railing. "It's in a safe place. What does it do?"

"Stupid child," Pavlina started. "Why are you bothering with these wolves? We could crush them under our heels if you would only—"

Kora spun around. "Greyson, shut her up."

Greyson clamped a hand over Pavlina's mouth. "This won't last."

Kora returned to Vittoria. "Answer me. Now."

Frustration clear on her face, Vittoria lifted her chin. "The stone gives all Rasputin vampires immunity from the sun."

Kora's mouth dropped open as the stunning news registered. "We could daywalk?"

"Yes," Vittoria answered. "Making your people unstoppable."

No wonder the wolves didn't want them to have it. What would it be like to feel the sun's warmth on her face? To see the world bathed in the brilliance of daylight? She had no idea.

She'd never been human. Never had that other life in the mortal world.

From the garden, Vittoria said, "You see why we cannot allow one sect of vampires to own such a thing?"

Kora was lost in a literal daydream, but pulled herself back to the moment. "I do. But what would the Brotherhood do with it?"

Vittoria's eyes narrowed. "Destroy it."

A moment before, Kora had been ready to side with the wolves. Now the idea of destroying the one thing that could grant her a normal life felt like sacrilege. She shook her head. "There has to be a middle ground."

"There isn't," Vittoria answered. "Where is the stone?"

"I told you. A safe place."

Greyson let out a growl. Kora turned in time to see him pull a bloody hand away from Pavlina's mouth.

She glared at Kora. "Give the stone to me, child. Join your true family. We will rule these dogs."

"Shut up," Kora snapped. "Greyson, what would you do?"

He frowned. "I already possess the privilege of walking in the sun. It wouldn't be fair of me to give my opinion. But I sure wouldn't give that stone to Pavlina. Or the Brotherhood. You're right. There has to be a middle ground."

She stared at a spot on the balcony just in front of

her feet. His words made her realize that she'd been silly to think there was a future for them. He could daywalk. She couldn't. That put a world of difference between them. And at some point, that difference would get old.

But if she possessed the Rasputin's Stone... She looked at Pavlina again. "How does the stone work? How do you activate it?"

Pavlina smiled. "It must be reunited with its master."

Kora almost rolled her eyes. "In plain language, please."

Pavlina huffed. "It must be added to the urn that holds Rasputin's ashes, which is at an undisclosed location."

But Pavlina undoubtedly knew that location. And yet, in that moment, Kora realized how tired of all this cloak-and-dagger stuff she was.

All she wanted to do was go home and live her life. Although, if that life wasn't going to have Greyson in it, how much was there to look forward to? Because the astonishing truth was, she loved him.

Emotion clogged her throat. She found her voice anyway. "Greyson?"

"Yes?" His quick response held a note of hope, which surprised her. In one word, he told her he was at her service, ready to do whatever she needed, and happy to help.

What a remarkable man.

"I can't daywalk."

He nodded, still holding Pavlina back. "I know."

"Doesn't that matter to you? Because you can."

"Does it matter to you?"

She shrugged. "Day and night are very different worlds. You can do things I can't."

"That's true. But that ability also allows me to protect you better." He smiled. "And that's something I'd like to keep doing."

Pavlina rolled her eyes. "Spare me the syrupy words, you low-born cretin. My daughter descends from a line of vampires you can only dream of belonging to."

Kora pointed at the woman who'd given birth to her. "Stop calling me your daughter. Stop acting like it suddenly matters. And don't talk to Greyson that way. He's worth a hundred of you. And what's more, I love him."

Greyson's mouth fell open, but Kora had more business to take care of before she could respond to him. "Vittoria, because I cannot trust you and your kind, a third party will have to be engaged and a treaty drawn up. The stone should be put into permanent storage, away from vampires and shifters, and sealed in place with unbreakable magic. I imagine the Vampire Council will be a part of this as well. Do you agree to this?"

The woman frowned, but seemed to realize it was the best she was going to get. "What third party?"

"I would suggest a very powerful and ancient witch by the name of Alice Bishop. She resides in the United States in a town called Nocturne Falls. A place the Brotherhood could learn a lot from."

Vittoria glanced at the wolves around her, perhaps to gauge their thoughts. Then she looked at Kora again. "When will this take place?"

"One week from today."

Vittoria nodded. "I must be allowed to bring several of my people."

"You may bring one. There's no reason for more than that at a treaty signing. You wouldn't want the Vampire Council represented by half a dozen, would you?"

"No." She frowned. "Agreed."

Kora gave Greyson a quick wink, then leaped over the balcony and landed softly in the garden below. She walked to the fountain, hand outstretched toward Vittoria. "Thank you."

Vittoria shook her hand. "I didn't expect this outcome. But then, I never thought a vampire would give up the chance to daywalk. You're a very unusual one."

Kora smiled. "I'm only half vampire. My father is a reaper."

"That explains it."

"How so?"

"You are already able to daywalk."

Kora snorted. "I wish. No, that ability wasn't passed on to me."

Vittoria's expression changed suddenly. "So you were born as you are."

"Yes."

"But that means...you've never seen the sun."

"Correct."

Vittoria stared at her. "And yet, you're willing to give up the stone?"

"For peace, yes." She glanced back at the balcony. "And because the life that's waiting for me is worth it."

"Then you're even more remarkable than I thought." Vittoria tipped her head back and let out a short howl.

A moment later, the scattered members of the Brotherhood formed up around her. Kora stopped counting at forty-three.

Vittoria then held up her hand. "A temporary treaty has been called between the Brotherhood and the keeper of Rasputin's Stone, Kora Dupree. She is granted free passage."

"And my partner, the vampire Greyson Garrett."

The wolves all nodded.

Vittoria took a few steps backward toward the gate. "I will see you in one week."

"One week."

She smiled, flashing large canines and glowing eyes. "Do not let this go wrong, or the Brotherhood will do whatever necessary to make things right."

"I'd expect nothing less, and I understand." But Kora also knew Pavlina wasn't a problem so easily solved.

When the last wolf slipped through the gates, Greyson released Pavlina. She did exactly what he'd expected her to do. Bolted over the balcony railing and down to the garden to confront Kora.

He followed behind her, ready to restrain her again if need be.

Some of the other vampires had wandered out of the house and now stood at the edge of the garden, looking very unsure about who Kora was and what had just happened.

Pavlina launched into Kora with a tirade. "How dare you assume you have any kind of right to negotiate our freedom away? What you did is paramount to treason. It's insanity. I cannot—"

"Hold up," Kora shot back. "You know that thing you were planning? The whole take-over-the-world thing? Let's rewind to that, shall we? Because if you want to talk insanity, that's a good place to start.

What did you think the Vampire Council was going to do? Just sit by and let it happen?"

"You are dead to me, Kora."

"So, business as usual, then?" She rolled her eyes. "You're unbelievable, although I give you points for consistency." She looked past Pavlina to Greyson. "I'm ready to go. There's nothing more I can do here."

"You're not going anywhere." Pavlina was beyond fuming now. "You gave away the ability to walk in the sun. Do you understand that? Can you grasp the loss of such a thing? Or has your reaper side made you incapable of comprehending such a simple idea?"

Greyson expected Kora to blow up over the dig at her father, but somehow she remained relatively calm. He was impressed.

Kora shook her head. "I can't grasp it, I guess, because I've never been human. Never known the warmth of the sun, or the feel of it on my skin, never seen the world lit up by its rays except on the rare occasions that there's been a UV filter to protect me. So maybe I don't understand it, but then again, maybe it was an even bigger thing for me to give up, considering I've never experienced it, while the rest of you have."

Greyson was so proud of her he thought he might burst. "You did the right thing, Kora. You saved the world from war."

Pavlina snarled at him. "Shut up. You're too blinded by love to see clearly. And you're not one of Rasputin's children, so your opinion is worthless."

If she'd been a man, Greyson would have knocked her out. "I think love has made me see more clearly than ever, but how would you know, Pavlina? Have you ever loved anything other than yourself?"

A slight smile turned up the corners of Kora's mouth. "She hasn't. And I don't think she ever will. Now, let's go. I'm ready to go home."

He nodded. "Me, too."

He stepped around Pavlina to join Kora, who was already headed for the gates.

But of course, Pavlina wasn't done. "You are *not* leaving with Rasputin's Stone."

Kora whipped around. "I would sooner go to ash than see that stone in your hands."

Pavlina's hands clenched, and a muscle beneath her eye twitched. "I should have left you to the sun when you were born, you ungrateful wretch. Would have saved me a lifetime of misery."

Greyson put his hand on Kora's arm. She was seething. "Misery? What misery have you had? I was the one left without a mother. And Lucien without a wife."

Pavlina snorted. "I only married him because he agreed to take you on. I never loved him. And I never wanted you."

Greyson watched the light in Kora's eyes darken. "You made that abundantly clear, but what do you mean that he agreed to take me on?"

Pavlina laughed. "Do you really think Lucien is your father?"

Kora's lower lip quivered in what looked like rage,

not impending tears. "You're lying. That's all you know how to do."

Greyson leaned in, his voice as soft as he could make it. "She's only saying that to get to you. Let's go."

Kora nodded and stumbled back a few steps.

Pavlina put her hands on her hips, her face a cruel mask. "That's right. Run back to your daddy. Ask him. See for yourself. Truth is, I don't really know who your father is."

Then she barked out a laugh, threw her hands into the air, and turned for the house. Suddenly, she stopped and spun around. "Don't ever come back here either."

"Don't worry about that," Greyson said. He wrapped his arm around Kora's waist and held on to her, guiding her to the gate and back onto the sidewalk.

Kora looked like she'd disconnected from her body.

He kept her moving and hailed a cab as soon as one appeared two streets over. She remained quiet all the way to the plane. Then stayed quiet after he got her on board and into a seat.

He left her side only once. To dig the tracker out of his arm, which seemed to help the pain immensely. After that, he sat across from her and one seat over so he'd be close, but not so close that she felt smothered. This was so out of his area of expertise, but space seemed like a smart move.

They'd been in the air twenty minutes when she finally spoke. "How's your arm?"

"Much better since I got the tracker out."

"Good. You should probably still see a doctor."

He shrugged. "I'm all right."

She frowned and a few more long minutes went by before she spoke again. "Do you think she's telling the truth?"

Greyson measured his answer. Lying might make her feel better, but it wouldn't do any good in the long run. "I don't know. But I do know that your father will tell you the truth."

Kora nodded, her eyes so filled with sadness that Greyson's heart ached for her. "I don't know if I want to ask him. I mean…" She stared at her lap. "Then he'd know I know. And I don't want that between us."

"He won't love you any less. If anything, it kind of makes him an even better dad than he was before."

She lifted her head. "I suppose you're right."

She wrapped one arm around her middle, then rested her other elbow on her hand and brought her thumb to her mouth so she could chew on her fingernail. That wasn't something she'd ever done before. She was always so perfect in the way she looked and acted.

But now she was staring into space, lost in thoughts that had to be painful.

He'd never seen her more vulnerable. More hurt. He wanted desperately to fix things for her. To make her happy again.

To crush Pavlina into dust.

He swallowed. "I meant what I said. Earlier."

She looked at him. "Hmm?"

"Maybe now isn't the right time, but then again, maybe it's the perfect time, but I have to tell you. I love you, Kora. I am in love with you. And I just want to make you happy."

Her gaze stayed on him, that same faraway look she'd had a moment ago present again. "You love me?"

He nodded. "So much that I can think of nothing else."

She covered her mouth with her hand, not quite stifling the sob that slipped out. "How can you love me? I'm a mess. My mother is a monster. My father is potentially unknown. I can't daywalk, while you can. My past is—"

"None of that matters. Unless you don't feel the same way about me. Just say the word, and I'll never mention it again."

She laughed. Or sobbed again, he couldn't tell. "Yes, I love you. But I am no good for you. Don't you see that?"

"You're all kinds of good for me. You might be too good for me."

A tear slipped down her cheek. "You know that's not true."

He kissed it away, taking her hands in his. "Kora, I know you're hurting right now, and I know there's nothing I can say to make it better, but if there is anything in my power that I can do to help, just say so."

She shook her head, and a genuine smile appeared. "Just tell me it's going to be okay."

"It is, I promise you." He kissed her forehead. "There is one thing I need to ask you."

"What's that?"

"Where on earth did you hide the stone?"

That got him a little laugh. "Nowhere." She reached into his jacket pocket and pulled it out.

He couldn't have been more shocked if she'd produced it out of thin air, but then it was the same thing she'd done with the locket, and he hadn't picked up on that either. "How did you...but you said—"

"I said it was in a safe place. And I put it there when we were getting off the plane." She shrugged. "I figured that way if Pavlina searched me, she'd believe me. And if you didn't know you had it, you couldn't accidentally give it away. Not that you would."

"Wow. Well played."

She pressed her hand to his cheek. "Do you really love me? You weren't just saying that to make me feel better?"

"I really do. But you know your father isn't going to be happy."

"I think, in light of everything that's gone on, he'll come around very quickly." She sighed. "I hope so anyway. After all, if I'm happy, shouldn't he be happy about that?"

Greyson wasn't so sure about that. "Well, Hattie likes me, so—"

"My father likes you. He just doesn't think I should be involved with anyone right now. Or maybe ever. Who knows?"

"Do you think it could be because he doesn't want you to end up like your mother?"

She shot him a look. "Are you implying that I'm going to go wild, sleep with more guys than I can count, and end up pregnant with a child I don't want? Because that is not going to happen."

"No. I just meant he doesn't want to see you in a situation where you don't have a lot of options. Right now, you're completely independent."

She laughed softly. "I don't know about that. I live in a house he owns, drive a car he paid for, rely on him for my paycheck...I am about as far from independent as you can get." She sighed. "I guess I see where he's coming from. I need to stand on my own two feet a little more."

"Kora, you're too hard on yourself."

"I'm just being honest."

"Then be honest a little more. What do you want?"

She stared straight ahead for a moment. "Surprisingly, just to live an ordinary life for a while. Drama is exhausting."

He nodded. "And maybe that right there is why your father doesn't want you to get involved with anyone. Relationships are a breeding ground for drama."

"But do they have to be?"

"No. But there's no guarantee either." He shouldn't be telling her such things. But to be anything but truthful would only hurt them both in the end. "I've witnessed it firsthand."

"I guess you have." Her gaze went to her hands in her lap. "So maybe we shouldn't go out. Despite our feelings. Maybe not getting involved is for the best."

He wanted to rage against that idea, to tell her things would be different for them, that a happily ever after was all that lay ahead, but he'd thought the same thing about his last relationship, and she was marrying another man. "I will abide by whatever you want."

Her subtle nod was his answer. Then, after a moment, a soft, "Okay."

He sat there a minute longer, his heart going numb with the loss of what might have been. Then he got up, went to the back of the plane, and took a different seat.

He drifted off as the sun was coming up, but there was no promise in the start of a new day. No fresh beginning.

Just heartache that he'd caused himself.

Kora immersed herself in work as soon as they got back to Nocturne Falls. All kinds of work.

To start with, she explained everything that had happened in Rome to Elenora Ellingham and Alice Bishop, who lived at Elenora's estate. That had taken some help from her father, since Kora didn't know the Ellinghams that well. Thankfully, Alice was more than willing to accommodate Kora's request, and Elenora seemed pleased to host the treaty. At least she seemed pleased once she made it clear that Sheriff Merrow, who was a werewolf himself, would be on hand to ensure the Brotherhood behaved themselves.

Although Alice could probably neuter them all with a single word.

Next, Kora immediately resumed her schedule at Insomnia, where she decided to make up for the time she'd been away by starting a cleaning and inventory project on a scale she was pretty sure had never been done before. In her opinion, the place needed it.

She also did some things that weren't work, but added to her increasingly busy agenda. Like making a vet appointment for Waffles just to make sure he was doing all right since recovering from the state he was in when she found him. Not only was he fine, but he'd gained some weight, putting him at a healthy twelve and a half pounds. Apparently, all his floof just made him look bigger.

Outside of work and Waffles, she also spent some long-needed time with Hattie, and in the spare moments that were left, she reorganized her closet and seriously assessed each item in it as to whether or not it still suited her.

She resolved not to wear so much leather when she wasn't at work. She could see how intimidating a look it was, and while that image might have been something she actively cultivated once upon a time, not any longer. She wanted to leave some of that past behind. She wanted people to like her. She wanted friends.

Along those lines, she even found time to meet Monalisa Tsvetkov for coffee.

But not once in the last six days had she talked to her father about the bombshell Pavlina had dropped. She didn't want to upset him, or bring such awful news into their relationship when it was going so well. She also didn't want to cause waves when she needed him to be in a good mood. Just in case things between her and Greyson changed.

Not that she'd spoken to Greyson since they'd gotten back, except to let him know the details of the treaty meeting.

Despite that, she thought about him constantly. Wondered what he was doing. If he was thinking of her. If he missed her like she missed him. If she was being a fool.

She almost called him twice. Almost texted him a dozen times. But what would that get her? They'd agreed not to see each other. That it was for the best. That they were better off as friends.

But were they still friends? Didn't friends hang out? Didn't friends talk? Truth was, she didn't know if she could have that kind of casual relationship with a man who made her light-headed and fluttery.

Things weren't supposed to get light-headed and fluttery in the friend zone. At least that's how she thought it worked.

And why did she care so much what her father thought about her and Greyson? Well, she knew the answer to that. She owed her father so much. Like her current situation. And without him, the life she was living would go away.

Not that she thought he'd be so petty as to take everything from her if she did start seeing someone. He wasn't Pavlina. He was as opposite as could be.

But he'd asked her not to get involved with Greyson, and the thought of disappointing him...that was heavy.

Still, Greyson was ever present in her head and heart. The constant push-pull between want and obligation made her feel so mixed up that staying busy was the only thing keeping her from breaking down, she was sure of it.

But if this was the normal life she'd dreamed of getting back to, it was miserable. In fact, her mood seemed to be worsening the closer the treaty meeting got. Maybe because she'd be face-to-face with Greyson again. And she'd be reminded in that very visual way about what she couldn't have.

She put a basket of clean laundry on the bed, then sat beside it, closed her eyes, and made herself take a few deep breaths in a weak attempt to get the unhappiness out of her system.

But Greyson was still there in all his charming, devilish glory. No doubt he'd show up to the meeting looking like his usual self. Hair a little too long and slightly unkempt, like he'd just rolled out of bed. A dusting of dark stubble accentuating his strong jaw. Dressed in some lace-cuffed shirt and black jeans with a velvet jacket as if he was on his way to audition for Sexiest Vampire of the Year.

Which he'd probably get, because honestly, was there any competition?

No. No, there was not.

She braced herself on her hands and leaned back to stare at the ceiling. Why did he have to be so handsome? So kind? So sweet? And the sort of kisser that made her stomach do flips and her knees go weak?

Why couldn't she stop thinking about him? And worse, about future things almost too embarrassing to admit?

Like marrying him. And buying a house with him. And having babies with him.

She'd never been that girl who dreamed of the big wedding with the white dress and the flowers, and now, because of him, she was.

Apparently, that's what a man like him did to a woman.

Her phone rang, startling her out of her head. She glanced at the screen. Hattie. "Hi, Mémé."

"Oh good, you're up. Hi, honey. What are you doing? Tonight's your night off, isn't it?"

"It is." She'd been up for an hour, but she supposed her grandmother still thought of her as a kid. It was endlessly endearing. "I was going to finish organizing my closet. I still need to go through my accessories."

Hattie made an unimpressed grunt. "I don't think so."

Kora laughed. "No?"

"No."

"You have something better in mind?"

"I do." Hattie paused for obvious dramatic effect. "Coq au vin."

"Oh wow. That does sound better." Hattie's coq au vin was exceptional and not to be missed. She really only made it for special occasions. Kora guessed she'd made it now because she knew Kora was in a funk. She was remarkably perceptive like that.

"I thought it would. You'll be here at sundown, then."

"Yes, ma'am." That was in less than half an hour. "Should I bring anything?"

"Just yourself. And fix yourself up. I know you're moping."

Kora shook her head. "I will."

"A little lipstick never killed anyone."

"Yes, Mémé. I'll see you then. Love you."

"Love you, too."

They both hung up. Kora looked at Waffles. "I guess I'm not finishing the closet tonight, then." She scratched under his chin, resulting in closed eyes and lots of purring. "You really need a buddy, don't you? Maybe next week I'll take a trip to the rescue and see if there are any suitable friends for you."

She kissed his head. "Right now, I need to get dressed. What do you think Mémé will accept as fixed up? Probably not pants. But I don't have a lot of dresses that aren't leather. Maybe I should get some."

She went to her closet, well aware of what was in it due to her reorganization. "You think I could get away with jeans and a nice blouse with a little sweater?"

She looked over her shoulder. Waffles had his feet in the air and was soundly asleep. She laughed. "Thanks for the input. I bet the sound of me opening your dinner wakes you up."

Picking something out didn't take long because there wasn't much left to choose from. She ended up with the new dark-washed jeans she'd just bought this week to add some depth to her new friendly wardrobe, a printed red blouse, and a navy cardigan. The latter two being gifts from Hattie that Kora had never actually worn. She slipped her feet into black flats, did her hair and makeup, then added a little jewelry and took a turn in front of the full-length mirror. "She can't complain about clothing she gave me."

After feeding Waffles, which did indeed wake him up, she jumped in the car and headed for her father's house. The car reminded her she really needed to talk to her dad about the vehicle. It was beautiful, but it wasn't practical. And it was silly for someone in her financial situation to drive something this expensive. A secondhand crossover would be just fine. Something she planned on buying herself.

The idea made her smile. What would it be like to make a car payment? Certainly about as grown-up as she could imagine. She didn't think her father would let her pay rent, but someday, she'd get her own place and do that, too.

Maybe she'd ask Greyson to go car shopping with her. That would be a good excuse to see him, wouldn't it? She didn't care one bit if taking a man along made her appear less independent. She was tired of not seeing him, and that seemed like a valid reason to reach out.

She sighed. It really was time to take her father aside and gently broach the subject of having a man in her life.

Her thoughts continued in that vein through one quick stop at the florist then on the rest of the drive to her father's house. Twilight was such a lovely time of evening. The faint purple light felt warm and promising. She took it as a good sign and clung to whatever that portended for the rest of the night.

After the week she'd had, she needed something good to happen. Something that stopped all the longing and uncertainty in her head.

Talking to her father would be a great way to make that happen. She hoped.

But as she pulled into the driveway and stared up at the house, a little of her courage slipped away.

She turned the car off and sat there for a minute. No, she was not going to let this go. She couldn't. Her personal happiness was at stake.

He had to understand that. Especially now that he was so happy with his new wife, new house, Hattie's return to the mortal world, and his new life that could be lived out in the open.

Maybe Kora hadn't exactly earned all that yet, but happiness was an inalienable right. Her father wanted her to be happy, she knew that. She just had to make him see that Greyson was a big part of that happiness.

She got out of the car, the flowers she'd bought for Hattie tucked in one arm.

Of course, all of that would hinge on one very important detail—Greyson still wanting to be a part of that happiness.

She walked up the steps to the front porch. This week apart could have changed things for him. Could have made him see that he was just fine being single. She hoped that wasn't the case.

The door opened as she lifted her hand to knock. Hattie smiled up at her. "Hi, honey. You look so nice."

"Hi, Mémé. Thanks." She held out the simple bunch of daisies and some little purple flowers. "These are for you."

"Oh, they're lovely. What a nice surprise. Come in." Hattie took the flowers.

Kora kissed her on the cheek as she stepped inside. "The house smells delicious. I can't wait."

"Your father and Imari are in the living room, if you want to say hi."

"I do, but don't you need help in the kitchen?"

"No, everything's done. You go on in. In fact, tell everyone to come to the table."

"Okay." She went into the living room while her grandmother went back to the kitchen.

Lucien looked up from the *Tombstone*, the local Nocturne Falls paper. "Good evening, Kora."

"Hi, Dad. Imari."

Imari put her magazine down and smiled at her. "Hi there. Are you recovered from your trip?"

"Mostly. After the treaty meeting tomorrow, it'll finally all be behind me."

"That will be good."

"It will be." She hooked a thumb toward the dining room. "Mémé says everyone should come to the table."

Imari put her magazine aside. "I should see if she needs help."

She disappeared into the kitchen, and Lucien joined Kora. "You all right?"

"I've been better. Can we talk after dinner?"

"Of course. You know I'm always here for you."

She nodded, smiling tightly. Knowing that and guessing his reaction to her decision were two different things.

How different remained to be seen.

Greyson paced when he had something stuck on his mind, when he was waiting, or when he needed to think through a problem.

At the moment, he had a trifecta going on.

His phone buzzed, stopping him in his tracks. He checked the screen, then nodded as he read the brief message.

She's here.

It was go time.

He took one final look in the mirror. Too late to get a haircut now. Why hadn't he thought of that sooner? He knew why. His brain was clogged up by a tall blonde who made everything else fall by the wayside.

Well, he'd had enough. Not of her. He'd never have enough of her. But he'd had his fill of just sitting around, abiding by her father's wishes. His fill of longing to touch her and hold her and kiss her and not being able to.

315

Being friends was worthless when it didn't assuage the needs of his body, mind, and heart. A useless platitude that meant they might see each other only by accident.

Screw that. He wasn't living in the same town as the woman he loved and hoping to occasionally run into her at the grocery store.

Neither one of them shopped enough for that to even happen.

Greyson was a man in love. A man who was done waiting around. Done feeling like this and seeing no end in sight. And Lucien was just going to have to understand that Greyson intended to claim Kora as his own.

Naturally, this was all with the understanding that she still wanted him. Because if she didn't, this could get pretty embarrassing for him.

Her rejection tonight would make tomorrow incredibly uncomfortable, too. He'd put so much in place, all because of the way he felt about her.

Not that he'd change anything he'd done.

But if she turned down his big gesture, he was going to feel like a fool. Granted, he'd live through it and get on with his life. Somehow. He'd managed after Jayne, but this...this felt different. Bigger. Much more like forever.

Maybe he'd move out of Nocturne Falls. Some time away could be good. He could spend the next century at Catherine's apartment in Paris, licking his wounds.

Because if Kora turned him down, he was really

going to need some time to figure out where he was going wrong with women.

No more thinking about all that now. Time for positive thoughts and action. He jumped in his car and sped through the streets of Nocturne Falls toward Lucien's new Victorian, getting to the house in what was probably record time. But then, he was a man on a mission.

He ran up the walk to the porch and found the door open just as he'd been told it would be.

The tantalizing smells of dinner and the chatter of harmonious conversation reached him at the same time.

Both suddenly crystalized what he was about to do. Intrude on a family event. The possibility existed that his interruption would not be well received. But there was no other way to do this. He needed to speak his mind, and he wanted the whole family to know at the same time what he was about. This was his moment. It would determine the course of his future. He felt as sure about that as anything.

He strode boldly into the dining room.

Hattie's smiling face was the first thing he saw, followed by Kora's confused one.

Her brows bent. "Greyson?"

"Hi, sweetheart." Every nerve in his body was electric with hope. "I need to say something to you, Kora." He turned. "And to you, Lucien."

The reaper set his fork down, wiped his napkin across his mouth, then sat back. "Go on, then."

Bright red courage flowed through Greyson's

veins with the same ferocity that blood once had. "I love your daughter." He glanced at Kora. "I do, you know."

She was smiling. That was a good sign. "I know. I love you, too."

Relief swept him. He approached Lucien again. "I know you don't think she should be seeing anyone right now, but you're wrong. I'm good for her. She's incredible for me. I'm asking you right here and now not to stand in the way of what's meant to be."

Imari clapped her hands together. "This is so romantic."

Lucien frowned at his wife. "You would think that."

"Well, it is, Lucien." She shook her head at him. "And honestly, why are you telling your adult daughter how to live her life?" Imari rolled her eyes. "Men."

Lucien opened his mouth, but Hattie spoke first. "You have my blessing."

Lucien's second frown was directed at his grandmother. "Mémé, please. You don't understand—"

Hattie's stern frown was everything. "I understand that Greyson is a lovely man with good manners, a firm financial background, and that he has on more than one occasion protected our Kora from danger. He loves her. He just said so. And she loves him. What else is there to understand?"

Lucien leaned forward, both hands on the table. "She is trying to establish herself. To get her life on track."

Imari crossed her arms. "I'd say having a man like Greyson as her partner would put her life on track about as firmly as one could hope for. The rest will come with time."

Greyson finally got a word in. "I have more than enough to take care of both of us. And Waffles."

Kora laughed softly, her gaze on him and him alone. "I've missed you."

"And I, you, love." He went to stand by her chair.

She took his hand immediately and finally looked at her father. "Dad, this is what I wanted to talk to you about after dinner anyway. I'm miserable without Greyson." She shook her head. "I'm not going to derail the progress I've made just because I'm in a relationship. Especially not with a man like Greyson. Something you should know very well."

Hattie nodded. "Very true. Who do you always call when you need something? How much better will it be to have him at Kora's side?"

Lucien grimaced. "I'm being railroaded."

Kora shrugged. "It's a little hard to get hit with so much truth all at once, I know. Kind of like what happened to me when I returned home to find you married."

Lucien sighed. "I suppose. But that was different. That marriage was to save Imari."

The genie snorted. "But look who it really saved."

Lucien reached over and took his wife's hand in a move that clearly showed how much he agreed with her.

"Dad, I just want to be happy. Don't you want me to be happy, too?"

A long moment passed, then he nodded. "Of course I do, Kora. But what if things don't go the way you hope?"

"I could say the same about you and Imari, and maybe I would have once upon a time, but not now, because I can see how much you care about each other. You'll just have to do the same for us. Let time show you the truth."

Greyson nodded. "And it will."

Imari smiled at them. "I have no doubt."

Lucien's frown softened. "I have reservations." He held up a hand. "But I will not stand in your way."

Kora let out a soft squeal, a sound of pure joy and not one Greyson ever remembered hearing her make before. It was a beautiful thing.

He wasn't about to express himself the same way, but he felt that joy, too. "Thank you, Lucien."

"Yes, thank you, Daddy." Kora jumped up and hugged her father. "There are still a few things I want to talk to you about. Like that car, for instance…"

Lucien stopped patting his daughter on the shoulder. "What's wrong with that car? Did you wreck it?"

She leaned back. "No. I actually want to give it back to you and buy something with my own money."

"You do?"

She nodded. "It's a beautiful car, but I haven't earned it. I'm not at that stage in my life. I shouldn't be driving a Ferrari. I'll get something I can afford."

Lucien gaze held disbelief. "You will?"

"Sure. An SUV or one of those crossover things. I have some money saved now." She shrugged. "Or maybe I just won't have a car for a while. It's not like I need it to get to work."

Lucien looked around Kora to make eye contact with Greyson. "Did you have anything to do with this?"

He shook his head. "Not a thing."

"He didn't directly," Kora said. "But I've realized a lot of things lately. About what taking responsibility really means and what being a grown-up requires, and I just want to make some changes in my life."

"I'm impressed," Lucien said. He took another beat before speaking again. When he did, he put his hand over Kora's. "I don't want you without a vehicle, but I can see your mind is made up. I approve. I don't know what happened on that trip, and I don't need to, but I'm proud of you."

"Thanks, Dad. I want to make you proud." She put her arm around his shoulders and turned to see Greyson. "We both do."

Greyson nodded. "And we will."

The weight of taking on a relationship with Kora was abundantly apparent, but at the same time, Greyson had never felt so light. He would do everything in his power to make this work and to keep her happy.

She was worth it. They were worth it.

And this time, it really was forever.

The two emissaries from the Vampire Council had arrived the evening before and stayed at Elenora's estate. Mitsuki, a Japanese woman who was rumored to be nearly five centuries old, and Nobis, a dark-skinned man with light eyes and a faint Nigerian accent, were already at the table with Alice when Elenora escorted Kora and Greyson into the grand ballroom. Multiple paper copies of the treaty sat in front of Alice, waiting to be signed, along with a fresh box of pens.

Elenora was as prepared as could be, and for that, Kora was grateful. She wanted this over and done.

So what if the room was a little large for a meeting? This wasn't just any meeting, and something about the scale of the ballroom underlined the seriousness of why they were gathering. Kora found no fault in it.

As they approached the table, the sounds of others arriving carried in.

Led by Wentworth, Elenora's part-time butler, the Brotherhood's Vittoria and her second, a man named Daniel, walked in with Sheriff Merrow. They'd been given rooms at a local hotel, and Kora had heard from Greyson that a deputy had watched the place all night.

Thankfully, they'd gotten this far without incident, and now all of them were gathered in Elenora's ballroom, where she'd had a large, round table set up.

Wentworth left them and took a spot by the door.

Kora thought the table was a stroke of genius. No one had a better seat, since it was round, and putting everyone on equal terms was exactly what this meeting needed.

Especially because the Brotherhood and the Vampire Council were staring each other down like someone might get hurt.

Kora hoped this could be done civilly, but she was starting to have doubts. Five vampires, three werewolves, and a witch in the same room? What were the odds no one came out unscathed?

Well, if something got started, Kora would not be the originator.

Elenora held out her hands. "Now that we're all here, why don't we sit? I'm sure everyone is eager to accomplish what they came here for."

Seats were taken, but the tension in the room remained. The Brotherhood had to know they'd never get out of here alive if they tried something.

Or maybe that was the cause of the tension.

Kora tried to keep a smile on her face. "Once

again, thank you, Elenora, for hosting this event. It was very kind of you to open your home."

She nodded. "My pleasure."

But Kora thought that pleasure was mostly due to Elenora also being chosen as the neutral party, which meant she'd been elected to hold Rasputin's Stone until the meeting. Elenora's love for rare and priceless gems had won that round.

From the pocket of her Chanel suit, Elenora lifted a black velvet pouch, and from that, she produced the stone. She placed it on the table before her on top of the little bag. "As you can see, the object in question is safe and sound. As soon as you sign the treaty, I'll turn it over to Alice, who will confine it according to the parameters set out in the treaty."

Vittoria said, "I would like to see the stone up close."

Greyson shook his head. "That can't happen. It's spelled out in the treaty."

Kora didn't know how Greyson knew that. She hadn't. But he seemed pretty adamant about it.

Daniel's lip curled, but before anyone could speak further, Mitsuki raised her hand to interrupt.

"He's correct," she said. "No one but the neutral party and the witch are permitted to touch the stone. It's written so in the treaty. It is a provision meant to maintain the impartiality of the proceedings."

Daniel made a face. "We didn't agree to that."

Vittoria leaned in and mumbled something to him in Italian, then spoke to the group. "My apologies, my colleague wasn't aware of that stipulation, or that we had indeed agreed to it. In fairness, it was added later."

Daniel looked like he wanted to bite something. Or someone. When he spoke, it was with the rasp of frustration. "I want a moment to look over the treaty again."

Elenora nodded. "A wise idea. Why don't both parties do that?" She passed copies around the table to the Brotherhood and the Vampire Council emissaries. There was no need for Greyson or Kora to look the agreement over. As was often said in this part of the South, neither of them had a dog in the fight anymore.

Although, that did make Kora wonder again how Greyson had been aware that touching the stone was off-limits. She could see the logic in it, however. Chaos would break out if someone decided not to give it back.

Daniel took more than a moment with his reading. Finally, after about ten minutes, he laid the treaty on the table.

Elenora's brows lifted. "Is everything in order?"

He nodded, still grumpy. He was clearly taking this change personally, but Kora had no clue why. Maybe he'd hoped securing the stone would bring him some kind of advancement.

Vittoria, who'd finished reading her copy much earlier, folded her hands on the table. "We're ready to sign."

Nobis looked at Elenora. "As are we." His deep voice seemed to boom through the open space.

Elenora passed out pens. "Well, then, let's make it official. Sheriff Merrow, if you would be witness one? Then we'll have Wentworth be witness two."

The sheriff grunted affirmatively.

Wentworth left his spot by the door and came to the table.

The signing took another ten minutes, with copies being passed to all, then the sheriff and Wentworth adding their signatures.

When it was all done, Elenora sent Wentworth to make more copies. "You'll each go home with two copies, and another two copies will remain here. In addition, a copy will be sent digitally to both the American and European Witches Association. And, of course, to any and all requesting councils, packs, and organizations that may be interested."

Daniel still didn't look happy. "Where will the stone be kept?"

Alice came to attention. "The stone will be donated to the National Gem and Mineral Collection at the National Museum of Natural History in Washington, DC. It's one of the largest natural red spinels on record. We had it assessed as such, and the museum has very graciously accepted it for their exhibition."

He crossed his arms. "You think that's going to stop a vampire from breaking in and retrieving it?"

"Perhaps not," Alice said. "But the spell of protection I place over the stone will cause it to be spirited back to me should a shifter or vampire touch it."

Vittoria frowned. "What if there's one working at the museum?"

Alice looked mildly bored with the conversation. As if the wolves were rather dumb for thinking she hadn't planned everything thoroughly. "A stipulation of our donation was that the stone only be touched with gloved hands due to the curse it holds."

Daniel's brows bent. "There's no curse on that stone."

Alice smiled thinly. "There will be when I'm done. It also won't be the only curse, but I'm not divulging everything that I'm doing to protect it. And the museum has agreed to the requirements, which is all that matters. Anything else?"

Daniel looked at Vittoria before answering. She shook her head. "No."

"Nothing from us either," Mitsuki said.

"Very good." Alice stood and held her hands out toward the stone. She whispered a few words, and for a moment, her eyes clouded over like they were covered with milky lenses. Then they went back to normal, and she lowered her hands. "It's done."

"Thank you, Alice." Elenora smiled at the group. "The insured transport will be here tomorrow. Until then, Alice will take possession of the stone. Unless there's anything further, thank you all for coming. Cars are waiting outside to take you to your planes."

Vittoria and Daniel left immediately, but the Vampire Council members remained, engaging Elenora in conversation.

Kora tried to catch the eye of Mitsuki or Nobis in the hopes of finding out what would be done about her mother, but she didn't want to be rude either. You didn't just insert yourself into the conversation with vampires of that standing.

She sighed.

"What's wrong?" Greyson asked.

She shrugged. "I was just hoping to get an update on my mother."

"Go ask. They won't mind the interruption." He tipped his head toward them. "C'mon."

Before she could stop him, he took her hand and started walking.

As soon as they approached, Elenora turned to include them in the small circle. "And here are our intrepid discoverers of the stone."

Kora smiled at the emissaries, hoping they could help. "Thank you for coming."

"For such an occasion as this?" Nobis said. "My dear, you and your partner have helped us avoid the kind of event that would have turned the supernatural world upside down. We are indebted to you."

"Then maybe you can help me with something?"

Mitsuki nodded. "Certainly."

"I was wondering about my mother. I know she's part of the Prosvita. I know she still wants the stone. And blames me for not getting it. What will happen to her?" Kora held her palms up. "I'm not asking for leniency or anything like that. She's never been much of a parent, sadly. I'm just curious, I guess."

Mitsuki glanced at Nobis with a rather guarded expression. He hesitated, then answered. "Your mother is being closely watched. And will be for a very long time. She won't be a problem for you or anyone else. And if she is...she will be dealt with."

Kora let that sink in. The Vampire Council wasn't a group you wanted to cross. "Thank you."

"Thank you," Nobis said. "Giving you that information in no way repays you for what you did. If you ever need something, beyond what's been done, you have only to ask."

"That's very kind." And completely unexpected. But she wasn't sure what he meant by *beyond what's been done*. She pushed it aside to ponder later.

Goodbyes were said, and the emissaries left.

Kora thanked Alice and Elenora again. "It was great that you both helped with this."

Elenora smiled rather oddly at Greyson. "Now would be a good time, don't you think?"

Kora looked at him. "A good time for what?"

His grin was equally curious. "Didn't you wonder what Nobis meant when he mentioned what's already been done for you?"

She nodded. "Yes, but I figured I'd understand it later."

"Well," Greyson said, "I can explain it now if you'd like."

With a little laugh, Elenora put her hand on Alice's shoulder. "Why don't we leave them alone?"

It took only a minute for Alice and Elenora to leave, but to Greyson it felt like an eternity. He'd been waiting for this moment since it had all fallen into place days ago, and now the kind of anticipation he hadn't felt in centuries coursed through him. Not since he'd been a child and Christmas had been hours away had he been so eager. His face ached from smiling. "I spoke to the council on your behalf and—"

"You did what?" Kora looked a little green.

"All good, I promise. I told them what you went through to procure that stone. I reminded them of where you come from."

She groaned. "Yes, I suppose the council knows all about my reputation."

"They do. But they're impressed by how you're working to change that. And they agreed that your actions with the stone deserve some kind of award. Especially because you weren't asking for one."

A little worry crept into her gaze. "What kind of reward? Greyson, what have you done?"

He stuck his hands in his pockets and shrugged. "I just thought it was time someone spoke up for you. And so they've deposited a rather large sum into the Bank of Nocturne Falls in an account in your name."

Her mouth came open. "Large sum? What's large?"

"It should be about two and a half million. More than enough for you not to have to worry for the next century, if you manage it right."

"Two and a half…are you serious?"

He nodded. She was trembling, so he took his hands out of his pockets to hold on to her. "There's more. Can you handle it?"

She nodded, then shook her head. "I can't believe you did that."

"I love you. Why wouldn't I advocate for the woman I hope to spend the rest of my life with?"

She swallowed, seemingly overcome by the moment. "Thank you." Her voice was strained by emotion. "So much."

He cupped her face in his hands and kissed her. "It's my pleasure. I mean that. So is the next part."

"I don't know if I can take any more."

He laughed. "You can. You'll see."

He dug into his jacket pocket and took out the best surprise of all, dangling the little black velvet pouch on its silken cord.

Her gaze went to it immediately. "What is that?"

"This bag holds a shard of Rasputin's Stone. A shard taken with approval, I'd like to add. Done by

331

our very own local gem smith, Willa Iscove. She's the one who appraised the stone to determine what it is. You were right about it being spinel, as you heard. Anyway, with this around your neck, you'll be able to daywalk."

"But how? I mean, that's incredible, but my mother said it needed the ashes of Rasputin to work."

"And thanks to the very appreciative council, there's enough in there to activate the shard."

She stared at the bag, then at him. "I've never seen the sun in person."

"I know, sweetheart." He slipped the cord around her neck. "I was hoping we could see it together for the first time."

Her head was down as she put her hand over the little pouch where it rested against her chest. "I would like that very much."

Then she raised her gaze to his, her eyes sparkling with tears. "You know what else I'd like?"

"What's that? Just name it. Anything."

She smiled a little shyly, then her demeanor changed. A boldness overtook her. "I want to marry you. And have lots and lots of—"

"Kids?"

"I was going to say cats, but we can talk." She threw her arms around him. "How did I get this lucky?"

He pulled her in tight. "Well, it wasn't clean living, so it must be me."

She laughed. "That's one of the many things I love about you, Greyson. You're so humble."

"We're well-suited, then, aren't we?"

"I suppose we are." She bent her head in, resting her forehead against his. "I never imagined all this could happen. I really do feel like the luckiest girl in the world." She picked her head up to look at him again. "But what do you think my dad is going to say?"

"He already knows about us."

"But getting married? That might push him over the edge."

Greyson kissed the tip of her nose. "Good thing I went to see him this morning to ask for his blessing."

"You did?"

Greyson nodded. "He wasn't thrilled at first, but Hattie straightened him out. She's pretty good at that."

"She is."

"And ultimately, he knows that I will protect you with my life. Then I told him about getting you the shard to protect you from the sun, and that did it. He gave me his blessing."

"You're an amazing man, Greyson."

"You're an amazing woman." He scooped her into his arms, making her squeal. "Do you think you're ever going to tell him about Pavlina and what she said?"

Kora shook her head. "I don't think so. What good would it do? It would only upset him. And as far as I'm concerned, he's the only father I want or need."

Greyson smiled. "Very wise. Now what do you say we get out of Elenora's house and go do something as a couple for the very first time?"

"I'm in. And as a matter of fact, there's one errand I need to run."

"What's that?"

She pointed toward the door. "You'll see."

Kora was giddy with life. Her cup had been filled and was now overflowing, and she wanted to share her good fortune with another deserving creature.

She also kind of wanted to see how Greyson would handle such a thing as finding Waffles a brother. Or sister.

It took only a phone call to have someone meet them at the Nocturne Falls feline rescue and open the facility so they could see the cats up for adoption.

Greyson drove, too, which surprised her because she hadn't been sure he'd want an animal in his Camaro. It was his pride and joy, after all, but then again, maybe it didn't matter as much to him as she'd imagined.

He parked and turned the car off. "This is a test, isn't it?"

"Sort of." She winked at him. "I'm sure you'll pass."

"I'm not."

"You're not? Why?"

He shrugged. "I've never had a pet. How do I know how to pick one out? Or what kind of buddy Waffles will get along with?"

"Well, nobody really knows that until we introduce them. But Waffles is pretty chill. I think he'd welcome just about anyone."

"Okay. But don't let me screw up. If I'm choosing wrong, say so."

She put a hand on his leg. "Trust your heart. You can't go wrong that way."

"True," he said. "That's how I ended up with you."

Laughing, they headed in.

The man who'd opened the rescue, Brent Tillis, greeted them with a smile. He was a secondary wizard and worked as a vet tech at Waffles's animal hospital. "Hi, Kora."

"Hi, Brent. This is my boyfriend, Greyson." The word *boyfriend* was going to make her grin like a fool for a long time coming.

Brent stuck his hand out. "Nice to meet you, man. Welcome to the rescue."

Greyson shook his hand. "Thanks for opening up on such short notice."

"So an animal can get a home? Anytime. Come on back." He led them to the cat rooms. "We don't have that many cats here right now. The citizens are pretty good about keeping us empty, but please take a look and see if anyone catches your interest."

"Thanks," Kora said.

"Sure thing. I'll be up front when you're ready."

He left them, and Greyson hooked his thumb toward the right. "How about I take this room, and you take the other one?"

"Sounds good. See you in a few minutes, then." If Greyson wanted to give it a shot on his own, she was fine with that. She got the sense he was nervous about this. Like, really nervous, which surprised her. He was such a cool cat.

No pun intended.

She went into the room, careful not to let any of the cats out, but Brent had been right. There weren't many, which was great. The three in there were all sleeping and didn't seem especially interested in doing much else.

Considering it was closing in on eleven p.m., she'd expected to see more activity from such a nocturnal group.

She stood in the middle of the room and put her hands on her hips. "You guys might not be active enough for Waffles. He needs a playmate, not a nap buddy."

The door opened behind her.

She turned to see Greyson slipping in.

He was holding a skinny white and orange tabby with one eye. "I probably did this too fast, but I don't care what you say, I'm not leaving this cat here."

"Whoa, hang on, I'm not going to say no. What's his deal?"

"Her. I think. I don't know for sure, but she's giving me a female vibe. But look at her." The little cat was pressing herself into Greyson's chest and purring up a storm like her ship had come in. "She's only got one eye. People are going to pass her over because of that. And she's too skinny. She needs someone to love her and feed her and get her healthy."

Kora's heart nearly burst. "I agree to all of that. She's a sweet little thing, isn't she?"

"She is. Very sweet. Came right over to me and curled up in my arms. Not afraid at all." Kora's approval seemed to placate Greyson, and his tone became less frantic. "And then there's her name."

"Oh?"

"It's on her collar."

Kora gave the little cat a scratch under the chin, then lifted the name tag to read for herself. She snorted. "Chicken?"

"I'm sure Brent could tell us the story behind it, but how can you pass up a cat named Chicken when your other cat is named Waffles?"

"Chicken and Waffles."

Greyson looked at Chicken, who had started to make biscuits on his arm, then at Kora. "Pretty great, don't you think?"

She nodded. "About as great as Greyson and Kora."

He smiled. "I couldn't agree more."

She kissed him, then gave Chicken a little pat on the head. "Let's take the new baby home to meet her big brother."

"Yeah, let's. I can't wait for them to meet." Greyson started for the door, then stopped. "Thanks."

"For what?"

"For this." He shook his head. "I've never had a pet. I didn't even know I wanted one, but I've never wanted to save an animal more than I want to save this cat right now."

"I love you, Greyson. So much it hurts."

"I love you, too." He snuggled Chicken a little closer. "Just tell me one thing."

"What's that?"

"Are we going to be that crazy couple with sixteen cats?"

Her brows went up. "This is just two cats."

His gaze went past her in the direction of the other cat room. "I know, but there was another cat in there I thought might be a contender…"

She put her hand on his back and gave him a little nudge toward the door. "Let's see how Waffles and Chicken get on first."

He kissed her cheek. "Okay, but I'm holding you to that."

She shook her head. "Greyson Garrett, crazy cat guy. Who knew?"

"Not me." He opened the door and went toward the front. "Is it weird?"

She was nearly overcome by the bliss of the moment. By the amazing heart of this man in front of her who was single-handedly making her dreams come true. "No. It's perfect. Just like you."

His eyes glowed with love. "Just like *us*."

THE END

Want to be up to date on all books & release dates by Kristen Painter? Sign-up for my newsletter on my website, www.kristenpainter.com. No spam, just news (sales, freebies, releases, you know, all that jazz.)

If you loved the book and want to help the series grow, tell a friend about the book and take time to leave a review!

Other Books by Kristen Painter

PARANORMAL ROMANCE:

Nocturne Falls series:
The Vampire's Mail Order Bride
The Werewolf Meets His Match
The Gargoyle Gets His Girl
The Professor Woos The Witch
The Witch's Halloween Hero – short story
The Werewolf's Christmas Wish – short story
The Vampire's Fake Fiancée
The Vampire's Valentine Surprise – short story
The Shifter Romances The Writer
The Vampire's True Love Trials – short story
The Dragon Finds Forever
The Vampire's Accidental Wife
The Reaper Rescues the Genie
The Detective Wins the Witch
The Vampire's Priceless Treasure

Can't get enough Nocturne Falls?
Try the NOCTURNE FALLS UNIVERSE books.
New stories, new authors, same Nocturne Falls world!
www.http://kristenpainter.com/nocturne-falls-universe/

Shadowvale series:
The Trouble with Witches
The Vampire's Cursed Kiss
The Forgettable Miss French

Sin City Collectors series:
Queen of Hearts
Dead Man's Hand
Double or Nothing
Box set

Standalone Paranormal Romance:
Dark Kiss of the Reaper
Heart of Fire
Recipe for Magic
Miss Bramble and the Leviathan

COZY PARANORMAL MYSTERY:

Jayne Frost series
Miss Frost Ices The Imp – A Nocturne Falls Mystery
Miss Frost Saves The Sandman – A Nocturne Falls Mystery
Miss Frost Saves the Sandman – A Nocturne Falls Mystery
Miss Frost Cracks a Caper – A Nocturne Falls Mystery
When Birdie Babysat Spider – A Jayne Frost short
Miss Frost Braves the Blizzard – A Nocturne Falls Mystery
Miss Frost Chills the Cheater – A Nocturne Falls Mystery

Happily Everlasting series
Witchful Thinking

URBAN FANTASY:

The House of Comarré series:
Forbidden Blood
Blood Rights
Flesh and Blood
Bad Blood
Out For Blood
Last Blood

The Crescent City series:
House of the Rising Sun
City of Eternal Night
Garden of Dreams and Desires

Nothing is completed without an amazing team.

Many thanks to:

Design & derivative cover art: Janet Holmes using
images under license from Shutterstock.com
Interior formatting: Author E.M.S
Editor: Joyce Lamb
Copyedits/proofs: Marlene Engel/Lisa Bateman

About the Author

USA Today Best Selling Author Kristen Painter is a little obsessed with cats, books, chocolate, and shoes. It's a healthy mix. She loves to entertain her readers with interesting twists and unforgettable characters. She currently writes the best-selling paranormal romance series, Nocturne Falls, and the cozy mystery spin off series, Jayne Frost. The former college English teacher can often be found all over social media where she loves to interact with readers.

www.kristenpainter.com

Made in the USA
Lexington, KY
10 December 2019

58386504R00192